Returning *Home*

Marcus Blake

Returning Home

A Mavericknes Media / Truesource Publishing book

Returning Home was edited by
Carol Felder and J M Almgreen

The story is fictional and any resemblance to actual people, places, and certain facts associated with the characters created by Marcus Blake is purely coincidence.

Mavericknes Media : Dallas Texas

Truesource Publishing : Dallas Texas

www.truesourcepublishing.com

ISBN : 978-1-932996-55-5

Printed in the United States of America
Published in Dallas, Texas

For More information on Marcus Blake go to....

www.marcusblake.net
www.facebook.com/themarcusblake
www.twitter.com/marcusblake
www.thatnerdshow.com

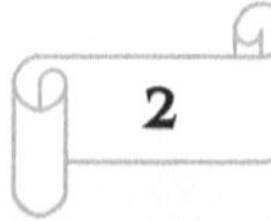

About the Author

Marcus Blake was born in Chicago, Illinois in 1977. He grew up in Chicago and East Texas. His education is in History, Literature, Psychology, and Religion & Philosophy. Marcus Blake has studied at many universities throughout the United States, but his Alma Mater is Stephen F. Austin State University in Nacogdoches, Texas, which is also where he wrote his first book, The Music of Life. Marcus Blake is a Poet, Musician, Comedian, Writer, and Historian. His books are The Music of Life, My Reflections, Returning Home. Sex Game. The Lonely Girl, Stories From Wrigley, 30 Minutes: Trust and Lies, 30 Minutes: Guilty Until Proven Innocent, 30 Minutes: A Soldier's Song, and 30 Minutes: A Badge of Honor. . He has taught in the public school system, served in the Army, and been a guest speaker at Education and Literary events throughout the world. Marcus Blake is also a Radio Host, his current show is Saturday Morning Nerd Show which can be heard on Saturday Mornings at www.thatnerdshow.com. He is a veteran of Rock and Roll shows as well as Political shows on the radio. Marcus Blake makes his home in the Dallas, Texas .

Other Books by Marcus Blake…

The Music of Life

My Reflections

Sex Game

The Lonely Girl

Stories From Wrigley

30 Minutes: Trust and Lies

30 Minutes: Guilty Until Proven Innocent

30 Minutes: A Soldier's Song

30 Minutes: A Badge of Honor

Ring of Warriors: Making a Fighter

This Book is dedicated to...

Keith and Eliza Felder

&

George and Barbara Almgreen

One can only be so lucky to have grandparents such as these. My life would not be what it is without the relationships I had with each of them.

The Idea of Family

What Makes a Family,
A merry band of characters
Trudging through life
Somehow staying connected
Fighting and reconciling in just a few moments
Getting annoyed with each other
Being the shoulder we lean on at three in the morning
A family can be people who let us down the most
But always there to pick us up when we have fallen.
They remind us that we are not alone
And that we can be loved despite our doubts.
The family is an eclectic band of people
Binding themselves to who we become
They can rescue us from the engulfing depression
That which come from being alone
Is it any wonder where we find true joy
It comes from having within our life loved ones
For who among us can truly be happy without a family
Everything in life is connected, since the beginning of time
For what connects us shall always be called Family

Table of Contents

1

My Father's Story

On the eve of my twenty-first birthday, my father sat me down to have one of those father and son talks. It's the kind of talk we get when we're young and it's usually about a subject that we think our parents cannot quite understand anymore. They are the times when we think that our parents remain too old fashioned and couldn't possibly know what we're going through even though they, too, were young once.

I think every child knows how parents can be when they want to talk to you about something important, but it wasn't one of those times for me. Instead, my father told me a story I had never heard before. It was a family story, the kind that we never hear until we're old enough because we could never understand it before.

My name is Sean Mitchell Collins; it's a stern Irish name, a family name. I was named after my great-grandfather whom I've never met because he died shortly before I was born. The irony of being named after him is that I didn't know much about him because it wasn't all that often my family talked about him, at least in front of me. While I was growing up, I only heard bits and pieces about him.

I never understood why my father nearly broke into tears when he was mentioned. I never even knew the struggles my family endured when it came to having a relationship with my great-grandfather. In addition, I was never made to understand why he was so loved and revered by so many, but mostly by my own father.

Even though I didn't understand all of this, tonight would be the night my father would make sense out of it for me. Unfortunately, I couldn't escape this talk with my father before I went out for the evening because I still lived with him and my mother. Living at home had serious advantages, home -cooked meals were always nice, and I could save a lot of money while I was in college.

At first, I thought my father's story was the one thing that could destroy my evening of celebration on what was to be a tremendous occasion for me, but as it turned out this was a story I could not afford to miss. In my Humanities class at the college I was attending, we had a project due on family history displayed through film, literature, or art; I still hadn't decided what to do yet. The timing of my father's story couldn't have been better with this project being due, and because the relationship between my father and I was strained.

I didn't understand my father at all. I never knew where he was coming from in his points of view or how he dealt with our family. I know I'm not the only man who has ever felt that way about his father, but the uniqueness of this story would explain, well, all the things I never knew but thought I did about my family. And to tell you the truth, I also thought my father didn't understand me or how I lived my life, but I couldn't have been more wrong.

Sometimes the relationships between fathers and sons are like that. They become tense and awkward to the point where all you can do is either yell at each other or not talk at all. Even though it seems the members of a family don't understand each other, that's when those same people understand each other perfectly.

My father, Jonathan Mitchell Collins, sat me down to tell me about a man named Mitchell Ryan Collins, who as it would turn out would be the most influential person in his life and the best man he ever knew. Of course you would never know this by the way my father talked about him or should I say never did.

Mitch Collins, as everybody knew him, was born in Boston Massachusetts in 1918. He was a fisherman's son, but unlike most Irishmen who followed in their father's footsteps, Mitch knew early on that this was not for him. From what I understand he was very intelligent and his intellect would grant him an academic scholarship to the University of Chicago in 1936.

Nobody remaining in my family knows much about his childhood except that he had a brother that was a couple of years younger than him who he was very close to. His brother Maxwell, Max for short, would be killed in action during World War II. He loved planes, so he became a B-17 Co-Pilot. His death was something that always haunted Mitch while adding to the mystery about his childhood.

Mitch told my father one time that his life really

began in 1936 when he went off to college, and this would also be how my family started in Chicago. Mitch loved this town so much that he really never left unless he was traveling on business, which I came to find out he did quite often after the War. Chicago was something different from what he had known, and it was a whole new world for him. It became a new life for him; something he needed at that time so he became reborn and never left.

Even though Math and Science were subjects that came very easy to him, college was the first place to challenge him in his thoughts and make him a scholar. It also opened the door to the world, showing him all the endless possibilities within it. In all total, Mitch would spend a total of six years at the University of Chicago, never returning to Boston except for his parents' funeral in 1948.

Mitch's field of study became Engineering and Physics while at the University of Chicago, and he even completed some of his post graduate work by the time WWII came around. Like many American men after the bombing of Pearl Harbor, he quickly joined the Navy and changed his life's plans forever, never completing his PhD.

He served as a Navel engineer overseeing the engine room on board a small battleship. He made it through four years of service while being decorated for heroism twice. My grandmother and father told me that he did not speak very often about his experiences in the war or the horrible acts of men he saw. According to my father he would always say that no human being should ever have to witness the acts of war.

He was like so many of the young men that went off to war and lost their innocence, but came home with a new respect and passion for life. My father said that Mitch once told him when he was very young that life is a profound and passionate thing and that life should always be lived with that in mind. This also would be his justification for many of the things he would do later in life.

Sometime during the war when wounded in Pearl Harbor Hawaii, Mitch met a beautiful young woman named Alice who was training to be a nurse at the hospital there. As if he had seen the face of an angel, Mitch fell in love with her instantly; at least that's what he always claimed. Although she was nineteen at the time, she seemed to have been grown up all of her life and the age difference never seemed to matter. They were just a man and a woman who loved each other, but as it turned out, they never had a lot in common. They were two completely different people and like their age difference it didn't matter at all because they loved each other. They both realized very early that they loved each other to the point that they couldn't live without one another.

Mitch and Alice corresponded through the last two years of the war, never missing a day to write each other. As soon as they were both discharged from the Navy, Mitch traded in his uniform for a tuxedo on his way to a wedding.

After the war, Mitch decided that the best job for him was a government job in the Atomic Commission traveling across the United States instead of stuck in some kind of science lab. When the war was finally over and they were married, my great-grandparents settled in Chicago.

Alice was from a small town in Oklahoma called Eagle City, which doesn't exist anymore except for a cemetery in which many of her relatives are buried in. She was a farmer's daughter who knew only of small dusty towns and the country side. She never saw a big city until she was sent to Los Angeles for training on her way to being shipped out to Hawaii for service in the war. When she settled in Chicago after the war, it was a scary place for her at first, but then her world was completely opened through all the glamour and excitement of the windy city.

From the time she and Mitch settled in Chicago, Alice never returned to Oklahoma except for brief visits and funerals. Despite the many generations of her family that had resided in the state, which they had help settle even before the land race of 1893, Alice never lived there again. She had been won over by the glamour of the big city.

As for Mitch, even though he was really working in Washington DC and in Nevada, he always said that Chicago was the place he always wanted to be because it was home. Mitch loved the city of Chicago and all it had to offer more than any other place he had ever been. Through the many travels that he and my great grandmother would have in their lifetimes, Chicago would always be their home.

Not too long after my great-grandparents were married their first child would be born, two years after they were married to be exact. They had a girl who they named Catherine and who would become one of the foremost important women in my father's life. Two years after that they had another girl named Laura who is my father's mother and she looked almost exactly like Mitch. Mitch never had the son that my father thinks he always wanted, but in the end he did get to raise a son and make the same mistakes that father's make with their sons.

Mitch was an active father even though he was an alcoholic who was rarely sober. He was very much part of his children's lives, even when they thought their father was a bit strange.

No matter what, he did the best he could for his family and provided a nice life for his wife and children, giving them the opportunity to be educated, independent women. Eventually his practical world would collide with the idealism of youth, and their differences would create a void between his children and him, something that is never uncommon between parents and children.

When my grandmother, Laura, was nineteen, she fell in love with a fellow student at the college she was attending. Soon after they fell in love and started seeing each other, he was drafted into the army during the Vietnam War. Before he left for his tour of duty, my grandmother became pregnant with my father, Jonathan.

My father never met his own dad because he died in Vietnam, but Mitch in no small way became the father he needed in life. At the time my grandmother and her boyfriend didn't get along with Mitch their generational differences were most of ideology. My grandmother's generation believed that America could not be trusted and the war in Vietnam was wrong. Mitch came from a generation that never had use for questioning its government and believed that service to one's country should happen with fervor and contentment. When all this was going on, it was the beginning of a strained relationship between Mitch and his two daughters.

Mitch had become by accident the father figure in my father's life and helped raise him until my great-grandparents separated. This was the unique nature of the relationship my father had with his grandfather, and the one thing my father would have to reconcile after Mitch would pass away. As with most relationships with fathers and sons, they tend to get strained, and their relationship was no different. It didn't get any easier when my father was sixteen. After nearly forty years of marriage Mitch and my great-grandmother Alice split up.

At the time of their separation Mitch had been retired from his government job for some time and he never quite settled down. He still liked to go out on the town and stay out all night playing cards with friends or drinking all night as full-blown alcoholics tend to do. In that lifestyle Mitch would also cross a line that that he could never come back from when it came to his devotion to his wife. Alice just couldn't handle it any more. She also couldn't forgive the unthinkable when it came and through him out of the house while clinging to some small hope that he would have settled down when he retired. My grandmother and my father were still living with Mitch and Alice in Chicago at the time.

If you asked my father at what point in time the relationship with he and Mitch was damaged, it was probably about the time of my great-grandparent's divorce. The thing is, even though Mitch might have been a hard man, always demanding discipline and order in his family and job; he was a very charming and well liked individual. Mitch was the type of person that always could make friends easily. That also included people from all age groups even young people that didn't have anything in common with older adults especially many of the women that were my father's age.

Mitch always had a very special persona around women; maybe it was because he liked them more than anything. It was widely known that the two great habits he never really parted with were women and whiskey. My father never went into great detail about why he and Mitch didn't have a great relationship during the last years of Mitch's life. However, he told me this incredible story of how the family was put back together while Mitch laid to rest his demons. Through this story I began to finally see what happened between Mitch and my father.

If you think a generational difference between people can be hard at times, then two generations can be impossible to deal with at times. Like every good story that involves family, love, and redemption, the story has to start with tragedy first. So when my father began his story he began with the most tragic moment of our family history or at least the most tragic as he saw it. My father sat me down in the living room with a couple of beers as we began talking as men for the first time and then he began to tell this incredible story.

2

April Sorrows

It was a cloudy and wet day on April 9, 1992, not at all unusual for April in Texas, as Mitch turned off the interstate on his way to the Baylor Medical Center in Dallas. He was on his way for a couple of medical tests that were not routine for a man of his age and to see an old friend, a fellow comrade in arms who had seen the same gory side of war. The waiting room was silent and cold with people hoping that it wouldn't be the inevitable, but most waiting rooms are like that. Nobody wants to talk or be friendly in a place like this, thinking that if they do it will jinx them and bad news will come.

Mitch tried to make the best of the situation by reading some out of date magazines on what women really want in men, waiting for the depressing information he knew was coming, but still hoping he could be wrong. A man with as much experience in life as he had always knew when something was wrong by the way he felt. As one gets older, one learns to trust their intuitions so the truth becomes revealed.

Sometimes we have to look deep within ourselves to find the truth by looking for the answers that we don't want to look for.

The nurse called Mitch's name and led him to a dressing room filled with medical paraphernalia for him to change into. When he was done he was led into a dark room with a MRI machine. As he was slowly being slid into the tunnel, haunting images of his war experiences started to come back.

Mitch couldn't help but remember friends and fellow soldiers dying all around him at different times in the war. Each one of his friend's faces were imprinted on his mind forever, screaming in agony on their way to meet the hereafter. He even thought back to a particular time in a navy hospital standing next to his friend Charlie Rogers as the doctors told the nurses around him that there was nothing they could do for him and he was going to die a death that was as painful as they come

It wasn't often that images of Mitch's war experiences that he so desperately tried to forget came back; it was only when he was very scared. He could not help but be scared of taking these medical tests or confirming the answers that he already knew. When Mitch was done dressing into his clothes, he was led into a doctor's office. Some of the pictures on the wall as he looked around were very familiar and somewhat comforting because he was in some of them.

There were pictures of his days in the Pacific or on his battleship during the war with some of his close friends. Some of them made it home and some of them didn't, but the pictures brought a comforting feeling remembering back to a time when Mitch and his buddies had only each other and hope to keep them alive.

The pictures brought back memories of the

worst of times, and of the best of times because all the men in pictures were filled with such innocence that most people all long to have again. Dr. Calvin Whitaker walked in and shouted to Mitch.

"Where's that rotten bastard that never keeps in-touch anymore, I mean not even a Christmas Card."

Mitch responded sarcastically, "Dr. Whitaker you haven't retired yet, God help all your patients."

The two men shook hands and embraced like brothers who had not seen each other in years. Whitaker started to walk back to his desk and asked Mitch, "Well what can I do for you, because I know this isn't a social call even though it's been too long since we've seen each or you wouldn't have come here to see me in my office."

Mitch took a seat on the other side of the desk and responded in a somber tone, "I needed to do a couple of tests for some problems I've been having and I didn't want anybody else telling me the bad news."

"Mitch, how do you know it's serious? Maybe you're just getting old."

Mitch laughed. "I've been old for forty years, Calvin. Now, I know there's something really wrong"

Calvin walked to the coffeepot on the left side of his desk and asked, "Tell me some of symptoms you've been having."

Mitch hesitantly gave him the rundown. "Mostly I've felt numbness in different parts of my body at different times; also I've been very sick one day and completely better the next. I've seen too many friends that I used to work with have similar symptoms and not too long after they started they would die from it. It sounds like cancer to me, or maybe that's just what I'm really afraid of."

"Well," started Calvin, "it could be that, and with your exposure to radiation over the years I wouldn't be surprised, but it can also be a lot of different things. I see they already did a MRI on the recommendation of the doctor at the VA hospital, so let's just wait for the films and results of the blood work they did and go from there. In the meantime, here's some coffee, and I even have a little bit of medicine that'll cure anything for you."

He reached inside his bottom drawer and pulled out a small bottle of Irish Whisky and poured a little into both cups. The doctor held his cup up and said, "Here are two real Irish coffees for two real Irishmen, and may it cure any ailment that we might have."

Mitch looked at the doctor with a cockeyed smile and said, "Don't mind if I do, but won't you get fired for drinking while on duty?"

Dr. Whitaker just smiled and said, "It's just old time medicine. Besides, what are they going to do, retire me? I should've been retired four years ago."

The two older gentlemen just laughed and talked about old times, remembering all the good times they had together as young men and some of the sad ones, too. They were men of experience that never bullshitted each other over what could happen. They looked at death as something waiting to happen, but lived each moment in life like it was their last because they truly knew from experience they might never get another moment.

They were men who respected the ones that had gone before them, but also lived life with the thanks for the chances that were granted to them. They knew the costs in life, they knew the sacrifices that had to be made sometimes, and they knew how to revel in the moment when it was all said and done, when peace had finally come because they were old men of experience.

About half an hour later, the nurse came in

with the results of the medical tests taken by Mitch. Dr. Whitaker took the pictures and posted them on the lightened board and carefully studied them. After a few sighs and what seemed an eternity, he said somberly, "Mitch, come on over here and I'll show you what we found."

Mitch got up and sarcastically said, "Well, I know this isn't good since you're smiling."

Dr. Whitaker smiled and said, "Mitch, you were right that it's not good; you actually have a couple of things that are wrong. If you look here, this huge mass inside your chest is cancer and it looks like it might have been there for a very long time just spreading very slowly. That would explain why you've only been getting sick off and on for the last few months, but there is another mass at the base of your brain, right above the tip of the spine."

Mitch looked at the picture regretfully and asked, "It's a brain tumor right?"

"Yes it is, and it is inoperable. I mean a good neurosurgeon could go in and try to get it, but the operation alone would probably kill you, especially at your age. The brain tumor would explain the numbness you feel at times, but there are options to help with your sickness."

Mitch slowly walked back to his chair with a saddened look that seemed to display a thousand emotions. After what seemed a long period of time he asked the doctor what could be done.

Dr. Whitaker said calmly, "You can undergo chemotherapy and it might shrink the tumor, but you would have to deal with the side effects from the therapy which could be just as bad as having to deal with the tumor itself. With the cancer, surgeons could go in and get most or even all of it, but with your exposure to radiation over the years working in the

Atomic Commission the cancer would probably come back. If you undergo the treatments, you might be able to prolong your life another couple of years, but you would be in such unbearable pain most of those two years. You have to ask yourself if it's really worth it. If you don't do any of the treatments, then you have anywhere from three months to a year to live; then it becomes a question of what will kill you first, the cancer or the tumor."

"Well I don't have a whole lot of choices because one or the other is going to kill me. What would you do if you were in my shoes?"

Dr. Calvin Whitaker sat back with a sigh and said as compassionately as he could, "First of all, start making some preparations for the inevitable. Guys with as much shit as we've seen know when the end is near. We have lived very full lives, seen a lot of places, seen a lot of horrible things, but we have seen a lot of beautiful things, too. When it becomes the winter of your life and the moments are not as many for you, then you live what moments you do have to the very fullest and be thankful for what God gives you. I can't really tell you what to do except to plan for the inevitable, but knowing you, you already know what to do."

Mitch just sat back and smiled and then spoke up with cheeriness in his voice, "Well, there are a few places I haven't seen for a long time, as well as some people I haven't seen for a while. I think it's time I take a trip and take care of all that."

Mitch got up and grabbed his coat and started for the door then he turned around and said, "Thanks for the truth, Calvin; you're a good friend as always."

"I'm sorry that I had to give you the bad news," he said. "Me too, but I'm glad it was a friend," answered Mitch.

"You take care, and if you need anything from your doctor then don't hesitate to call. Oh, by the way, say hi to Alice for me."

"Calvin, we've been split up for nine years and I haven't talked to her for at least three years."

The doctor just laughed and said, "I know that, but say hi to her for me anyway."

Mitch just laughed and asked, "What makes you think I'm going to call her up and tell her I'm dying?"

Calvin smiled satirically. "I'll see you in June. Until then don't have too much of a good time, doctor's orders."

Mitch walked out laughing and thought to himself that he wasn't done yet, not with this life anyway, and he was going to finish before he was gone. He wasn't going to stop living until God finally brought him home.

Mitch sat in his car and thought for a while, wondering what he should do next. He was tired and it had been a couple of weeks since he had been home in Chicago, but since he hadn't been keeping busy lately like he usually did, a long extended trip seemed to be the right thing for him.

He reached under the seat and grabbed the small bottle of whiskey that he always kept with him just in case and took a sip. Whiskey was always a sweet taste for him and it always made him think of happier times. Mitch closed his eyes and thought back to the first time he ever danced with his wife, Alice. It was at the hospital where he had first met her.

∞∞∞∞∞∞∞

Mitch remembered seeing her a few times while he was recuperating at the hospital; she even tended to him a few times. One particular night there was a dance outside on the shoreline across from the hospital. Mitch had been in his hospital bed for weeks, not moving around all that much even though he was supposed to be to gaining his strength back. He wasn't too anxious to return to the war because it was always hard for any soldier to return from the peace and comfort that could be found in a hospital to the nightmare and madness of war.

When he heard about the dance and that all the medical personnel were going to be there, he started walking around that morning with the intention of being well enough to attend the dance. Mitch was able to walk on his own and attend the dance that night, and he didn't waste any time asking her to dance. As he remembered, Alice looked like a flower blooming and pouring forth all its radiance beneath the moonlight.

He remembered thinking to himself at the time that he didn't know whether she was an angel or an actual human being from the way she looked within the glimmer of the moonlight that was being shown; she was a celestial mixture of fire, the stars and the moon, and the waves of the sea.

He asked her to dance as she toyed with him. "I thought you were still in too much in pain to get out of bed, sir."

"Well, I heard you were going to be at this dance tonight and I was all of a sudden feeling better. What can I say? You offer the best medicine than any of the doctors do."

It was a smooth line that a playboy might use on the innocent and young, but it had enough charm in it that any woman would believe it. It was one of those great gifts that Mitch had; he could charm anybody into liking him.

Alice just smiled at him and said, "Since you're mysteriously feeling better, I think you should dance to help gain your strength back. After all, that's what the doctors have said for you to do and I would only be following their orders as a nurse."

What Mitch may not have known then was that Alice had noticed him as well, and she hoped that there would be a moment when they could introduce themselves as people and not just a patient and a nurse.

They danced under the moon and stars forgetting about the world around them and time had no meaning for these two love-struck souls. Mitch could remember the first time he ever touched her, for she felt like the finest silk. Her skin was as soft as the grass in a meadow where the flowers danced in the wind and the deer play with the butterflies; a place where only peace can be known. It is a place of simple times, a place where the insanity of this world cannot find its way and the perfect moments of peace are hidden away for special times.

Mitch danced with Alice most of the night and didn't want to let her go as if she was an angel of God sent here only for him. After a long stroll along the countryside where they watched the sunrise signaling the beginning of a new day or the start of heaven's awakening, they parted. It wasn't too long after that night that Mitch had to go back to the war, but he was filled with love and the one thing that makes life truly worth living.

He could also remember that their letters were the only thing to bridge the gap between heaven and hell or the distance from each other's hearts. He thought back to a time of innocence, a time of madness, and a time of pure happiness. It is a simple place where the poets dream about lover's sleep, where for him he could find the true image of Venus. It might have seemed too much like an infatuation for this man, but through all the things at that time that didn't make sense, his love for Alice was the only thing that could make sense.

It was true, Mitch had never known a happier time in his life than when he was with Alice, and yet after one chance meeting, he somehow knew that although he might be happy with his life, life for him could not be any better without her. After a long stroll down memory's domain, Mitch woke up and decided what he should do and where he should go. He was on his way to a journey that he knew was probably his end.

It's a type of journey that is made in the heart and that causes us to dig deep into our past to confront those demons that we push into the shadows; a journey that is usually made in the winter of our life when all we are is stalked by death.

Mitch went by the store to get a few supplies and then got back in his 1955 Cadillac convertible; the only thing he had ever kept in vintage condition. He headed southeast into the very Deep South to a city that held more fun and great music that any place in the south. It was a place with more history, culture, and dark places within city walls lasting for hundreds of years.

This was one of Mitch's favorite places to visit and a place he had always garnered fond memories or the lack thereof. Music on every street corner and a celebration of masks every year; there was no place like it. Mitch could think of no better place to start his journey, and the first person he had to meet along the way would probably be down there anyway. Mitch took a slow drive down the interstate with the top down as the sun started to break

3

Making a way to the Past

When the night had finally descended upon
that part of the world, Mitch entered the city limits of
New Orleans, Louisiana, a place he was very familiar
with, but had not always been kind to him. He found
a motel that he had been to quite often in the last forty
years and that was in the heart of the city. New
Orleans was a place where every form of excitement
was possible; it was a place where the inhabitants
would be welcomed by the sounds of Davis, or
Coltrane, or Armstrong.

After settling in he decided that a drink was in
order and set out for a nice dingy Cathouse where the
whiskey was always good and the music was even
better. He found a place called *The Blue's Nile Café* in
the French Quarter because it was the place where his
estranged grandson would be. He sat himself at the
bar and ordered a crown straight up. He immediately
recognized the piano player who was playing some old

jazz tune that he had learned as a kid when he first started taking piano lessons.

Mitch looked at this kid at the piano with amazement and sorrow, thinking back to all the years he had known him. The kid was a young vibrant man in the awakening of his life with so much ahead of him and yet so much behind. The young man who sat at the piano knew very little of deep, forgotten regrets and the reasons why some people live life to their fullest and why some people don't. The innocence still surrounded him, but only in a thin cloud that was soon to be pushed away in a journey that he was very much unaware of.

As Mitch sat at the bar and watched the young man he fell back into memory again. This time the memory was one of his most regretful moments; a time where he let his temper get the better of him with his grandson.

∞∞∞∞∞∞

Mitch stumbled around the garage drunk, looking at the mess that Jonathan had left. A garage that was clean and organized with nothing out of place.   He was furious and he wasn't thinking straight; the only thoughts that consumed him at that moment were finding his grandson so he could scold him for the mess he left.

"Jonathan, get your ass out here in the garage! Jonathan you better get your goddamn ass in here now or you'll get the beating of a lifetime!" Mitch yelled in a drunken rant.

A few moments later his thirteen year old grandson came from the house into the garage. He replied, "What is it grandpa, why are you so mad?"

"Look at this mess, are you some kind of idiot,

you can't put things back? How many times have I told you to clean up when you're done?"

"I was coming back to finish fixing up my bike. I was going to put your tools away then."

"Look here, when you're done even for just a little while, then you clean up shit. That's what civilized people do."

"I told you Grandpa," Jonathan replied back in an angry tone, "I was going to put everything back when I was done."

Mitch didn't say anything for a moment, he just let his anger build up inside and then he back handed Jonathan across the head, hard and fast. Jonathan didn't know how to respond as he gathered his balance from the hard blow because his grandfather had never hit him before. Mitch could lose his temper quickly, especially when he was drunk, but he had never hit Jonathan.

Mitch just looked at him in anger then replied, "Don't get a tone with me, I keep telling you to pick up after yourself, but you never listen. It's like leaving water all over the sink counter when you wash hands; it's not hard to clean it up. You're just lazy. "

Jonathan gave his grandfather a dirty look and then replied back, "Screw you, I'm not lazy." After he yelled at Mitch he stormed off in anger kicking whatever was in his path while he walked out the door.

"Get back here you lazy jackass!" Mitch yelled in his drunken angry rage, but Jonathan never came back. He stood there looking at the mess thinking about the last few moments while his anger subsided; he just grabbed another beer and went back to watching the ball game in his recliner. It wasn't until the next day when he sobered up that he remembered what he had done. He couldn't believe that his drunken anger had gotten so bad that he actually hit his grandson.

He never really apologized for it; he and Jonathan didn't say a word to each other for a few weeks and eventually they both forgot about it because if certain incidents were never talked about with Mitch and his family then it was never to be brought up again. However, it never stopped Mitch from feeling horrible over what he had done to his grandson.

∞∞∞∞∞∞∞

As Mitch sat there sipping on his whiskey, he remembered that scene vividly with Jonathan; he remembered how regretful and hurt he was that he could have done that to him. Their relationship from that point would start to become strained, and it was at that moment that Mitch knew his drinking was the problem. Every time that he looked at Jonathan from that day forward, all he could see was his regret and the mirror of a troubled man.

When the set was over with, one of the cocktail waitresses brought the young piano player a drink. She looked at him with a smile and a surprised look, as if to discover something about her friend that she had not known before.

She said to him, "Here, this is from the older gentlemen from the bar; he said that he was family."

Jonathan the piano player looked at his friend and replied, "Thanks for the drink, but anything that man tells you check with me first to see if it's the truth."

"Oh, he *must* be family to get an angry response like that from you," she said. "I guess he's not the well-liked kind."

Jonathan didn't respond and just walked past her on his way to the bar, as if to settle an old score.

In a way, an old score was about to be settled with him, although he didn't know it. It was a score that had nothing to do with money or any earthly possession, but one of haunting memories and a longing that lost in a dark journey.

Jonathan slowly walked up to the older gentleman and asked coolly, "Thanks for the drink, but what are you doing here, Mitch?"

"Well, I was driving through the south and heard you were in New Orleans; I thought we might have dinner since it's been a few years since I last saw you."

"Why do you want to see me when I haven't heard from you in all these years?"

Mitch looked at him with a cocked smile and said, "It's nice to know you haven't changed, but I'm still your grandfather whether you want me to be or not. Besides, I need to talk to you."

"Mitch, I don't want to rehash old memories with you. You have your life to live, and I have mine, okay?"

Mitch replied harshly, "It's very important what I have to tell, and you could have enough respect for an old man to at least give him five minutes."

Jonathan paused for a minute in contemplation and responded, "Alright, I'll give you a few minutes. There's a diner around the corner that's actually pretty good; I'll meet you there at nine o'clock in the morning."

With that said Jonathan turned around and walked back to the piano to finish his last set. Mitch finished his drink and walked back to his hotel to have another drink. He knew that his encounter with Jonathan would probably not go that well, but he also knew that he wanted him to know what was happening with him.

No matter what harsh feelings were between Mitch and the family, his family did have a right to know about his illness. As far as he was concerned, nobody should have to wake up one day to find that a loved one has died and then find out that person had been dying for a long time.

Surprises like those are not easy on anyone, no matter what the feelings were about a certain individual. As Mitch lay in bed with a glass of whiskey flipping through channels on the television, he faded back into his memories once again. They were not sad memories this time, but of some of the best times of his life. He could remember like yesterday all the moments that surrounded the births of his children and the smile that his wife carried with her on those occasions.

He remembered the day Jonathan was born and how he felt being a grandfather for the first time; much like a father feels on the day his son is born. Jonathan had been born in a time of confusion, idealism, division, and a time of awakening for the family. It was a time when 1960's youth idealism collided with their parent's post war belief system, and the two different generations didn't seem to understand each other.

Jonathan's birth didn't come from a pure like old-fashioned wedding of two young people starting their lives together, but from two young people who challenged life at every turn when they didn't fully understand anything. None of that mattered at the time, though, because amidst all tension between family members, Jonathan's birth was an endless delight to Mitch.

Mitch thought back to all the holidays spent with his family when it seemed that everybody was laughing with joy. He could remember the smell of

Alice baking holiday treats in the kitchen. The smell
of his favorite holiday treat was Alice's sour cream
sweet rolls, a blend of cinnamon twists with sweet
sour cream icing on top, was always etched in
memory. Christmas did not officially begin until Alice
made those, something her mother taught her to
make on the farm.

At the same time he remembered many times
when his children and grandson were growing up that
were not joyous, but times of sadness and anger.
Through the barrage of memories that floated through
his mind he shed a few tears and wondered what
happened to those times and how he ended up here
and now.

He thought to himself, sometimes we do not
realize the mistakes we make until it is too late, until
the full effect of those mistakes seeps though. As he
thought back to his actions and tried to take stock of
them he became very tired and drifted off to sleep,
lulled by the low sounds of the television. This was
not uncommon for this lonely and haunted man, but
these times were changing like the seasons that come
and go. The times where he could ignore the things of
the past were limited now and no amount of whiskey
could help him forget

At five minutes after nine Jonathan entered the
diner looking like the long night had won him over.
He was greeted by a waitress that he had never seen
before who made the comment, "It's about time you
showed up, your grandfather is already starting to
complain about your sense of time."

Jonathan just looked at her with short smile and
replied, "There's just no pleasing that man." No matter
how much he might have hated him, he could still find
humor with his grandfather.

He walked over to the booth to where the older

gentleman was sitting who was already on his second cup of coffee. Mitch looked up from his newspaper and said, "I see you are still as fluent with time as you used to be."

Jonathan replied, "I make up for it in other areas so you can't complain too much."

Mitch quickly changed the subject to avoid an argument and started asking Jonathan about how his life had been the past few years. After both men had gotten their coffee and ordered breakfast they went through the usual small talk of catching up with one another before they got very serious.

Jonathan finally asked, "Okay Mitch, what is it that you wanted so desperately to tell me? We might as well quit the small talk and get right to the point."

"There isn't any way to dance around the issue so I'll just say it. I stopped in Dallas the other day to see an old friend of mine who is a doctor and to get some tests done. It wasn't good; I found out that I'm dying."

Jonathan was surprised and paused for a few moments, not knowing what to say. It wasn't the thing he expected his grandfather to say. It's one of those things that we never expect someone to say.

Finally, Jonathan asked, "What are you dying from?"

"I have a tumor that's inoperable and I'm in the beginning stages of cancer. The simple truth is that no matter what I do one of them will eventually kill me. Because of this, I'm not going to do Chemotherapy. I don't want the last moments of my life being in pain while trying to find a cure for something for which there is no cure."

Jonathan sat in the booth drinking his coffee staring at his cup in disbelief like a man who just saw some cosmic event for which there is no explanation.

He tried to take full measure of what he was hearing despite all the anger he felt; anger directed at Mitch for walking out on the family so many years ago and anger for not being able to do anything for this man whom he still cared about despite the past.

"What are you going to do with what time you have left?" asked Jonathan.

"The doctor has predicted that I only have about three months to a year to live, so I'm going to live every moment I can to its fullest. I've decided to take an extended trip and see a few people and places one last time, and maybe see some things I've never seen before. While I'm still fit, I'm going to keep driving and see where the road takes me, but I don't want to do it alone. Part of the reason I wanted to talk to you is to see if you might be willing to go on this trip with me. If money's a problem, I'll take care of all your expenses."

Jonathan just sat back with an astonished look on his face and replied, "Let me understand this, you want me to go along with you on your trip and play some kind of nurse to you? How long do you want me to do this - until you eventually die?"

"No, it wouldn't be like that; if I wanted a nurse to take care of me then I would hire one. I just want a travel companion; someone who can share this journey with me and who might understand why I'm doing this. You never know, you might learn something from it, and you and I can share something together as adults and as family."

Jonathan started to feel angry again about what he was hearing.
"Look," he said, "I'm sorry that you're dying and you feel like you should have one last show before your part from this life, but I don't have time to take off for a couple of months and be your travel buddy. I have gigs all summer long and even one playing keyboard in

my friend's band in Las Vegas. This is how I make my living, Mitch, and frankly I just don't want to go strolling down memory lane with you anymore. What's done is done with us and we live our own lives now; I think we should just leave it at that," Jonathan started to stand up and continued talking "I'm sorry I just can't do this with you anymore; my life is too short to waste."

"Jonathan," said Mitch in his hurt and gloom, "I'm sorry you feel that way, but whether you like it or not we're still family. There isn't anybody that I would rather share this journey with. I'm not asking for a lot, just a few months, and you never know, you might need something like this. If you change your mind, I'm leaving about eight o'clock tomorrow and I'm staying at the 6th Street Inn."

Jonathan finished his coffee and looked at Mitch with a little satisfaction and said, "Yeah well, you may think we're family, but family doesn't walk out on one another. Enjoy your trip Mitch, you can send me a postcard."

With that said Jonathan turned around and walked out of the diner, never looking back. The hurt was still there between Mitch and Jonathan as well as the rest of the family. It's the kind that runs deep inside the heart and divides generations. It seemed that no matter how much Mitch had tried to keep on good terms with Jonathan in the last nine years, Jonathan was determined to keep hating him for the hurt that he caused his mother, his aunt, and his grandmother. Jonathan did not want anything to do with a man that could cause so much pain even though he still didn't know fully what had happened years ago.

All Jonathan saw when led down memory lane was a lot of pain and suffering. Dealing with our past is not always an easy, but the things that could be the most rewarding are never easy. Mitch finished his breakfast and last cup of coffee and then started walking around New Orleans not exactly knowing where he was going, but it didn't matter.

The sun was shining in brilliant radiance over the Mississippi; it was the promise of a new day. Mitch was beginning an Odyssey, one that begins in the heart of a man. He didn't know whether he would travel this journey alone or with a companion, but all he could do was embrace his journey for all that it would be.

4

Meetings of Chance or Fate

After walking around for about an hour, Mitch stumbled onto a bar that had its front door open, but wasn't quite open yet. He was getting tired so he needed to stop and rest a bit. He walked in and looked around the little rustic joint that still had the feeling of great music constantly being played, the feeling of home to any music lover. It was a place true of New Orleans, where music of the purist soul was played every night into the wee hours of the morning. It was a place that had heart and a quiet restless soul that appealed to Mitch.

He walked in and saw a short but attractive young woman behind the bar cutting fruit. She had medium long dirty blond hair that covered part of her face and whisked with a breeze as she walked or turned around. Her face had small features and was slightly freckled underneath the eyes and above her blushed cheeks. Mitch noticed that out of all her attractive features it was her deep green eyes that radiated her beauty.

Her eyes were as green as an Irish meadow during a clear spring day, and when you looked inside her eyes you knew that you were home. She was simple and serene; she had the look of the everyday girl, the girl that never disappoints and is always the best thing for you. This is why he liked her immediately, and because he could sense she was pure of heart.

She also reminded him of his mother when she was a young woman raising two stubborn and rebellious sons; before age had caught up with her as well as the toiling hard work of an Irish immigrant.

He spoke up in his usual charming tone, "Hello there."

She looked up at him and replied, "Hello to you sir. I'm sorry were not quite open yet, but we will be in an hour."

Mitch gave her a charming smile and said, "Oh, I'm not here for a drink, I just wanted to know if I could sit down for bit. I've been walking around for about an hour trying to collect my thoughts and wore myself out. I've discovered the hard way that I'm not sixty-five anymore."

The lady behind the bar just smiled and casually laughed. "Sure, I don't see why not, you look harmless enough."

Mitch took a seat at the bar not too far from where she was and asked her, "So are you always this trustworthy of strangers that walk into your bar before you open?"

The woman replied in a sarcastically, "Well, I'm not too worried about a charming old man robbing my bar and harming me when there is a bank right down the street that's more lucrative."

Mitch just laughed and replied, "Ah, you're very intuitive; that's one of the most attractive qualities of a woman."

After a brief smile, she finally offered Mitch a cup of coffee that was for the employees who were unfortunate enough to have to be at work early. The lady behind the bar was a very sarcastic and blunt woman; qualities that might not please most men, but to Mitch added to her beauty.

She was only about five feet three inches, but seemed to be very strong willed and was not afraid to fight anybody if necessary. Her simple dirty blond hair made her very pretty, but it was her piercing green eyes that made her even more beautiful, like a porcelain doll that had to be handled with care only to preserve its beauty.

The bartender continued cutting fruit while partly paying attention to Mitch just to see if he had a hidden agenda. Mitch seemed harmless enough to her as a friendly stranger who just happened to pass by her door, but she was very cautious of any man. It was a quality she had developed early on in her life, for she was one who hadn't had very much luck with men from her childhood on to the men she had dated while as a young woman, which she was not anymore.

Mitch started to read the newspaper that was nearby, but he still watched this beautiful woman in front of him. Mitch was one, as he would always say, that admired great beauty in this world even though he might not partake in it. He loved women and thought that they were the greatest gift that God could have ever given the world. Mitch took notice that she did not wear a wedding ring and wondered what kind of woman she was, being in her mid to upper twenties and not being married.

He finally broke the uncomfortable silence

between them and asked, "So are you one of these
women who are married to their work? I see you're not
wearing a wedding ring."

It was an unusual question to ask a stranger,
much like a question that would be found in a bar as
a pickup line, but Mitch was simply curious about
people and loved to find out about them.

The bartender smiled and said, "Why, you're not
going to propose to me are you?"

Mitch laughed. "Oh no, being married once was
good enough for me. No, I'm just curious; I like to find
out about people that I talk to, but if it's too personal
of a question for you then you won't hurt my feelings
by not answering."

The bartender looked at him cautiously, but
answered the question anyway. "No, I have never been
married, but I thought I was close once. So now I
devote pretty much all my time to my work just like a
nineties woman would I guess."

"I would venture a guess that the guy probably
was a real idiot and never realized what he had until it
was too late. He probably took for granted having you
as a girlfriend, which is a common tale for most men
who have lost their lovers."

"You're not too far off," she began, "but I have
to know something. Who are you? This is not the
typical conversation I usually get in the morning."

Mitch laughed and said, "We probably should
introduce ourselves; my name is Mitch Collins."

The bartender gave him a surprised look and
began to realize why he looked so familiar to her. After
a long pause she finally spoke, "Now I know why you
seem so familiar to me. You're Jonathan's grandfather
from Chicago."

"Oh, you know my grandson?"

The bartender asked Mitch, "You don't

remember me do you? Jonathan and I used to date years ago and we spent Thanksgiving together in Chicago with your family about fours ago. You dropped by the house to see everybody on Thanksgiving until they all got mad at you and asked you to leave."

Mitch replied, "Unfortunately, I remember that day, not one of my best. I can't remember every girl that my grandson has ever dated, but I do remember you. For whatever reason you stand out among all the women he has ever dated that I've met, but at my age it is hard to remember names."

"I'm Sherry Melissa Felder, but everyone usually calls me Melissa."

Mitch smiled and said, "Wow, now that's a unique name, but I think that it's a very beautiful name. With a name like that and your looks I can understand why you would stand out among any group of women."

"Now I really remember you," she said. "Jonathan always said that you're charming around women."

"Can I help but be a little excited among the greatest gift God could have put on this earth?"

The two of them spent a long time just talking and catching up on each other's lives. Even though Jonathan had great discontent for his grandfather, Melissa had always liked him as well as all of Jonathan's family. Maybe it was for the fact that she had never had the closeness with her family that Jonathan had with his. She quickly fell under Mitch's spell when it came to people warming up to him.

Despite all his faults he was a man you couldn't help but like and be friends with. He was prince among people of all ages and someone who always told you the truth even if he never searched out the truth in himself. Mitch was always better when he was around people and he had the chance to know other people on a personal level. He had a unique way of bringing out the best in the people around him; the type of person that the world needed more of.

After a while Mitch finally asked Melissa, "So if you don't mind me asking, what happened between you and my grandson? I thought you two were pretty serious with each other."

"To be honest I think it was too much anger on both our parts. With me, I didn't have an easy life with my family so there's always been anger on my part with the idea of a family. I never knew my father and my mother was an alcoholic up until she died. Jonathan had a lot of anger toward what happened with him in his childhood, especially with you. In the beginning when we first met each other bartending together he was great and we had a lot of fun together. He was the first guy who really cared about me as a person and didn't just want to sleep with me. That seems to be the kind of people we meet in this business, and when I first met Jonathan he was a great piano player with a warm soul who was just different than anybody I had met."

She laughed to herself, bringing out a stubborn smile then she continued, "I have not always been an easy person to live with; I put on a tough exterior trying to hide my bitterness towards people who let me down, but my anger and cynicism always comes through that. In the last six months that Jonathan and I were together he became a lot angrier about the things that had happened in our lives. Some of those things were issues with his family like with you, and for me it was my mother dying on me. Through it all we both went through our little depressions. Instead of, as I realize now, trying to comfort and love each other through the rough times in our lives we let our anger get the best of each other."

Melissa turned away from Mitch for a moment, acting like she had to do something behind the bar as a few tears ran down her eyes. Mitch finally spoke up and said, "I think that's the most truthful way of explaining something I have ever heard somebody do. I have to admit I know how much anger Jonathan carries with him and that I am the cause of a lot of it. If it makes any difference, I know for a fact that Jonathan loved you very much during the years you were together and probably still does. You were a good thing for him."

"You don't have to say that just to make me feel better about what happened between us."

"I'm not saying that just to make you feel better, I mean what I say or I don't say it at all."

"Well then thank you for the compliment. I will say this, I do think Jonathan is a good person even if there is still anger between us, and a lot of his good qualities came from you and the rest of his family. Maybe it was not meant to be for me and Jonathan, but we did have some good times together and I am glad that he was a part of my life for a while. No matter what's happened in my life, I try to find the good in life and he was certainly that for me."

The two people in the bar just let the moments pass as if to reconcile all that had been said. Finally, Mitch spoke up to break yet another uncomfortable silence.

"I have a favor to ask since we do know each other and it's kind of a strange one," he said seriously. "I'm taking a trip throughout America and I need a travel companion, so I was wandering if you would join me. The thing is, I just found out the other day that I'm dying of cancer and have an inoperable brain tumor, so I'm going to see some things for the last time and maybe do some things I haven't done before. I would like somebody along with me to do some of the driving and maybe a friend to experience this journey with me."

Melissa looked at Mitch dumbfounded, not believing what she was being asked.

Melissa replied, "You know I have been asked a lot of strange things being a bartender, but I think that this is the strangest thing I have ever been asked...So let me understand this, you want me to take time off of my job and go with you on a trip because you're dying and need a friend to experience some things with?"

Mitch just looked at her with a big grin and replied, "Yes I do and I know it sounds crazy, but sometimes the crazy is the most exciting thing about life. Maybe true happiness is about doing the things that don't make much sense and taking the road less traveled."

After a long pause Melissa finally said, "That's very poetic and I'm very sorry that you're dying. Even though it has been nice to see you again I just can't take off for a few months and go with you on a trip. Its sounds exciting and interesting at the same time, but I really don't think I'm the person to do that with."

"If you're worried about money, then all your expenses would be taken care of and I do mean everything. I have plenty of money and I might as well use it on people who could really get something useful out of it. "

"Why don't you ask Jonathan or one of your kids to go with you? I would think they would get more out of it with you since they're family."

"I would love for Jonathan to take this trip with me, but the truth is he just doesn't want anything to do with me anymore, and my daughters just about feel the same way.   I don't think they will ever forgive me for the things I've done to them, and because of that I know they won't do this with me. Maybe someday I can make amends for all that I have done and be forgiven, but right now I just want to do some last things that I haven't gotten around to yet."

"I tell you what," she began, "you've made me smile and laugh today so I won't be a heartless bitch. I'll think about it and give you an answer tonight. I'll probably be leaving about eight, so come back in before that and get a drink; I'll let you know my answer then."

"Sherry Melissa, I promise that if you choose to take this journey with me, it will be the best one you have ever taken in your life up to this point. It will be filled with more wonder and surprise than any journey you might have ever encountered. This may be crazy, but it's what's crazy that leads to the exciting journeys of life."

With that, he grabbed her hand and softly patted the top while giving her a joyful smile. He then turned around and walked out. Melissa just shook her head and smiled, feeling like she was in a dream as the sunlight slowly faded into the windows over the flower pot of lilies on the big window sill.

Later that night, it was busy at the bar where Melissa worked, more than usual for a Wednesday night. Melissa was finishing up some paper work in the office as the owner of the bar walked in to gather some things. Her name was Stacy and she was a tall thin woman in her forties who preferred running a business instead of raising a family. She liked being on the go, and in her mind making good paying customers happy was always better than pleasing a family. She was truly a modern day woman who did not give in to stereotypes.

Melissa looked up from the desk at Stacy and said, "Stacy, I have something kind of funny to tell you. I had a very strange thing happen today. Jonathan's grandfather Mitch, from Chicago, came in and asked me to go on a trip with him. He found out he was dying and wants to see some things for the last time while sharing it with someone. The thing is none of his own family is very fond of him these days so nobody will go with him, that's why he asked me."

Stacy replied, "Jonathan's grandfather came in, really? Out of all the people that would walk into this joint he did, that's kinda strange." She paused for a moment and with a smile said to Melissa, "I know you probably think it's a strange request, but I had a similar experience happen to me a few years ago. When my grandmother found out she had cancer and since we were very close, we took one last trip to the beach in Florida before she died. It was the most rewarding and memorable time that I had ever had with her and it changed my life in a good way. If he's good friend, someone that you care about, then I think you should consider it because a trip like that is one you will never forget. It could just be a life changing experience for you."

Melissa just sat there and pondered for a few moments without saying a word. Her friend could tell that it was a tough decision for her and also something that she needed to do because of all the things that had happened in her life over the past few years.

"I can't make this kind of decision for you," said Stacy, "but this is what I can do for you. Take off whatever time you need, because Lord knows you could use it, and help this guy out. I don't believe anybody should waste time with people that they care about."

"Thank you, I thought when I told you all this you would think it was crazy."

"Oh, don't get me wrong," said Stacy, "it's probably a little crazy, but that's not always a bad thing. Sometimes I think there's not any logic to dealing with friends and family, but loving someone doesn't always make sense. Here's my advice, take the trip because it will do you good."

At that moment one of the waitresses walked in and told Melissa that there was an older gentleman there to see her. As Melissa was walking out Stacy said one last thing to her, "When you're done with what you have to do, give me a call."

"I haven't even told you what I'm doing yet."

"I know what you'll end up doing. I'm your friend and sometimes I know you better than you know yourself."

With that, Melissa walked out and saw Mitch at the end of the bar. Mitch looked with a smile and said, "Well how has your day been? Good I hope."

"My day hasn't been too bad. Listen, I still think this is a little crazy, but I will go with you because your own family won't do this. I will help you and I could use the time off anyway."

"Well that's good. I didn't know what I was going to do about a travel companion if you said no. I might've had to ask the waitress who was so helpful when I came in tonight."

Melissa laughed and said, "Look at you, you big flirt, I don't know if her boyfriend would like that too much...I can already tell that this is going to be an adventure with you, but I'll try to help you out anyway I can."

"Thank you and I promise I won't be too much trouble. This is where I'm staying; I'll be ready at nine o'clock, so don't be late.

"So where are we going first, anyway?"

Mitch grinned at her and said, "Well we'll figure that out tomorrow. Until then, have a good night."

Mitch got up from the bar and started to walk out. As he got to the entrance of the bar he looked at the waitress who had helped him before; he smiled at her and said, "Karen, you take care and stay out of trouble."

Karen smiled and said, "Mitch you have a wonderful trip and don't be a stranger in here."

Karen walked over to where Melissa was and asked her, "So you've known that guy for a long time, huh?"

"Yes you can say that; I take it he was pretty nice to you?"

"Yeah, most of the old men that come in here just want to grab my butt, but Mitch was pretty nice and he made me laugh. He seems like he's very charming around the ladies."

"Yes he is, but he is also a good man. So after only a few minutes you and him are already on a first name basis?"

Karen replied, "Oh yeah, it's like I've known him for years and he's one of my best friends."

"That's Mitch Collins for you; you can become best friends with him in only a matter of minutes, or in one conversation."

∞∞∞∞∞∞∞∞∞

Mitch arrived back at his hotel to settle in for the evening. As he started to unlock his door he looked up at the clear bright sky. He looked at the stars that seemed to light up the night and go on forever. He just stood there staring at the sky and trying to pick out a few of the constellations that he knew off hand, then he looked at the three-quarter moon shining with brilliance against a dark backdrop looking like a broken down movie screen.

The moon seemed to be staring back at him with the most serious and sorrowful of looks. Mitch could see his memories being played across the moon in all its radiance, and as he stood there he remembered back to the last time he ever saw his brother before he died. It was at an airfield in England in April of 1945. Mitch got to have a nice quiet drink with him and they talked about what they were going to do when they finally got home. He remembered as he was walking his brother to his plane that he embraced him and told him to keep safe, it was a protective charge not uncommon from older siblings before his brother Max was about to leave on a mission.

As Mitch walked back to the Airbase he turned around to see his brother charge down the runway and salute him from one soldier to another and then he was gone against the fading skyline. For Mitch it was a fading memory of eternal youth and innocence, a time long since passed.

Mitch walked back into his room and poured himself a glass of Whiskey from a half-empty bottle that he had only bought the day before. He stared at the glass and the glass stared back with deep brown eyes as if to comfort a grieving widow. Mitch started to cry. He knew deep down what he had never admitted, where the tragedies in his life had really started and had continued for the last forty-seven years. It seemed that he had been grieving ever since then, but then never having the chance to grieve. He finished his drink and finally fell into a long sleep.

∞∞∞∞∞∞∞

People were starting to clear out at The Blue
Nile Club where Jonathan played, and the waitresses
were busy cleaning up to the sound of clanking
glasses. Jonathan started to put his music away and
clean up around the stage when Janet, one of the
waitresses, walked over to him.

"Did everything with your grandfather go okay?"
she asked. "You seem a little withdrawn tonight."

"Yeah, everything went fine," he said.

"So what's going on with him that's made
you distant tonight?"

"He's dying and wants me to take care of him,
but I can't do it anymore. I can't pretend that we have
some great relationship and he didn't hurt me a long
time ago."

As he got up and started to walk past her Janet
replied, "You know, if he is dying, maybe he's just
trying to get back what he lost before it's too late. It's
not uncommon for someone to do that if they know
they're going to die soon."

"What are you talking about?" he asked.

"Maybe he just wants to put things right
with you."

"You know, that's what he said to me, but he
missed that chance a long time ago."

"You're the one who will miss a great
opportunity if you just walk away angry because
you're still going to be alive with only your regret to live
with after he's long gone. I'm only telling you that as a
friend."

She walked away before he had a chance to
reply, so he just sat down and continued to be angry.
It wasn't that he was angry with himself or Mitch, but
just at the way life had turned out with his family, the
people he really did love the most.

Jonathan shook his head and went back to emptying his tip jar and then walked back to the bar to get a drink. Before he could even say anything his boss asked, "So did everything go okay with your grandfather, with him dying and all?"

Jonathan stood there shaking his head and replied, "How did you know about that when I haven't even told you yet?"

"Hey, it's a bar. You can't keep a secret around here. Besides, Janet just told me."

"I love how my personal life remains personal around here," said Jonathan.

"If there's anything you want to talk about, then feel free because there isn't a person here who wouldn't listen to you if you needed to get something off your chest."

"That's okay; I really don't feel like discussing anything with a panel of people around here."

"If you don't want to talk then maybe you could listen, because I have some friendly advice for you. When I look at my family I see this: a wife who I don't think really understands me and has to be liked by everyone she meets. I have a father who is never happy and has never been pleased with me for owning a bar in New Orleans since both of my brothers are doctors. I have a neurotic and very Catholic daughter who is married to a very Jewish man. Then I have a son who has no common sense and can't decide what he really wants to do with his life except spend his money on hookers. For some people, they would look at all that and drink their life away, but I wouldn't know what to do without them, and in a sense that's my reason for living. I love every one of them, and if I would have walked out many years ago like I had the chance, I would have missed out on a lot. That would have been more of a tragedy than anything else that's ever happened to me."

"You're catholic daughter is married to a Jewish man, how's that even possible?"

"Don't ask, because I still can't believe it. At this point I think she must have lost a bet or something, but who knows in this crazy world."

"Well you got that right, but what are you really trying to tell me with this story of yours? You think I should help my grandfather out and go on this trip with him?"

His boss replied with a laugh, "I'm not telling you that you should do anything, I just thought you should hear my funny story just to hear it."

The boss then walked off from where they had been standing. Jonathan started shaking his head and thought to himself that everybody around him had lost their mind, but then he started thinking about something else. He thought to himself about what he really had to lose by going on the trip and about what he'd really do if he received a call one day about Mitch's death. He gathered up his money and his things and told his boss that he would be gone for a while and left his car in the back for safe keeping. Jonathan just walked out with one thought, "what the hell." With that thought in mind he took his leave of the club he had been playing piano at and went home to his place to pack.

The streetlights shined with a radiance that was unlike the French Quarter as Jonathan walked down the street to his place. Like something out of a Capra movie there was something magical in the streets of New Orleans that Jonathan couldn't figure out, but he just smiled and hopped a trolley back to his place.

The sun was finishing its last descent over the skyline as Mitch packed his vintage Caddie. It was a beautiful day and he was going to take advantage of it with the car top down. As soon as he closed his trunk a taxi pulled in front of the motel. Melissa got out of the car with a very surprised look on her face as if she had just woken from a long dream.

Mitch smiled at her and said, "Oh good, you're here early, I would hate to leave you behind, especially with such a beautiful day ahead of us."

"Well I'm here, I still can't believe it, but I am here."

"Good, because you have started something that I hope will be an amazing adventure."

"Yeah, you keep saying that, but I still have my doubts."

"Indeed you should, but you can also trust me little lady."

Mitch winked at her, not an uncommon trait for him, and Melissa gave him a sarcastic grin. After they shook hands, still trying to be polite as possible while under the circumstances, another taxi drove up. Both Melissa and Mitch looked over to the taxi astonished, especially at the person who began to climb out.

Mitch could hardly believe it as Jonathan grabbed his big duffle bag from the trunk.

"I thought you weren't coming because you didn't have the time to stroll down memory lane," said Mitch, as he shot a childish smile toward his grandson. He hadn't smiled like that for a long time.

"I wasn't planning on it till about eight hours ago, but I figured what the hell, there might be something good about this trip after all."

Mitch replied, "I'm glad you feel that way, and just to let you know we will have another travel companion, but if I am correct you two have already met."

Jonathan glanced around to the front of the car

and saw a woman putting a small bag in the front seat. When she looked at him they both got an astonished look on their face, then Jonathan looked at Mitch with a look of shock.

"What is she doing here?" he asked. "Is this some kind joke?"

"You know, you can just look me and ask that question since I'm the one you really want to ask in the first place," said Melissa angrily.

As Jonathan whipped around to say something Mitch intervened. "I invited her to go with me after you said no, but at the time I started to talk with her in her place of business I didn't realize that you two had dated years ago. I wanted a travel companion and she seemed very nice and agreed to go. She's a friend of mine as well, and if you can act like an adult then you shouldn't have a problem with it just because you two at one time were a couple. Besides, I can invite whomever I want to, and if you have a problem then you better chase your taxi down."

Melissa shot a look at Jonathan that said there wasn't anything he could do or say. Jonathan knew her looks all too well and he knew by her looks when to play nice.

"Well," he said, quite defeated, "there isn't anything I can really say to that, so Melissa it's good to see you again. I hope you're doing well."

"If you're coming then you can drive," said Mitch.

Jonathan looked surprised at the offer. "What, you only let me drive your car once and then you said never again after I nearly killed you."

"Hey, I'm dying, so I might just have a little bit of a change of heart. Besides, I'm sure there's much better things to complain about at this point. Anyway, I have a hangover and I'd rather sit in the back and stretch out beneath the gorgeous sun."

Jonathan shook his head. "I can already tell this is going to be a strange trip."

Melissa laughed and said, "Oh, this is going to be an interesting trip with you two, but I'm very curious to see how it's going to turn out."

They all got in the car to leave with Jonathan and Melissa in the front and Mitch riding like a king in the back of his royal blue '51 Cadillac. As the car turned onto the road leading through the center of New Orleans there was a tape in the stereo playing Sinatra softly; it was the song *Fly me to the Moon.*

Mitch just sat back and smiled, for he knew that one of his favorite times in his life would be this moment. He was taking a trip like many times before with his family by his side. They headed west not knowing what they would find, but searching for that one thing that makes the difference in any idealistic soul.

The sun was bright and the clouds conveyed such joyful whispers for the three misguided souls, like the man's footprints within the sand who disappear for a while, but soon are there again. Mitch looked back briefly at the city that is New Orleans for the last time as they passed the city limits, to one of the best places he had always known and one of the worst.

5

Every Journey has a Beginning

The sun was shining bright with a light breeze that lightly whisked through Melissa's hair. As the Cadillac drove down the interstate, all three passengers were in their comfortable silences. Mitch had drifted off to sleep enjoying the fact that for first time in nearly fifty years, he had a driver. He still liked to drive and rarely ever let someone drive for him, but since he was dying he thought he might as well let someone caddie him around.

Jonathan and Melissa had not said a word to each other since they all left New Orleans three hours before, and even though neither of these stubborn souls would admit it to each other, it was beginning to be annoying just having complete silence.

Melissa finally looked over to Jonathan and noticed a look of boredom on his face.

"Okay, I'm finally bored," she said, "let's talk so we can get this being pissed off at each other out at of the way. After all, it's going to be a long trip."

"I don't think we really have all that much to talk about," said Jonathan.

"Look, I don't want to spend this trip fighting with you over our past," said Melissa. "I mean, whatever happened between us is over and we should just go on with our lives, right? So what have you been doing with yourself lately? And before you ask me if I really care about what's been happening in your life, the answer is yes I do."

"How do you know that's what I was going to ask?" Jonathan asked with a funny look on his face.

"Oh come now, don't you think I know you better than you even know yourself by now? So honestly, tell me what you've been doing lately."

"I haven't really been doing anything different than what I've always been doing; just playing piano wherever I can, and I am still a part time bartender at *The Blue's Night Café*. I still love the life and I guess it's too hard to give up. What about you? What have you been doing lately?"

Melissa smiled that smile at Jonathan that always let him know that it made her feel good for him to care about her life, even the most mundane details. It hadn't always been that way in their on and off again relationship. Jonathan was one that could be very withdrawn and not care about anyone around him when he got angry. It must have been a common trait in stubborn Irish Men.

"Oh, my life hasn't been all that exciting since you left," she replied, "but I am still bartending and managing The Cat House. I can't say that I go out and party like we used to. I guess both of us are still doing what we have been doing for years, except it's not with each other."

Jonathan laughed and said, "Yeah, I guess we're still living the same life, but now were beginning to get old and we're trying to hold on to our old ways!

"I wasn't talking about our jobs, I meant we're still hiding behind those shadows in our personal life, but speak for yourself on being old, I'm still as young as I ever was. There's one simple truth that we can't ignore: we're not kids anymore, and we have to grow up."

"Now that's a frightening thought," said Jonathan. "Nope, not me. I refuse, I won't let that happen."

Melissa glanced toward the back seat at Mitch sleeping and then looked at Jonathan with a smile. "Yeah, right, but good luck with that, Jonathan."

Jonathan just smiled at her, saying without words that she was right, that they both still hid behind the shadows of their own destructive soul and he was too much like the old man sleeping in the back seat of the car. They always knew how to flirt with each other very well, even when there was tension between them. Jonathan could be funny in the way he handled his frustrations with Melissa and they always came out in his sharp flirtations with her.

It was a sarcastic and charming quality he had inherited. The relationship between the both of them had always been a complicated one because it was complicated by them. This also seemed to be a common trait among human beings when it comes to relationships and between people. One could only wonder if other species ever went through such trouble trying to love each other. It seemed that you had to be completely crazy to love someone other than yourself with all the torture you could put yourself through loving someone else.

They seem to love and hate each other more than anybody else, but that was always a quality in very stubborn people. Jonathan and Melissa were always trying to get at one another, but at the same time they depended on each other more than two people probably could. It was these things that seemed to make their relationship with each other work, even though they acted like they were not together anymore and had to get away from each other for a while. Sometimes couples are never really broken up or separated; they just take a break from each other.

After a long silence Melissa finally asked Jonathan, "So what made you change your mind and go on this trip with your grandfather?"

Melissa always referred to Mitch as "your grandfather" when speaking to Jonathan even though Jonathan called Mitch by his name instead of grandpa or even grandfather. It was her little way of still recognizing the fact that both men were still family even though they might not think of each other like that anymore. It was her way of trying to show Jonathan could not change the fact that Mitch was still his grandfather and he might still love him despite all that had happened in the past.

Jonathan replied, "I knew you would eventually ask me that, and to be honest I don't know if I have the answer to that. I figured what the hell, I really didn't have anything to lose by going on this trip with him and I just wanted to see if he really was dying instead of trying some stupid scheme just to get me or anyone in my family back into his life again."

Melissa looked at him in disappointment. "No, that's not the real reason and you know it," she said. "You're too damn scared to admit what you know to be true."

Jonathan was visibly angry. "What the hell are you talking about? If that isn't the reason, then what is it, since you seem to know?"

"No, I'm not going to give you that; if you can't figure out the truth behind your own feelings then I sure as hell am not going to do it for you."

Jonathan just started shaking his head and went back to watching the road and ignoring Melissa. It was something that was never uncommon for him when he got mad.

After a few minutes of complete silence and the both of them ignoring each other, Jonathan finally asked her, "So what made you come on this trip with an old man you hardly know?"

Melissa looked surprised. "It was because I felt sorry that the one person he had originally counted on who wouldn't do it."

Jonathan started to say something mean, but she cut him off.

"I'm also doing this because he made me laugh and it's been awhile since any man could do that. It's true I was really laughing at the proposition he made to me, but nonetheless he still made me laugh and that's all I need right now. Besides, I could also use a bit of adventure in my life."

Jonathan shook his head, obviously angry and disappointed with her.

"You too, huh? I guess you're just another lonely soul he put underneath his spell."

Melissa looked shocked. "See, you've never understood me and what I really need in my life. Maybe it's some kind of Irish thing, maybe all Irish men are like this."

Before Jonathan could reply, Mitch spoke up, "Hey, speak for him and not all Irish men. I don't want to be lumped in the same group with him. And just so you know, I was having a pretty good nap until I heard you two fighting."

"You heard all that?" asked Melissa.

"Of course I did. I may be dying, but I'm not deaf. Besides, I'm surprised the whole countryside didn't tell you to be quiet."

"So you want to tell me exactly where we're going, or will we just keep driving until we see the ocean?" said Jonathan.

"Were heading to Paris, Texas so I can see an old friend, and you can see someone I know you haven't seen in a long time," said Mitch. Jonathan looked surprised and said, "Wow, I haven't been out to that farm in over fifteen years."

Melissa looked clueless. "What's in Paris Texas?" she asked.

"A very dear friend and one of the most beautiful places upon God's green earth," said Mitch.

The day was beginning to end as the sun slowly faded beneath the skyline. The old car pulled onto a country road that seemed to lead nowhere, but it was the picturesque sunset fading over the rolling Texas hills that made everybody in the car forget about where they were. Mitch was driving and humming softly to himself while taking in the familiar place he was in because he knew there was a good chance that he would not see it again. It was one of his favorite places to visit because he could escape into a place within himself that he never visited enough.

Melissa finally spoke up after a long silence had captured the passengers and asked, "So where is this place and who is it that we are about to see?"

"We're heading to a farm just down this road a ways and we're going to see an old family friend. I've known him since the war and we have watched each other's kids grow up. His name is Thomas and this farm we're about to visit is one of the most beautiful places you will ever see. I haven't seen him or his wife

Rebel in about a year.

Melissa looked at him and said, "I guess he hasn't heard the news yet so you figured you would start your journey by telling your oldest and dearest friend."

Mitch gave her a half smile and replied, "Something like that."

Jonathan was taking his turn sleeping in the back seat and Mitch looked back at him while continuing to talk.

He said to Melissa, "It's a pretty interesting story how Thomas got this farm. He's a Texas native and worked for Kraft Foods for forty years. The State of Texas had this deal for Texas Veterans where you could get hundreds of acres of land by just paying something like fifty dollars a month. Now this was in the fifties, so there was a lot of farm land to be given away. Anyway, he did this for a lot of years and when he was close to retirement he built a farm house on his land and became a rancher."

Mitch took a moment and laughed to himself about how everybody used to say Thomas was crazy for buying a bunch of useless land then he ended up proving everybody wrong by building a beautiful spread and successful ranch. His friend got the last laugh and even Mitch was one of those people that had to admit he was wrong.

Mitch continued his story, "It took a lot of years, but he built this land up and made a beautiful place out of it, and I believe that even though he doesn't ranch anymore he still rents out the land. Alice and Rebel have been best friends since before the war, and it was her and I that introduced Rebel to Thomas, so we have been for the most part family to one another. Rebel and Alice still talk to each other at least once a week. They're the best friends I've ever had, and part of the reason I'm starting here on this journey is because I want to tell them about me in person and see them again. I haven't seen them in a long time and it's about time that I do because I may not see them again. Anyway, it's a beautiful place to visit so it's a good place to start a vacation, so to speak."

Melissa didn't say anything and just looked at Mitch with a somber look, for there was nothing to say. They both knew that just talking was only a way to try and hide the sorrow of the situation, but in the end they were not that successful because no matter what, nobody in the car could get past the fact that Mitch was dying and this would be his last trip to Paris, Texas. The two passengers in the front seat sat in silence, staring out at the cold black night trying to forget the seriousness of the trip, but they did so with no avail.

Finally, the car pulled up into the driveway of the farmhouse. The farmhouse was simple; it was rustic and made of earthly things adding to the simplicity of the old farmhouse. It was the perfect place for two people who didn't care about having luxuries; it was perfect for those who only wanted the simple life where you would not be consumed by what was unimportant in life. Mitch drove the car up to the front porch of the house which connected the long and winding driveway. He honked the horn which had a very distinctive sound; the sound of something from a long time ago.

The outside lights came on and two older looking people came walking out of the house. The old woman, full of energy, shouted with excitement,

"Well I'll be, after a year he finally decided to show his face around here again. Come here and give me a hug you old man."

"I figured a year was long enough keep a pretty gal of mine waiting," said Mitch. "I thought you might need to see me again."

The old woman known as Rebel responded, "You could at least write or call once in a while."

As he hugged her, Mitch replied, "Hey, you know I like to be full of surprises."

The old man known as Thomas looked at Mitch sarcastically and said "Old timer, you better not be messing around with my wife, I couldn't offer a drink to someone who did that."

"Hey, I'm too goddamn old to be denied a good drink, so how about we just call it even and get a drink anyway."

Thomas replied, "Now you're talking, but if you're buying then I guess we can just forget that it's been awhile since you've written or called."

Jonathan and Melissa got out of the car and laughed with each other over the satirical greetings by the old friends. Rebel finally spoke up after Mitch and Thomas were done shaking hands and laughing with one another.

"Okay Mitch, what's with the surprise visit after it's been so long since we've heard you, and what's with the two strangers?"

"What can I say? It's been far too long since I've been down this way to see you guys and I thought I would surprise you. As for the two strangers, I know you don't recognize him anymore, but this is Jonathan, all grown up and this woman is a friend of ours; her name is Sherri Melissa."

Rebel looked at the both of them with surprise and joy then walked up to give Jonathan a hug. As she hugged him she said, "My God young man you have grown into a good looking man and it's been far too long since you've been here. "

"Hello, Rebel. It has been too long," said Jonathan.

"Yes sir it has and you shouldn't take so long to come back and see me."

Rebel walked over to Melissa and looked her up and down. She looked at her as trying to figure out why two men she had known for the longest time would want somebody like her along with them on whatever journey they were on. Finally she smiled as she realized there was a stubbornness and grace about her that could help make better men of them.

It was a maternal instinct, a bond between two feisty women, or perhaps it was both that allowed Rebel to see this in Melissa. Finally, Rebel smiled and hugged Melissa as if they had been oldest friends.

"I can see why they like you and why they would want you along for this trip. I would guess that you and Jonathan were in a relationship once."

"You can tell all that by just looking at me?" Melissa asked.

"Oh Yes, its woman's intuition, and I already can feel a connection with you. Besides, I can tell that you and Jonathan once had a thing by the way he still looks at you"

Melissa shot a surprised look at Rebel and then Jonathan intervened as he was starting to get agitated before anybody could say anything.

"Okay Rebel," he began, "my love life is not the issue, nor do we need to put any ideas in people's heads."

"Jonathan, don't get rattled, I have no interest in pursuing anything with you again," Melissa replied.

"That's not what I meant, but it's good to know for future reference," Jonathan shot back.

Mitch finally spoke up as Thomas and Rebel

were laughing at Jonathan's insecurity. "Can you two quit flirting with one another, it's too hot out here and I am seriously in need of a drink. I think it's time we go inside. If you two want to continue this little farce, then be my guest."

Jonathan started to say something, but Melissa just pressed her finger against his lips to shut him up. Everyone else just laughed as Jonathan was left there sort of dumbfounded by what happened and then everybody went inside the house.

It wasn't long after the three visitors were settled in and they could begin to rest from a long day's journey. Jonathan took a long hot shower, finally finding something refreshing after a strange trip down memory lane while Rebel and Melissa talked. Rebel wanted to know all about her and how she came to be in the company of two men she loved very much, but she really wanted to know what it was about her that made Jonathan love her even though he would not admit it.

The two talked one another as if they were old friends catching up after being away from each other for many years. Mitch and Thomas retired to the study so they could drink a very good glass of brandy and talk as if they were young men again, a time that sometimes became a little too truthful after a few drinks.

Thomas handed Mitch a glass of good bourbon and asked him, "Okay Mitch, what are you really doing here, not that I mind seeing my best friend, but you wouldn't just show up here out of the blue if it wasn't serious."

"I think you're being a little presumptuous. Maybe I just wanted to see you since I haven't been here in about a year; did you ever think of that?"

"I doubt that's the reason since you have

Jonathan with you. You two haven't spoken to each other in a long time and I don't think it's him trying to patch up your relationship. Something's going on with you or you wouldn't be traveling with him and some girl, so what is it."

"Okay, you're half right," said Mitch. "I am trying to make the effort with Jonathan and I have good reason to. The truth is that I found out about a week ago that I have cancer and an inoperable tumor on the tip of my spine and the base of my brain. There's no way I can escape dying this time, one or the other is going to kill me."

Thomas stared at Mitch with concern and surprise for a few moments before responding. "Can you do any kind of treatment to stop it or help you in any way?"

"No, not anything that would help prolong the pain in my life, and that's why I'm not going to do anything. I just want to live out what I have left of my life."

"How long do you have?"

"About six months to a year, if I'm lucky."

"Do Jonathan and that girl you're with know?" asked Thomas with sadness in his voice.

"Yes they do, and I really couldn't hide it from them anyway. They would find out eventually while I was hunched over in pain sitting in the car."

"Yeah, you're right, but more importantly does Alice know yet?"

"No she doesn't, nor does Laura or Catherine, but I will tell them in due time so I would appreciate if you or Rebel didn't make any phone calls on my behalf."

"I won't, but you're going to have to tell them soon because there's no way I can keep Rebel from saying anything for very long."

"Well I'm going to have to tell all them soon because once Laura finds out what he's doing with me on this trip she'll know something's wrong with me or Jonathan wouldn't have made the effort. "

Thomas took another sip of his whiskey and gave Mitch a peculiar look. Then he finally asked him, "How did you get Jonathan to go on this trip with you? I thought he still hated you after all these years."

"Oh, he still does to a good extent and never lets me forget it, but I think it was his curiosity of what could really happen on this trip that made him come."

"Maybe he's finally grown up enough to realize that this trip is truly his last go-around with his grandfather. You know, whether you want to believe it or not he still loves you and he still needs you," said Thomas.

"I know that, but like a good father figure I still have to let him figure that out on his own, or at least let him get to the point to where he can admit it."

"So what's the story with the girl, how did she get involved with all this?"

Mitch laughed a bit to himself and replied, "As it turns out she and Jonathan used to be in a pretty serious relationship years back. I just happened to wander in the bar she works at one day in New Orleans. While I was there I convinced her to come along with me on this trip before I knew Jonathan was going to come along. I needed a travel companion and she needed a vacation so it worked out, but then Jonathan decided to come, too. Now they just seem to be at each other's throat, but they're slowly working it out in their own way."

Thomas gave Mitch a funny smile. "You just happened to wonder into her bar and get Jonathan's ex-girlfriend to come along, huh? You've got something up your sleeve don't you?"

"Honestly, I didn't have any intentions of secretly throwing them together, I just met her by accident and my charm worked on her so here she is with us."

"We both know what happens when you start pouring on the charm," said Thomas. "Interesting things tend to happen and people's lives change forever."

Mitch laughed and said "Sure, people's lives may change, but it's usually for the best."

"Hey, if you want to keep living under that delusion while you live out your final days then go right ahead," began Thomas, "but I'm not going to lie for you when everybody finds out you're not that charming."

Both men smiled at each other, took another sip of bourbon and laughed out loud. Their laughter was the laughter of schoolyard friends doing anything they could to fight away their boredom, but at the same time strengthening the ties of lifelong friends.

After Jonathan got done with his shower and got dressed, he walked down the long hallway of the farmhouse and noticed many pictures hanging on the wall. It was like a museum; pictures marking the timeline of family history. Melissa and Rebel were in the big living room talking and looking at old pictures; Rebel was trying to get to know all she could about her in the short time they were spending together.

She wanted to know why a person like her would be allowed to take a trip with these men, but the more she talked to her the more she realized that she was right, there was something about her. There was something inside of her that could bring out the best in these two lost souls she has known for so many years.

Jonathan was caught in memory lane while

looking at the pictures on the wall. Some were very familiar to him because his grandparents had some of the same pictures. He also noticed all the familiar faces of the people in those pictures, Thomas and Rebel's grandchildren who he had played with in his youth while spending part of his summer vacation on this farm. There were also many pictures of Thomas, Rebel, Mitch, Laura, Catherine, and Alice, when they were all young and the whole world was right before their eyes. For the first time since this trip had started Jonathan was enjoying remembering the past.

As he was still looking at every feature of the people inside those pictures, Rebel and Melissa came to find him, as well as the other two men, to let them know that dinner was ready.

"Well come on young man, its time you get some food in you. Round up the other two troublemakers, I can't let anyone in this house go hungry," Rebel said to Jonathan.

"Young man? I think I've been past that for a long time."

"Probably, but you will always be a young man to someone my age, and I wouldn't argue or you might just find yourself without dinner,"

Jonathan just smiled at her while she wandered into the kitchen. Melissa gave Jonathan a weird smile and said, "So I hear you would get caught skinny dipping quite a bit around here when you were a kid."

"Oh Lord, the stories are going to come out tonight, I can already see that. By the way, no matter what gets said by the three senior citizens tonight, I'm not as bad as they like to make it out to be."

"I already know how bad you are, remember. We dated for a while. I just think it's funny that the problem of keeping your clothes on started when you were a kid. I thought it was just around me, so I don't know if I should be insulted or just laugh at your nakedness," Melissa said as she walked into the kitchen.

Jonathan just stared with confusion at her comment and then he heard the laughter of Mitch and Thomas from all the stories they had been telling. It was that moment that Jonathan finally understood why they started this journey on a farm in Paris, Texas. It was so that they could all be familiar with what family means, because it would the most important part to this trip.

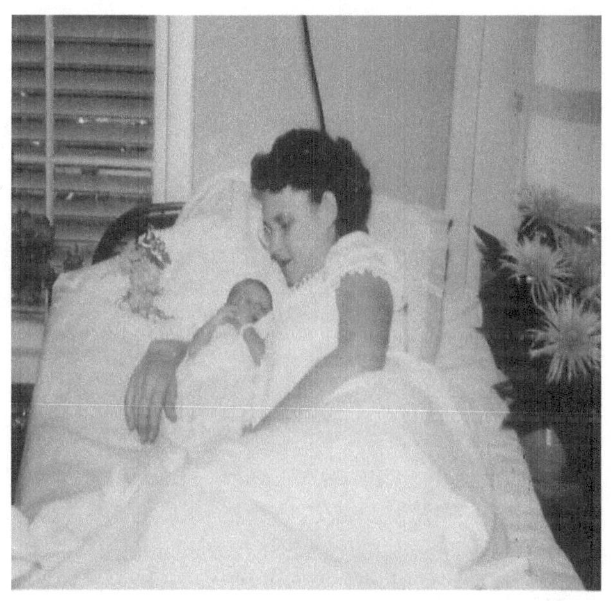

6

Taking the Long Road

The next morning Mitch, Jonathan, and Melissa were treated to a typical farm breakfast; hearty and big enough so one could never go hungry. It had been awhile since any of them had eaten that good or slept in really comfortable bed. The hospitality of Thomas and Rebel was just one more reminder of what home feels like, of what family should be.

They all sat around and let the time pass away in the early morning without notice, laughing and enjoying each other's company before it was time for the travelers to go. Mitch and his companions left about mid-morning after a good night's rest. As they finished loading up the car everyone stood on the big front porch of the farm house saying their goodbyes and then Rebel hugged Mitch long and hard.

It was a solemn moment and Rebel began to cry as she continued hugging Mitch.

"So Thomas told you last night," said Mitch.

She talked and cried at the same time, "Yes and I don't know what to say about this."

"You don't have to say anything," said Mitch. "I'm dying and there's nothing that anyone can do about it. The difference between us now is that I know that I'm going to die soon and you and Thomas can't honestly say that."

She let go of him and replied, "I know you're right, but I'm not ready to think about a world without one of my most beloved friends in it." The five people standing on the front porch didn't say anything to one another for a few moments.

Thomas finally spoke up and said, "Well come on, let's not linger around acting like he's already dead. Mitch, we've got to get you on your way so you can take care of the things you need to take care of before it's too late. "

Mitch smiled at his friend and shook his hand. They were men of hard lives and experience, the kind of experience that tells you the truth. It was the plain simple truth that there is nothing we can do about a death that is soon to come. Both of them could be honest about such things and that's why they could laugh about it.

Mitch replied to Thomas, "Don't have too much fun without me...I'll see you soon."

"Well you're going to have to; a long time doesn't seem to be in the cards for you."

Mitch laughed and replied, "Unfortunately you're right, so I guess I'll have to make a point of seeing you soon."

The two men shook hands again and everybody hugged one another again before the three travelers were driving the long and winding drive away from the farmhouse. Jonathan didn't understand the morbid playful banter between the two older men, but it was not something a young man in the prime of life could understand, only those coming to the winter of their life could understand this.

As the car drove away Thomas and Rebel drifted

away out of sight and the three travelers were once again left to the excitement of the open road and a final journey being made. Jonathan didn't know quite what to make of all this yet and the understanding that the two men had of one another so he just sat quietly.

Melissa finally spoke up and asked, "So where are we going now, any place exciting?"

"We're going to Oklahoma, to a town that doesn't really exist anymore," said Mitch.

Jonathan raised his eyes at the response and then asked, "Are we going to Eagle City?"

"Yes we are," said Mitch. "I always make a point to stop there on my way through Oklahoma and then make a stop in Canton to see your grandmother's sister Mary Ann. "

"What's in this town that we're going to visit?" asked Melissa. "I thought you said that it doesn't really exist anymore."

"Well, it doesn't really exist, but there is still a graveyard there and that's where we're going."

Jonathan began shaking his head as if he understood why Mitch would want to visit this place and didn't approve of it, but the truth was he didn't really know why. His anger at Mitch over the years had clouded his understanding of all the stories he had been told of his family so much so that the only thing he could see was the discontented version of the truth he wanted to see.

"So why are we going to a graveyard?" Melissa asked.

"I need to visit the gravesite of Alice's father, Lee. I have been doing this for a long time. It's my way of paying my respects to a man I loved and hated equally."

Melissa looked confused at his response and

vague answers, but didn't say anything. After a moment of quiet to the low rhythmic sounds of the Goodyear tires on the soft country road Jonathan finally had to ask a question. "I thought you quit visiting this gravesite when you and Alice split up? I mean, I don't get it. You never liked Lee Abshire, so why keep visiting his gravesite?"

"There are a lot of things you don't understand and so you know just because me and that old man didn't always get a long doesn't mean I hated him," said Mitch, sounding rather grandfatherly. "He was a miserable son of a bitch, but he was still a good man, one worthy of respect."

"You said he never liked you and there wasn't a day when you two weren't around each other that you didn't fight about something," said Jonathan.

Melissa and Mitch both kind of chuckled and then Mitch said, "That's true, but we had respect for one another and no matter how much we might have fought, we never crossed the line of disrespect. He was a hard man, but he was a true man. He worked hard to achieve what he did and knew how to respect someone without having to like them."

"Well I don't think that makes sense, but maybe there is something to that. After all, he did help you get a great deal on this car. That was him wasn't it?"

"You're correct, he helped me and your grandmother get a great deal on this car and its one of those reasons why I have kept it all these years."

Melissa looked at the two men in the car with curiosity and asked, "So are you guys going to tell me the story of this car?"

"I guess if you're going to ride in it with us across the country then you should know the story, "Mitch replied.

"Melissa, just keep this in mind," Jonathan

began, "no matter how much he doesn't want to admit it, my great grandfather never liked him, so that's why it's kind of a big deal when it comes to him helping my grandparents get this car."

"Jonathan's right for once. I'm probably sugar coating it too much. Lee hated me and I think his one decent act towards me was helping me and Alice get this car. This is probably why it's so special and why I still hang on to her," Mitch replied

"You mean there are actually people that don't like you?" Melissa asked jokingly. "I would have thought you would have me believe that you're the most likeable person on this planet. Now can you please tell me this story?"

Mitch laughed to himself and then started his story. "Like I said, Lee never really liked me and I'm still not quite sure why he gave his blessing for me to marry Alice. Sometimes I think it was for the fact that Alice would never speak to him again if he said no, and he loved her so much that bitter old man would've just dropped down dead if his little girl never spoke to him again, but he probably took pleasure knowing that if I screwed up in any way he would be justified in killing me and burying me somewhere on the farm just like he did with that one man that tried to harm his family when Alice was growing up."

Both Melissa and Jonathan gave a look of shock as Mitch finished his sentence. Not even Jonathan had heard this story before, but there were a great number of things he didn't know about his family that he was beginning to find. The one thing Mitch had always been was a storyteller, not in the written word, but more in an oral tradition as true Irishmen were prone to be, especially with a few drinks in them. Mitch could tell great stories, funny stories, and almost all of them had a piece of morality attached to them; it was this kind of quality that people liked most about Mitch because they could learn something from him and he could always find someone to teach.

"I told you Lee was a hard man, and I'll tell you why some other time."

"I've never even heard of this before and I definitely would have remembered it if I did," said Jonathan.

"I've told you about him before, but it was probably when you were a teenager and in your phase of hating me. When you get that way you tend to not listen and let your anger get the best of you," said Mitch.

Melissa smiled knowingly because she knew Mitch was right and she had experience with it as well when it came to Jonathan. He, on the other hand, just smirked as if he had just been scolded, but he, too, knew that Mitch was right.

Mitch continued his story, "Anyway, Alice and I had only been married for about five or six years, and with two children money was a little tight. I was in the habit of drinking and gambling my paychecks away so there wouldn't be much money to go around. One summer Alice was down in Oklahoma seeing her parents and I was supposed to meet her there when I was done with my business trip. I was so drunk most of that particular trip and lost the car playing poker to some hot shot Army General and didn't even have the money to get to Oklahoma so I had to hitchhike to the Abshire farm."

Mitch started shaking his head and letting out a little bit of laughter because he still couldn't believe that he did it. After a moment of silence he continued his story.

"I had to tell her at her father's place, and I was certain that he would kill me in the middle of the night and bury me on the farm then just tell Alice that I ran off for good. Needless to say, Alice was furious over the matter and I nearly got a divorce right then and there, but as mad as she was she really wanted to find a solution to our problem. She just wanted us to get another car and get home with a little money in our pocket. Lee didn't do anything that I expected and to his credit he helped me out for the good of his daughter and his grandchildren. A friend of his owned a car dealership and there was a fellow from around the area that had to get rid of his 1955 Cadillac convertible so he sold it to the dealership. It was in great condition and somehow Lee was able to work out this great deal on it so that it wouldn't be a lot of money for the both us. I honestly believe that this guy owed Lee a favor so that is why he was able to get such a great deal, which doesn't surprise me because Lee was always helping people out of jams so people owed him a lot."

For a moment there, Mitch drifted back into his memory, remembering that day very clearly when he showed up to the farm and had to tell his wife and her father that he lost the car in a poker game. He was still a little drunk when he got there and Lee wanted to kill him at that moment, but as mad as Alice was she wouldn't allow it. She just told Mitch to fix it or she would leave him and take his family with him.

After a few minutes of silence had gone by Jonathan asked, "So what happened after that?"

"It was Lee's deal that allowed him not to have to put a down payment on the car and drive it right off the lot. His credit was a firm handshake and his word. Anyway, I got this car and was made to promise not to ever bet my car or my paycheck in a poker game ever again. Over the next few years I bought the car from Lee who bought it from the dealership, and he even gave me a little money to get back home. There have been a lot of promises I've broken, but I never broke the one I made to Lee. What he did was the one true descent thing he could do for me, so that is why I have never gotten rid of the car because I'm still reminded of how I was saved by the least likely person. It's also why I have true respect for him and why I never miss an opportunity to pay my respects when I pass through Oklahoma. The other thing is," he said as he chuckled to himself, "I think he did this for me so his little girl didn't look like she was married to a complete bum and maybe his grandchildren wouldn't be so ashamed of their father when they were riding in a Cadillac. That man had a weird sense of humor; he also had a strange sense of irony."

Jonathan looked as if he'd been caught by surprise by the story. "I thought you said Lee never talked to you after you and my grandmother got married?"

"Well, he didn't and he didn't say much to me when he gave me the Cadillac. He just handed me the keys and the only words out of mouth were 'this is your last chance'."

Melissa asked Mitch, "So you're saying you two never had any conversations from the time you got married to the day that he died."

"A few words were spoken from that man to me," said Mitch, "but he was the type of man who could say everything with his eyes. Perhaps that's the way hard men are when they're from Oklahoma."

Jonathan stared at him with complete surprise. "I can't believe this is the first time I'm hearing the truth about you and Lee. I feel like I really don't know you at all or know my family for that matter."

"Perhaps you will take a chance to get to know your family on this trip," said Mitch. "Maybe now that you're older you'll actually listen instead of being mad at me." Mitch winked at Jonathan like he had done when he was a kid. Jonathan smiled at him then, just as he had done all those years ago. Mitch took it as a sign that there was hope for them after all, no matter how slight it was.

For the next few hours there was silence in car, the three passengers just sat listening to Frank Sinatra's greatest hits. It was the perfect soundtrack to a life lived of sorrow, of joy, of heartache, and for being able to remember when times were good.

∞∞∞∞∞∞

In the early afternoon the passengers arrived in Canton, Oklahoma. Jonathan had once been here when he was little, but he was too young to remember so the town was as new to him as it was to Melissa. It was like being somewhere for the very first time. It was a place filled with an eerie sense of anticipation of when life's greatest secrets were about to be told.

The first place they went to was Alice's sister's place. Jonathan's grandmother Alice still had one surviving sister living in Canton, Oklahoma. Her name was Mary Ann and she had never left this part of Oklahoma. The only time she had been away from Oklahoma was when she was serving as a nurse just like her sister during World War II in Europe.

Since the city of Eagle City didn't really exist anymore and the closest town to where it had once been was Canton, that's where she lived. When the town of Eagle City ceased to exist in the late 60's, what used to be the town folded into a suburb of Canton so that is where Mary Ann resided to this day.

Mary Ann was a short and feisty woman despite her deep stubbornness. She was an Oklahoma girl

91

raised on a farm, raised by a hard man so she knew how to fight her way through life. She knew that the only way to truly be successful in life was to work hard every day and fight to earn what was your right to have. She was almost the complete opposite of her sister Alice, where Alice was the sweet and innocent one Mary Ann was the hard to handle one.

Mitch always kept in contact with her because they had always liked each other and had a deep respect for one another. They pulled up to a quaint corner street house on a street that intersected the border between where Canton is today and were Eagle City used to be. The house that Mary Ann lived in was not too far from the farm that she and Alice had grown-up on.

As the travelers walked to the front door they were greeted by a short stocky lady known as Aunt Mary Ann. She was excited, but surprised to see Mitch and didn't even recognize at first the young man that stood beside him. After giving them a big smile and a big hug she finally said, "My God, Mitch, you sure do take your sweet time in coming back to see me."

"But at least I didn't forget about you as I was passing through Oklahoma, so you see, you're missing the whole point of me being here," said Mitch.

"And what's that?" she asked.

"That I'm here seeing you even after being married to your sister for many years."

"You've really got to stop flirting with me."

"Well, you're single and beautiful, why not?"

"You always were a charmer", she said as she looked at Melissa. "Honey, don't ever get mixed up with men like this. They will just leave your heart broken and feeling good about yourself all the same time, which is never a good thing."

Melissa smiled at her and decided to introduce herself before the two men she was traveling with had a chance to make up something about her so Mary Ann would not think she was his hitchhiking across Oklahoma. "I'm Melissa by the way, and I'm just a friend of these two men before they say something leading you to believe I'm some untrustworthy stranger."

"Well, with words like that you must already know how charmers like this can get people into trouble," Mary Ann replied.

"Oh, I've already had a few moments with these two and unfortunately I've had the pleasure of dating the younger one."

Mary Ann just smiled at the girl who she already liked and then she finally realized who the younger gentleman was.

"Well Jonathan, you are all grown-up and it sounds like you've developed some of your grandfather's bad habits when it comes to wooing women."

"Mere rumors Aunt Mary Ann, and I would like to think I inherited the good habits instead of the bad ones," he said, and then he smiled the sarcastic smile that he inherited from his grandfather while everybody laughed out loud.

Mary Ann let everybody into the house and then went into the kitchen to prepare coffee. Mitch followed her into the kitchen because he wanted to go ahead and tell her why he was passing through and to tell her the bad news. A few minutes later Mary Ann brought coffee out and she had a sad look upon her face. She told everybody to help themselves, and then she and Mitch went into the dining room to talk a little more in private.

Melissa and Jonathan drank their coffee and

walked around the house looking at all the pictures on the walls and the antiques Mary Ann had collected over the years. Jonathan was surprised to see some of the pictures that were still hanging in her house. He thought that with all the grief that he gave his grandmother Alice's sister wouldn't want any pictures of Mitch in her house, but they were pictures of good times. They were times when the family was closer and it was becoming clearer that Mary Ann just didn't want to let go of those good times, that's why she chose remember.

Now her husband had been dead for about 20 years, so it was just her living alone in this house staying as active as she could and becoming the neighborhood's surrogate grandmother. Most people that had lived in Canton or in Eagle City had known of her family history in Oklahoma. One of those was she and Alice's grandparents running in the Oklahoma land race and claiming land that would be the Abshire farm that they grew up on.

This was a piece of family history that Jonathan never knew, but he was learning as he stared at a picture of distant relatives just moments before the gun was shot to start the land race.

Melissa walked over to where Jonathan was and looked over her shoulder at the picture he was holding and asked, "What are you looking at?"

"This is a picture of my great great-grandparents on the Abshire side. The family with this huge group of people in the background and it appears to be the land race in Oklahoma; the bottom of the pictures are dated 1893," he replied

"What does that mean?" Melissa asked.

"Apparently my family ties to Oklahoma go back to when the land race happened and it's how my grandmother's family came to be in Oklahoma.

I guess my family helped settle Oklahoma,"
Jonathan replied

"You never knew that?" she asked. "You didn't
know much about your grandmother's side of the
family."

"I know very little about this side of the family.
When I was growing up, I was never told too much
about my grandmother's side of the family, and the
only thing I know about my grandmother's side of the
family is what Mitch would say in his drunken rants.
Mitch would stay drunk most of the time in those
days, and the only conversation that I'd really hear
from him regarding family history was bits and pieces
that were skipped over. My mother told me some
things, but everybody didn't really know what to
believe from my grandparents. He stayed drunk and
she would complain about him constantly so we all got
a shaded view of the truth."

"Looks like there's a lot of family history within
these photos on the wall. Perhaps you should take the
time to ask your Aunt Mary Ann and Mitch about
some of the things that you don't know. I think family
should take the time to pass down their history no
matter how good or bad it really is. I wish I could have
had that with my mother instead of the drunken
version she always displayed."

"Perhaps you're right," he replied.

Melissa and Jonathan walked around the rooms
looking at all the photos trying to get a sense of
nostalgia that was within those walls. It was a long
time before Mary Ann and Mitch came into the dining
room. When they did, she had tears in her eyes, but
she still had her great smile that was always full of life.

Jonathan asked her about the land race and
how the Abshire's came to be in Oklahoma, so over
coffee she sat and told the tale of how her family was

one of the founding members of that state.

Basically what happened was Mary Ann and Alice's grandfather Joseph Abshire and his wife Catherine were farmers from Kansas when a serious drought had plagued the Midwest in the 1890s. They, like many farmers all over the country, decided to take advantage of free land being offered in Oklahoma. Joseph and his eight sons and three daughters, along with his wife, piled into covered wagons with all their belongings and migrated nearly 100 miles to the border of Oklahoma to claim their land.

His eldest son was Lee, and at the time of the land race he was at the tender age of 21. Lee would become what was known as a Sooner, men who in the middle of the night snuck across the border illegally to put down their flag and claim their land before the race would begin.

Two days before the land race began; Lee made it across and traveled halfway through Oklahoma, finding a huge meadow of flatlands overlooking a steep ravine with a wild river passing through it. He knew that this would be the place they would stake their claim and where they would build the family farm, and that paradise would finally come to their family. It was in this area of Oklahoma that became Eagle City, and later on it would become Canton.

Canton actually began as a town with two general stores a few miles away from Eagle City and it was the town that serviced all the neighboring farms. With the growth of commerce in Canton, the town grew bigger over the next 40 years. As the farms died after World War II, Eagle City slowly disappeared. It has only been in the last 30 years that Canton stretched out beyond its former city limits and took over the old town of Eagle City.

Mitch sat quietly in deep reflection sipping his

coffee and listening to the story that he had heard a thousand times before, while Jonathan sat with a curious look listening to a story that he never knew. Melissa was just fascinated to hear the story for the first time. Jonathan listened to the story, but also wondered why men who were so much alike didn't really know each other. The three of them only stayed for another half-hour before they took their leave.

Mary Ann hugged both of the men like it was her last day on earth. She didn't want to let go because she knew that it would probably be the last time she saw Mitch before he passed on and she was already missing her friend.

The three of them headed to the graveyard, and wasn't easy to find because it was a place that time had long since forgotten, a place that was like an abandoned forest where all the life had disappeared years before. Although with this place it was very true and it was the graveyard that allowed for the only existence of this old farm town in Oklahoma.

They found this gated area with weathered stone and smooth cut marbled slabs sticking above the ground surrounded by weeds and wildflowers.

Melissa and Jonathan wondered if Mitch actually remembered where the grave was, and like a seasoned pro, Mitch found a flat bottomed slab marking the plots of Abshire. Along the way to the graveyard, they'd stopped to buy some flowers for to Mitch lay down on the plots as a sign of respect. Mitch didn't say anything for quite a long time, and the other journeymen could tell that he was in reflection. Finally, he spoke.

"You know, as hard of a man as he was and as much as I knew he didn't like me, he was still one of the best men I ever knew. Lee Abshire knew who he was and didn't apologize for it.

He did the best he knew how in taking care of his family and to protect them from the dangers in this world. Really, that's all you can ask of anybody, especially of a family man."

"It occurs to me," Melissa said after a long silence, "that with all the stories you have told us about how he didn't like you, he did, however, have enough respect for you, and that's all you can ask out of the father of the woman that you married."

"You're right, and the Cadillac is proof of that. I learned something over the years, and it's one of the things I've tried to teach Jonathan. It's the small things that count because it's what we really need the most. I believe it was the small things that he did for me and that's why I pay my respect."

The three of them stood in silence and Mitch drifted off into quiet reflection again. What Mitch was saying didn't make much sense to Jonathan at the time, but in the years to come he would understand perfectly what Mitch was saying especially in being married to my mother.

∞∞∞∞∞∞∞

It was in the winter of 1945. Mitch and Alice were in Oklahoma and Mitch was meeting her family for the very first time. The most important reason for Mitch being there and visiting her family was that he was going to ask Lee if he could have Alice's hand in marriage. As with most big families in that time people returned from a long journey there is always a big celebration and since the war was over there was no better time to welcome old friends and heroes home. Cousins, friends, and neighbors were all in attendance this one particular crisp, beautiful Sunday afternoon in the Oklahoma countryside.

Mitch had been nervous all day, and as his usual habit when he got nervous he took to drinking to calm his nerves. He sat in the living room quietly listening to stories that Alice's relatives and friends were telling about childhood and days long since gone in Oklahoma. Finally, Alice came over to Mitch and whispered into his ear that now would be a good time to go talk to her father, for he was alone in the barn and it was in the barn and her father felt most peaceful.

Mitch made his way to the barn and found Lee working with some wood. Lee knew he was there without having to turn around to look at him. With his back to Mitch he said, "Well, my boy, I reckon I already know why you're here. I have already heard that you and my daughter have been spending time with each other and writing each other the past two years."

"That's right, sir," replied Mitch.

"Before you get any crazy idea of asking my blessing on your marriage proposal to my daughter, there are a few things I would like to talk about. I hope you have treated her with the utmost respect and wouldn't take advantage of her good graces.

Mitch was about to respond before he was cut off by Lee, and that's when he finally turned around to face him. "Let me finish before you say anything. As the father here, I'm quite certain I've earned that right. I really don't care how this relationship between you and her started, and all I have is one important question to ask. Do you love her enough to stay faithful all your life? If you can't honestly answer that question then you have no place when comes to her being happy."

Mitch didn't hesitate a bit before he answered. He looked Alice's father directly in the eye and replied,

"There is no one that I love more than Alice and if you really want to know, I will do everything possible to make her happy."

"Okay you can marry her," said Lee after a short pause, "but if you do anything to make her unhappy or hurt her in any way, I'll kill you."

That was all Lee ever said about the matter of marrying his daughter. He walked over and shook Mitch's hand and that was the last word that he spoke to him on that particular trip.

∞∞∞∞∞∞

Mitch could remember that day like it was yesterday. He remembered how he was so nervous and how it was his intense love for Alice that got him over that, not the alcohol as one might think. Throughout the course of the rest of Lee's life he never spoke much to Mitch as the years went past, and Mitch finally figured out it wasn't that he hated him that much, it was because he did the one thing that fathers never want done, he married his daughter.

Mitch came out of his moment of reflection and spoke to the others, "I remember the day that I asked Lee if I could marry Alice. He said if I ever hurt her, he would kill me, and I believed him. This was a man who was only one person and took on the Ku Klux Klan when they threatened to burn down his farm for paying black men the same wages as white men. Lee told the guys hidden behind white sheets that if a black man was going to work the same as a white man that he get paid the same as a white man. I bet you didn't know that, Jonathan."

"No, I've never heard that story before," said Jonathan.

"He was a remarkable man," said Mitch, "and he

never backed down from anybody that threatened him, his way of life, his land, and most importantly his family. When they came one night to threaten Lee he walked out singlehandedly with a shotgun, fired once in the air, and told each one of those sons of bitches that they may succeed at their task and kill him in the process, but he was going to take most of them with him; it was only a matter of who wanted to be first. After that night he was never bothered again by anybody. "

Mitch just laughed to himself, while Jonathan stared in disbelief at the story he told. They didn't understand why he found it so amusing, but he simply replied to them that they had to know this man to understand why he was laughing. After another long pause and quiet reflection, the three returned to the car and left Oklahoma to continue their journey.

7

The Journey West

"**S**o where are we going now, Mitch?" Melissa asked as the trio drove down the Oklahoma country road.

"To the Grand Canyon, and if you've never seen it then you are definitely missing out," Mitch replied.

Jonathan looked at him like he was crazy and then said, "The Grand Canyon? Out of all the places you can visit you want to go there, it's just a bunch a rocks."

Mitch gave Jonathan a dirty look and after a long pause he replied, "You can ridicule me all you want, but the Grand Canyon is more than just a bunch of rocks, it's one of God's unimportant wonders. Travel Brochures can never do it justice, and even though it might seem boring, it's one of those things that you have to see at least once in a lifetime. "

Melissa asked, "So how many times have you seen it in your lifetime?"

Mitch replied. "I've seen it about 278 times, give or take; I always made a point to see it when I had to come out this way for business. It reminded me where I was and what I was getting myself into when I came out here and to remind myself that I wasn't in control out here, only God was."

"I still don't understand what the obsession is about the Grand Canyon," said Jonathan.

"That's because you only see it as a huge rock formation and if it doesn't have any music playing then it's not worth seeing," replied Mitch.

Melissa just laughed at both men and said, "I admit I don't really see the obsession either."

"If it's not some new fingle-fangled technology like this Nintendo I hear about, then it's not something of interest. Although you've never seen it either, how would you know what beauty lies within it?"

"Nintendo? What are we, 12 years old again? And how do you know what it is anyway? Did you hear about it on TV or something?" Jonathan asked.

"Well, I don't know what you kids use for fun anymore, and yes I've actually seen one. I'm not that out of touch with things as you might think," Mitch replied

Melissa interrupted before Jonathan could say another smart ass remark.

"Mitch, it's okay to admit that you don't know much about people our age. You act like we're kids again and angry that we're not going to an amusement park. Just so you know, I actually read for fun."

"And just to let you know, Mitch" began Jonathan, "I like to write and compose music for fun."

Mitch just shook his head and gave his two passengers a dirty look. "I know you're all grown up, but I still think of you as kids. When you get to be my age everybody younger than you is a kid. I'm a grandfather and I can still think of you as a kid; it's one of those special privileges a grandfather has."

Jonathan laughed. "Well, if I'm a kid my birthday is coming up. Can I get a Star Wars birthday party with a Star Wars birthday cake?"

"Ooh, my birthday is coming soon as well," joked Melissa. "Can I get a Barbie birthday party?"

Mitch looked at them sternly; he was not amused, but sarcasm was just part of being in this family.

"You know, it's not nice to mock an old man, but I will tell you something about the Grand Canyon. It's one of those places that you learn to appreciate, but it can change your life if you let it. Being kids, you might not understand that yet. "

They smiled at Mitch as he drifted off into quiet reflection again. They weren't making fun of him at all and they understood what he was trying to tell them. Sarcasm was a two way street with him and he welcomed it. This was important to Mitch because it's what a family does with one another and it was the first time in a lot of years that he had that family connection with his own family.

As he drifted off into quiet reflection there was a half cracked smile on his face while driving down the road. He could hear the sounds of laughter from Jonathan and Melissa fade into the laughter of his wife and two girls from years ago when he brought them out on vacation to see the Grand Canyon.

∞∞∞∞∞∞

"Dad is there anything fun to do at the Grand Canyon?" Catherine asked her father.

"What do you mean is there anything fun to do? "It's the Grand Canyon honey, of course it's fun," Mitch replied.

Catherine just shook her head at her dad and continued to read her magazine while her mother Alice laughed at her sarcastic and curious question. Mitch took another sip of his Irish coffee as he drove his blue Cadillac with the top down along the winding Texas road. Laura picked right up with her sisters line of questioning of her dad and asked, "Dad is it going to be fun like Disneyland?"

"It can be, and there will be some rides for you, honey," Mitch replied.

Alice gave him a dirty look. "Mitch, don't tell her that, she'll think it will be exactly like Disneyland."

"Alice there really are rides at the Grand Canyon. You get to take a tour down into it and ride a jackass at the same time," Mitch replied to her.

"Can you please refrain from using that kind of language in front of our girls? And riding a donkey into some caverns is not the type of ride that's going to thrill them, so you can't tell them that."

Laura and Catherine looked at their father with confused and disappointed looks, and both of them at the same time asked him, "Dad are there any other rides besides riding animals?"

Before he could answer them, Alice beat him to the punch. "Girls, what your father means is that there are rides at this place, just not rides like at Disneyland, but this place is going to be fun anyway."

Catherine looked sternly at her parents. "What's fun about riding on a donkey along a path of rocks?"

Mitch shook his head. "I'll tell you what's fun about that! You don't get to ride on a jackass, I mean donkey in Chicago, and you certainly don't get to see things like this in the city. The Grand Canyon is one of God's greatest wonders and something like this cannot be built by man, so you are truly getting to see a great work of art."

"I thought you always said good art only comes in the form of paint or clay," said Laura.

Alice laughed at her daughters' questions because she knew there was no way Mitch could convince them that where they were going was a fun place. Their girls were only little kids and not yet old enough to appreciate something so magnificent. "You're not going to convince them," she said to him. "I told you that this would be wasted on them."

"Well, by God, they are going to get the experience of a lifetime and learn to appreciate a god-like wonder such as this," Mitch responded.

The girls just laughed at their dad and started to sing. They were singing about Disneyland and then they started singing the Mickey Mouse Song. Alice laughed and told the girls to be quiet as Mitch took more sips of his coffee while mumbling to himself. Alice rubbed his shoulder and told him that it would be okay, that someday they would actually think their father's ideas were good.

Hours later Mitch and family arrived at the Grand Canyon as the sun was beginning to set. The evening light was already beginning to cast a pinkish orange shadow over the magnificent formation of rocks. Everybody got out of the car to go see the great formation of stone and rock; the girls were less than impressed, but then their dad brought them to the edge where the railing stood and made them look out.

The scene they were looking at was perfect; it was like something out of a movie or the perfect photograph. The girls stared off into the distance as the last sunlight was fading over the cliffs of the Grand Canyon, and for first time since they left Chicago on this trip they were happy. The perfect scene they were looking at finally got inside of them and they knew for the first time in their life that maybe their dad knew something that they didn't. They began to wonder if their dad might be smarter than they were and it took something magnificent like the Grand Canyon to do that.

This was also another reason Mitch like this place so much; he got to mesmerize his daughters with true beauty, something that can't be created by man. Mitch put his arms around the love of his life, letting her know without having to say anything what she really meant to him.

∞∞∞∞∞∞∞

It was already late in the evening when Mitch, Jonathan, and Melissa arrived at the Grand Canyon. It was already too dark to see anything and the tour would not be open till the next day, so they decided to get a hotel room and get some sleep. This was the first time on the road trip they had gotten a hotel room so it was a little awkward with the sleeping arrangements. Jonathan and Mitch shared a room while Melissa had one to herself. There weren't any long conversations between them when they got settled, they were so tired that they just went to bed and drifted off to sleep.

The next morning, Jonathan was the first to wake up. He went and got a morning paper and some coffee for the others. When he arrived back at the rooms he found Melissa basking in the morning sunlight as it was turning out to be a beautiful day, a perfect day for a tour of the Grand Canyon. No words passed between them as Jonathan handed her a cup of coffee. There had always been this unspoken rule between the both of them ever since they had started dating many years ago, neither one of them would speak to each other until the first cup of coffee had been drunk.

As they both stood alone outside in the quiet reverence of that beautiful day, Mitch was getting up, but not very well. He was already starting to have his battles with the cancer, things like dizziness and loss of balance, and he would also be prone to vomiting. He barely made it to the bathroom when he collapsed on the floor, and that's when Jonathan and Melissa heard the loud noise of him struggling. They both rushed to the bathroom to find Mitch slumped over the toilet barely moving and looking like death had already become him.

"Mitch, are you all right, what happened?" asked Jonathan.

In a ghastly tone Mitch replied, "Well, it looks like it's going to be a tough day for me and if I were the both of you I get used to me having days like this. They're only going to get worse until the end."

"Do we need to get you to a hospital?" Melissa asked.

"No, I'll just need to get some of my medicine. The hospital is the last resort for me at this point. Don't worry, I'll function." Mitch gave her an ailing smile. It didn't make her feel any better about his condition.

Melissa and Jonathan helped Mitch get off the floor, which was tough because he wasn't exactly a lightweight. They helped him get to the bed and Jonathan went to his suitcase to grab the bottle of pills that were prescribed for moments like this. Mitch was in such bad shape; Jonathan had to hold the glass of water to his mouth while holding his head tilted just a bit so he could take a drink.

Mitch had always been a very athletic and strong-willed person, he had always been very active and it was very hard for him to accept that this illness was going to do this to him; the illness would take away his energy; it would take away the life force that had always been in him over the years. He was getting weak and the more active he was the weaker he would get.

The medicine that he was on was not a cure for his disease; it more or less took away the pain for a little while. His medicine had such a drowsy affect that it could literally make a person sleep for 24 hours and it always had an immediate effect so Mitch drifted right off to sleep.

While Mitch slept, Jonathan and Melissa walked to the nearest diner and had breakfast together. They didn't say anything to each other for quite a while, still shocked by seeing Mitch as weak as he was. It was the first time since this trip had started that they had seen him so weak, and finally getting to see what his disease was going to do him. They finally realized that the hardest part of seeing a life-threatening disease take effect was to see it beat down the most strong-willed of people, to see it make the most active of people fragile and limp with weakness.

Jonathan sat for the longest time stirring his coffee and not saying a word. Melissa was quiet too, but she decided to break the silence and asked him, "So seeing your grandfather this way has made you finally realize the seriousness of everything. You finally now know that he is going to die and there is nothing that you can do about it."

"Yeah, you could say that. I have never seen anybody like that before and it's more of shock to see him that way."

"Why?"

"I have never known him to be weak. He always seems to be able to do anything. I always figured his feisty stubborn Irish attitude would never allow him to be weak."

"You really understood how weak and fragile a person could become from a destructive disease. You never understood it when I told you about my mother, but now you know."

"I guess you're right, but it can happen and there is nothing we can do about it."

"No, and that's the really hard part. It's never easy to watch someone wither away until they're nothing or dead, but the hardest part is not being able to do anything about it," she replied with some tears coming down her cheek.

"Is that what made you the saddest with your mother?"

"Yes it was. There is a part of me that will always hate her for what she was, an alcoholic that could never beat the disease. Then there will always be a part of me that will love her because she was my mother and we had a few sweet moments together that I will never forget. Although the thing that makes me more angry with her is that I couldn't help her, by the time I was old enough to do something she was already too far gone even though she wasn't dead yet. All I could do was watch her self-destruct."

He looked at her trying to hold back the tears that were forming in his eyes and with a look that said he finally knew all she had been through and finally understood he said, "I guess that's the way it will be with Mitch and I won't be able to help him. "

She grabbed his hand and squeezed it. "Yes and no. Yes he will wither away and eventually die and there is nothing we can do about it, but no we don't have to just watch him destruct. We can help him with the things he needs to put right."

"That may be true, but I still feel that this is some cheap ploy have a relationship with the family he lost a long time ago," he said.

"Why would you say something like that? He's trying to reach out to you and his family. In case you're wondering you know you can never really lose your family, just forget about them for a while."

"Look," said Jonathan, "he lost that a long time ago. If he wanted to get us back he shouldn't have walked out years ago. You weren't there so how would you know?"

"You're right I wasn't there and I don't know all the details, only what you have told me years ago when we were still dating. I'll tell you what I do know, if Mitch lost his chance to put things right with his family then you wouldn't be here now."

"Whether you agree with me or not, he lost us as a family when he walked out years ago."

"You can't lose someone by just walking away. It's something you have to choose to do. The reason I know that is because you never lost me when you walked out on us a few years ago."

"What the hell are you talking about? When you threw me out, we were done, our relationship was over with."

"I never threw you out, you left and you never lost me as a friend or a companion. You just chose not to see me or talk to me anymore. Don't you remember you dumb jackass?"

Her harsh words sent Jonathan back into his memory of long ago. He remembered the day he walked out from Melissa and why he left.

"That's it, Melissa. I'm done. You don't want me here anymore then I'm gone," Jonathan said to Melissa as she stood in front of him holding an empty bottle of Jack Daniels that he had finished off in a day.

She looked at him with tears in her eyes and said, "I never said that I didn't want you here, I just don't want you to be this way. I've already lived once with an alcoholic, I don't want to live with another one."

"I have a few drinks so I'm alcoholic? It's not like it's an everyday thing."

"Drinking a bottle of whiskey is not a normal thing and I want to know why you do it."

"It calms me down when I'm stressed out."

"What are you stressed out about? You're doing what you love, we both have enough money, and we have a great relationship, or at least I think we do."

"Okay it's fucking stifling around here and I do it to get my head clear, is that what you want to hear," he said in drunken anger.

"It's not really me is it? You do this every time you get some letter from your grandfather or something bad happens with your family."

"So what, I deal with it in my own way. I can't help it. I can't change who I am."

"It's not that you can't change, because that's bullshit. It's that you won't change; you won't even try to change. That's why I feel sorry for you, but I don't want you to leave."

"But you don't want me the way that I am and because of that I am leaving," Jonathan replied as he hit the lamp shade out of anger and started to walk out the door.

With tears running down her face she said,

"You can leave, but it doesn't mean that I'm done, it doesn't mean that I will stop loving you."

Jonathan didn't even turn around as she said that. He just kept walking until he was long gone from the house he lived in with her.

∞∞∞∞∞∞∞

Jonathan sat there in the diner booth remembering what happened that day and then he finally knew that truth of that day. He looked at her, surprised that she had responded the way she did and that he finally remembered what happened. He chose to walk out on her and leave the relationship for good because he was hurting inside, but that had nothing to do with Melissa. He had been reminded of a deep seeded pain that he always tried to ignore with a bottle of whiskey.

He didn't respond to her for a while and just went back to drinking his coffee. She was familiar with this action by Jonathan. He would have long pauses in his conversation when he knew somebody was right and he wasn't. When they were dating and they would have these kinds of arguments all he would do was walk away for a while. Later come back to finish the conversation when he wanted to.

She was always annoyed at this, but she also knew that it was better for him when it came to sorting out his thoughts and blowing up in anger right in front of her. Like his grandfather, Jonathan had a very stubborn Irish temper and on occasion it would get the best of him in conversation.

Over the years he had learned to control it before it got out of hand by just walking away or stopping his conversation. He wasn't one that liked to be wrong, especially when it was somebody that he did

114

care about and they were pointing out something about his family.

Jonathan still cared about Melissa even though he would not admit it out loud or let her know it in any way, but she knew him very well. She could already see this in him. He had become an open book to her very early on. It wasn't that he was very easy to read as a person or that she was for that fact, from the first days that they had known each other they fell in sync with each other right away. She cared about him as well and that had never stopped since they quit dating.

She wondered if they might ever try being with each other again, but there were still too many things that Jonathan had to let go; there were still too many hurts he kept on his shoulder, never letting them fall away. Melissa didn't know what the end had in store for them except for one thing; she knew all she could do was be there for Mitch and Jonathan when they were hurting.

After a long silence she finally spoke. "You know, the night before we left I had my dream again."

"The one about your mother dying."

"Yeah, and I haven't had it in years. With all this time gone by I thought it might finally be gone for good, but I guess not."

"Why do you think you had the dream again? You haven't had it since, well you know."

"Yeah, since we quit seeing other. Actually, the last time I had it was the night you left."

"Not exactly my finest hour," Jonathan replied.

"It wasn't exactly 'our' finest hour, but yeah that was the last time I had it. I'm convinced that the only time I have it is when some big life changing event happens. This trip would probably qualify.

"Is there more detail in the dream this time?"

"Not really, but no matter what it's the same exact dream and I can see very clearly my mother killing herself after staring at a bottle of Gin for a very long time. She just gave up, knowing that she couldn't beat the disease. I can see plainly her cutting her wrists and the blood pouring out like a waterfall while she lies in her pool of blood for hours until I finally find her."

Jonathan looked at her sadly. "You know, I have always thought your reoccurring dream was God showing you what happened with her until you finally found her and maybe there is yet something you still have to deal with before you finally quit having it."

"It's funny you should say that and I'm quite surprised you remembered the dream. I thought you were always too drunk to remember anything," she said with a laugh.

"Hey, there were a few moments that I was listening," he said. "I can't believe I'm going to say this considering I don't like to admit anything is wrong about me, but we all have things we can't let go."

"Maybe you're right. Maybe we both have things to deal with before we can finally be happy," Melissa responded.

Jonathan smiled and nodded at her to let her know that she was right. He also knew that part of letting go of the things that caused their own self destruction was with each other. She grabbed his hand again and squeezed to let him know that she was there for him. The two of them didn't say anything else while they just exchanged glances from across the dinner table and finished their breakfast.

For the better part of the day Mitch was asleep, letting the medication take its full effect on him.

Melissa and Jonathan just hung around the hotel watching TV and playing cards until he woke up and needed something. Late in afternoon/evening he finally awoke not exactly sure where he was; Mitch had always been very aware of his surroundings and the medicine he was on would take a lot out of him to the point that he would be confused. It was the downside of the medication and taking the pain away.

"What time is it?" Mitch asked.

"It's about 4:30, you've slept for most of the day," Jonathan replied.

Melissa brought him a glass of water as he sat up in his bed. He looked at the both of them graciously and a little embarrassed because they had to see him this way. He knew it would be more of a shock for Jonathan because he had never seen him this way, but the look on Jonathan's face was surprisingly not of shock but of concern. That is when he knew that Jonathan had begun to let it inside, to let in the harsh reality of what life had become for the both of them as well as the effect it would have on the people close to them.

"Are you hungry?" asked Jonathan. "We could get something from the diner for you."

"Not really. I don't want to sit here for the rest of the evening so let's do something," Mitch said.

"What do you want to do?"

"I don't know, but anything is better than sitting here."

"If you're up to it, you can take me to see the Grand Canyon since I have never had the pleasure," Melissa said to both of them.

Mitch got up out of bed and smile at them both. "I'm sure they're still doing tours, and if not, then we will make it worth their while because for you it is definitely worth the experience."

The three of them left the hotel and went to the Grand Canyon. As luck would have it, there wasn't another tour and the park was going to be closed for a couple of months due to excavation and some repair. It sounded strange that this would be happening at the Grand Canyon, but they all knew that life had its interesting surprises. There was nothing they could do and by the time the park was open again Mitch would probably be gone.

An elderly gentleman came walking over to the trio and smiled at the sight of Mitch. He looked to be about the same age as Mitch and it also appeared the two men knew each other. The older gentleman spoke up and said, "Mitch Collins, you old dog, it's been too long since you've been here, how are you?"

Mitch and the older gentleman shook hands and Mitch replied, "Daniel, it's good to see you and I'm doing fine, how about you?"

"I can't complain too much, I'm still here and I just got made a grandfather again so there goes even more of my retirement to spoiling another grandchild," Daniel replied.

Daniel was an old friend of Mitch's who had been working at the Grand Canyon for over 45 years since he first came home from the War. He and Mitch had first met when Mitch was making one of his visits to the place when he was out this way on business. He was one of Mitch's oldest friends and they always made it a point to go out for beers when Mitch was out this way. Daniel was still going strong and had no intentions of retiring, unlike Mitch who had been retired for some time.

"So what the hell is going on around here, why can't we do the tour?" asked Mitch.

Daniel frowned and replied, "Oh, they have

some damn archeological dig going on with one of the universities and let me tell you it's playing hell on the tourist season."

"Well, I guess that's just my luck, isn't it?" replied Mitch.

"You never have been the luckiest son of bitch have you now…so who did you bring with you this time?" asked Daniel.

Mitch kind of chuckled because he knew that Daniel wouldn't believe what he was about to say, for even Daniel knew a little of the family history with the Collins'. He replied, "This is Jonathan and a friend of ours Sherry Melissa Felder. "

"Well I'll be, the boy in the picture has grown up into a man. There must be something going on if the both of you are here," said Daniel.

Jonathan looked at the both of them with a funny look. He was surprised to hear about a photo of him being kept by Mitch, but before he could respond to anything Mitch said, "I do have something to tell you and if you will let me buy you a beer then I'll let you know what's happening with me and why I'm here again.

The four of them went to the nearest bar which was not too far from where they were. The bar they went to was the typical rustic joint that would be found in Arizona, filled with Indian and Old Western artifacts for decoration and a bar that looked like it was actually built in the 19th century. It was a place that had been worn down by time, but was still filled with the same warmth of home that could bring comfort to traveling strangers.

Mitch recounted his tale to Daniel over a nice cold pint, and he told his old friend that he was dying and that this trip for him was his last hurrah. For Daniel he knew that this would be the last time he would see his friend at the Grand Canyon and the last that they would share a beer in Arizona. The old friends caught each other up on family and talked of old times just like college mates returning home from school.

For Jonathan and Melissa it was yet another chance to hear stories about the man that they were both getting to know. Jonathan was beginning to see something that he had never seen from the stories Daniel told. They weren't the most glamorous of stories because all they were about Mitch and his visits to the Grand Canyon while having good times with Daniel, but they brought out one thing for Jonathan, the picture of good and decent things that he had forgotten through all the years of hating him.

As the evening passed by the two friends said goodbye to one another knowing as all old men know that the end was near and this would be the last time they saw each other. Daniel hugged his old friend and wished him Godspeed on his journey. Hoping he would find what he was really looking for.

Daniel walked over to Melissa and Jonathan; he said goodbye to her with a kiss on the cheek and told her to take care of the men she was with for they were good men. He shook Jonathan's hand and told him, "Listen and learn from your grandfather while on this journey with him because your life will be changed forever, don't let the past keep you from really knowing him for that will be the biggest regret you will ever have."

As they got back to the park Mitch was disappointed that they could not go on the Grand Canyon tour, but mostly for Melissa because she couldn't see what he had always seen in the place. The excitement about this part of the trip for her was being with good and caring people and it made this part of the trip worth it. She wasn't upset about it because somewhere deep down she knew that she would be back. She could see the images in her mind; she was showing a child the long and winding view of rocky cliffs and caverns as a tall man brought them something to drink.

As she looked out at the view of the Grand Canyon she closed her eyes and could see the image clearly as if they were real and happening now. Melissa just smiled for she had not been happy in a long time, not as much as she was right now. She just looked at the two men she was traveling with as they tried to talk the tour director into letting them go on a tour; Mitch even played the dying card hoping God would show a little favor upon them for telling the truth, but it was no use.

Melissa just laughed at the family she had seemed to inherit by going on this trip and then thought to herself that this was she had always wanted. She wanted a family that was always there for each other and would spend time with each other even if they didn't like each other. The family never had to be perfect, but they loved each other no matter what and that was enough. She knew that even though this family would have to work through all the hurt that had been building over the years they still loved each other deep down. For Melissa this was perfect because she had never had it.

The three of them went to the edge by the railing that led out to the Grand Canyon and watched the sun set over the dessert red cliffs. For Mitch it reminded him of the time he took his family to the Grand Canyon all those years ago. The three of them stood there looking out as the sunset cast a shadow over them and it became the same scene from years ago.

Mitch finally knew that it was this, the time he

spent with his family that made him complete. Through all the years he was away on business, out for the evening when Alice didn't want any part of his excitement, or even when he drowned his memories in the bottle, it was still the times that he spent with his girls, with his wife and with his grandson that made him the happiest.

This was it for him, the last time he would see this place. It was one of his favorite places on earth and as sun was closing over the canyon Mitch began to see it close in on his life forever.

8

Catching up with the Past

$\mathbf{T}$he next morning the three passengers slowly woke and joined each other at the diner around the corner for breakfast. Mitch was feeling better from the day before, ready to continue his journey even though he knew it was going to be harder this time. The men were the first to emerge from their hotel room and arrive at the diner while Melissa took her time in her own hotel room waking up and getting ready before she joined the others as was common with women. Where Jonathan never understood why it took so long for women to get ready Mitch knew all too well from his years of being married and raising two girls.

"What takes women so long to get up and get ready?" asked Jonathan.

"Let me give you a little more knowledge that you may not have figured out. You know that women are the most complex creatures on earth and that complexity is never seen so clearly as when women are first rising out of bed and preparing to start the day. I've learned a lot in my time, but that's one thing I have never figured out myself and the one time I inquired about it with my stubborn attitude I almost made it to my own funeral, so I've learned to let the curiosity go. I recommend that you do the same."

Jonathan shot him a confused look, for he was not ready to accept that kind of answer. When Melissa finally arrived at the diner for breakfast, Jonathan started to say something sarcastic. Mitch quietly put his hand on his arm, looked at him with a stern look and shook his head at Jonathan to tell him no; it was better not to say a word.

Melissa smiled at the both of them. "Well, I hope you both had a good night's sleep, I know I did."

"My dear, was your first experience at the Grand Canyon worth it?" asked Mitch.

"It was. I wish we could have gone on the tour, but I know that I will eventually come back," she replied.

"I had a feeling you would enjoy it. Just to let you know, I have never seen a better sunset than the ones that settle over the canyons here; definitely one of God's greatest wonders."

"I would have to agree with that," she said.

Jonathan smiled at them and said, "I think the sunset here only matches that of a truly beautiful woman."

Mitch chuckled, shook his head and replied, "I'm glad to see that you're finally learning something."

Melissa couldn't help but laugh at the two men sitting with her and their sarcastic masculine sense of humor. "You two are awful, but I'm glad that the both of you are smart enough to recognize that simple truth," she said.

The three of them just laughed and ordered while enjoying each other's company. They had a great time together the night before, and seeing something so beautiful and magnificent was having a profound effect on the both of them. It was becoming easier for Melissa and Jonathan to be on this trip, even though they had finally reconciled the fact that the end would not be a happy one. It was especially becoming easier for Jonathan because he was seeing something different in his grandfather that he had never seen before.

After a long pause, Mitch said, "Well, now that we're done with this part of the trip it's time to head through the mountains and make a stop in Las Vegas. If you think it's beautiful here, then you definitely have to see the Rocky Mountains; those are truly some of God's wonders."

"Rocky Mountains?" asked Jonathan. "I think that medicine's getting to you. The Rockies aren't on the way to Vegas, at least not from here."

"Well, my boy," said Mitch, "I never said we were going the shortest way, did I? No, we're going to double back and go through Colorado.

"I thought you were about to say Vegas is beautiful, and if you did I was going to question your sanity," Jonathan replied.

"No, not Las Vegas; it's one of those places that's really exciting and strange at the same time, but not beautiful. Don't get me wrong, seeing Vegas is worth the experience, but don't hold it up as some great work of art. You can have fun there; I saw Elvis Presley and The Rat Pack there."

"So what's your motivation for going there again if all those guys are gone now?" Melissa asked.

"I just want to see it again, one last time, and

there's something else I have always wanted to do, so I guess I better do it now since I don't have much time left," Mitch replied.

"It's good we're going because some old band mates of mine are playing in Vegas. I was supposed to go with them before I signed on for this, but it will be good to see them while we're there and see if they can be successful," Jonathan said to the others.

"Who's playing in Vegas that you used to play with?" Melissa asked Jonathan.

"Barry and Mike. They had that little band that used to play at the *Krazy Korner* and I would fill in for the keyboard player once a week," Jonathan answered.

"I guess forgot about them, I can't keep up with all the gigs you had when we were seeing each other. What are they doing in Vegas?"

"Their new band that they put together got some gig playing at some casino so they could also get recognized and make their first album. They ask me to go along and be their keyboard player while doing background vocals," Jonathan replied.

"Who was going to sing lead vocals for the band, Barry?" she asked Jonathan.

"Yeah, and I know what you're going to say, and that's why I didn't take the gig," he replied.

"I would hope not, Barry can't sing to save his life; I think Bob Dylan could do a better job. If you would have taken the gig then you would be officially prostituting yourself when it comes to music," Melissa replied.

"I know, I like Barry and Mike, Mike writes great songs, but Barry has delusions of grandeur when it comes to singing," Jonathan responded.

Mitch had a confused look on his face as if he had missed something. He had no idea what they were talking about and was beginning to wonder if it was the medicine causing this, but he knew in reality that he just didn't have any frame of reference on their conversation.

"You know, sometimes I just don't know what you are guys are talking about, maybe I'm finally too old and out of touch with everything," he said.

"Well, how could you know what we were talking about when we are talking about places and things that us two at this table would know about?" Jonathan replied.

"I thought you might be talking about something that included all of us and what we were doing; didn't know if the medication was really taking a toll on me," Mitch responded.

Jonathan shook his head and gave a halfcocked smile to Mitch then replied, "I think this is your way of trying to be a part of every conversation we have or at least be the topic of every conversation we have."

Mitch laughed. "No, but now that you mention it, there is something you should understand. When an older person is in your presence they should be the topic of conversation so as to show reverence for all their years of experience."

Melissa laughed and Jonathan just stared in disbelief at the comment Mitch had made. He couldn't tell if he was being serious or if it was part of the man's dark and demented Irish sense of humor. Finally, Mitch winked and smiled at Jonathan just to let him know that he was being harassed a little bit by his grandfather.

Melissa laughed at them as she was becoming accustomed to by now, but she was especially laughing at Jonathan for getting a little angry for the harassment he was enduring by his grandfather.

As Jonathan was giving his grandfather a mild

dirty look for being the butt of his joke, Mitch replied, "Sorry my dear boy, but you'll have to just put up with my little indulgences. I have to catch up with my jokes from years of not seeing you."

"I don't know why you feel so compelled," Jonathan replied.

"It's just one of those little things about having a family; you get to harass each other. After all, its family, there's not much else you can do with them and if you must know the truth, it's a grandfather's prerogative when it comes to his grandchildren so just get used to it." Mitch sat back in his chair and winked at his grandson.

Jonathan couldn't help but smile as Melissa was laughing at him because she knew that Mitch was right and part of it was making up for lost time. He stayed silent as Mitch went into a tale about Jonathan as a kid with Melissa. It was a story about Jonathan and rain puddles when he was little.

He told her about how he never could stay out of them no matter how much his mother and grandmother tried to keep him away from them, especially when he was dressed up in his nice clothes. According to Mitch, the rain puddles and Jonathan were like magnets and somehow, someway, they were going to be brought together. Jonathan was a little embarrassed, but he was even happier to see Mitch laughing and telling stories while not suffering from the effects of his disease and the medication that couldn't cure him.

"So I guess this trip is a little strange for you considering everything you went through with your mother," said Mitch.

She looked surprised that he knew about her mother. "How do you know about my mother?" she asked. "I've never said anything about her to you."

"Jonathan told me a little bit about her and your relationship with her. I'm very sorry you had to endure that with her. I don't think any child should have to experience that with a parent, I know mine shouldn't have." Mitch looked at Jonathan when he said the last sentence.

Jonathan didn't know how to respond because he was still trying to work out whether he should hate this man sitting across from him or forgive him, but he also knew that Mitch was trying. Mitch was trying to make the effort; he was trying to mend his own broken fences.

Melissa was visibly angry. "With all due respect, you shouldn't know anything about her because it's a private matter. And Jonathan, you shouldn't even be telling him about my mother. It's nobody's business but my own. I thought you would have more respect for me than that."

"I'm sorry," said Jonathan. "I didn't think it was that big of a deal for me to tell Mitch. He was asking what your story was so I told him a little bit of your past. I never thought you would be upset."

"That's the problem. You never do, you never think what other people might want. You have always done what you wanted to do without any regard for anybody else's feelings. Mitch, if you wanted to know about me then all you have to do is ask me and maybe I'll tell you."

"Melissa, I wasn't trying to offend you. I wanted Jonathan to tell me a little bit about you, from his own perspective. Before you get really angry, I think you should know something. I already knew that you were guarded when we first met and I knew that you probably wouldn't tell me if I asked you since we don't know each other really well, so that's why I asked Jonathan. Maybe I should have asked you instead, but

I wanted to know about you from somebody who knew you really well."

"I guess both of you are the same when it comes to having courtesy for someone else. But damn it Mitch you should have just asked me what you were curious about."

Mitch and Jonathan both just stared in disbelief at Melissa for being angry and hurt. With tears in her eyes she stormed out of the diner into the parking lot. Both men didn't know what to do and after a few minutes Mitch finally spoke up and said that one of them should go outside and talk to her, he suggested that Jonathan should do it because she was mostly angry with him.

Jonathan walked outside to find her sitting on the bumper of the car crying. He walked over not knowing what to do and even tried to put his hands on her shoulders to comfort her, but he couldn't do it. He didn't know why, but it just felt like it wasn't right under the circumstances. Finally, he spoke up and said "Look, I'm not trying to hurt you, but he asked and I thought he should know."

"Why does he have to know about my past?" "This trip is about him and his own life. It certainly isn't about me, and that's why I don't want him to know about my mother."

"You think it's very fair for the rest of us to open up and be honest while you get to hide behind the shadow of your own guilt?" he asked.

"The shadow of my own guilt? If there's any guilt I have over my mother's death then it has nothing to do with this trip that your grandfather is taking us on. I'm not the one who should be bearing my soul around here anyway."

"What does that mean?"

"You want me to be so honest, how about you?

I haven't seen you be completely honest yet. Why did you really come on this trip? Did you want to see if your grandfather was really dying or to finally watch the man you've hated for so many years finally keel over and die just to satisfy your vengeance for him hurting you years ago?"

"I'm on this trip for him and you know that," said Jonathan.

"Are you sure that's what it is, or are you just saying that because you know I'm right and don't want to have to admit it? Remember, I know your arrogant attitude when it comes to being right."

Jonathan started to walk away, but then he turned around and said angrily, "Fuck you, if that's what you want to believe just to get back at me for telling Mitch about your mother then fine, but I'm not the one who's been living with deep down regretful guilt for not being able to stop her mother's death. So if you want to be angry at me for what I did then let's get something straight. If this journey is about so called redemption and dealing with the past as you keep pointing out, then we are all on it together and that man who is paying for your way has a right to know the truth about you."

Melissa wore a look of shock on her face as she walked up to Jonathan and slapped him across the face for his comments. She tried to walk away mad, but she, like him, always had to have the last words. She replied, "You can go to hell you selfish son of a bitch. This trip shouldn't be about me, it's about fixing whatever you have between you."

Before she could finish Mitch walked out into the parking lot. "Before we all march off to hell I think I should say a few words."

Melissa and Jonathan both tried to say something and before they could get a word out Mitch held up his hands to quiet them. "Both of you shut up and let me finish. I don't think any of you have a clue about what you're talking about. So let's understand something about this trip, it's not about redemption although I'm sure that will play its part. This trip is about me getting to see some people and a few things for the last time. This trip is about me saying goodbye, I want you here because I didn't want to do it alone."

"Do you even know what we were talking about out here?" asked Jonathan.

Melissa started to say something as well, but Mitch cut her short and continued, "Don't mock me, jackass. I want the both of you to shut your mouth for a change and listen to me. If you two want to rip each other's guts out then go ahead, but do it when I'm not around; I should be dead soon so you won't have long to wait. Melissa I wasn't trying to get into your business, and if you don't want to talk about the past with your mother, fine. You have every right not to if you choose, but I think there is a concept you better learn to understand. It wasn't your fault and there wasn't anything you could have done for her."

Melissa started to interrupt, but Mitch held his back up to stop her from talking. He paused with a discerning look towards her, looked her directly in her deep green eyes, and repeated, "It wasn't your fault and there was nothing you could have done. That's the thing with alcoholics, they make choices that usually hurt the ones they love while they go on destroying themselves with the poison of their own choice. I should know, my father was an alcoholic and I watched him abuse my mother while sometimes taking his anger and frustration out on my brother and me.

Also I know from experience when it comes to being an alcoholic and when I became one after the war I finally realized that everything I did just like my father was my choice and I made them without any regard for the feelings of the ones I loved."

Melissa started to cry again. "I could have stopped her from killing herself," she said as her head hung low. "I could have gotten her the help she needed so she could have finally gotten better. I know I could have done that if I had been stronger, if I had cared about her a little more instead of hating her for what she was."

Mitch reached down and put his hand on her chin and brought it up to face him.

"Maybe you might have been able to do more, but our guilt always makes us think that when in reality we did all we could have done. Hating your mother for what she was is natural, but it doesn't mean you hated her. I know that because you were with her right up to the end. If you had really hated her then you would have abandoned her long before she died."

Melissa continued to cry and hugged Mitch like he was her own father. Mitch held her as if she was one of his own daughters and told her, "I can't tell you to quit feeling guilty; because that is something you will just have to work through on your own. However, I can tell you that it wasn't your fault and you need to accept that. The truth is not always what we want it to be, but when we finally realize it then we'll finally find peace."

Jonathan didn't know what to do or what to say. All he could do was walk over to where she was and put his hand on her shoulder, squeeze it to let her know that he cared and then let her be.

Before he could walk off Mitch stopped and said in a very serious tone, "Now for you this all I have to say. You may not completely understand this trip, but understand this. I am doing it for me, to say goodbye and to see some things for the last time. I have a right to die in peace and in my own way; I think I've earned that right. Now I don't want to do this with anybody else but my grandson, despite our past. My hope for you is that by the end you'll have a better understanding of what I did and why."

Jonathan didn't quite understand what he meant by this, but he was already figuring out that this journey for all of them would be about finding complete understanding about who they really were. Jonathan and Mitch just let Melissa be by herself around the car. They both went in and finished their meal. When Melissa was ready about an hour later the three travelers left Arizona, heading towards Colorado by way of a mountain pass.

∞∞∞∞∞∞

Over the next thirty six hours Mitch and his passengers traveled up interstate 25 into Colorado. They didn't do much talking and Melissa did not say but maybe three words to Jonathan. This was her way; when she was mad and had to find a way to get over it she had to be left alone for a while. When she and Jonathan had been dating it would be days before she would speak to him when she was mad, and even though they lived together for a time he would not see much of her when she was this way.

Melissa mainly slept and read a book while they all traveled to Colorado. Mitch and Jonathan talked baseball, which was always the one thing they could talk to each other about and not get mad at each other. Baseball for them was the calming force; they would debate about teams, players, and stats, but never really fight to the point that they couldn't speak to each other.

Mitch had grown up as a Red Sox fan since he was from Boston, but when he moved to Chicago he decided that he needed a National league team so for him the Chicago Cubs became that team. He always said that it was only right to cheer for two cursed teams because if one could stick it out then their faith would be unbreakable even more than some religions, which he thought religion was very questionable.

As Jonathan was growing up he and his grandfather would always spend their summers at Wrigley Field. It made such an impression on Jonathan that all he wanted to do with his life was be a baseball player and a piano player. When he was born, a friend of Mitch's by the name of Jack Hall placed a small Cubs baseball hat on his head to baptize him into the Cubs family as a fan. Nobody but Jack and Mitch thought it was very funny and thought that this baby was too young to be involved in such foolishness. After everybody had their complaints Old Jack Hall just said that it was too late, Jonathan Collins was going to be a Cubs Fan until the day he died.

So this became true for Jonathan, and by the time he could walk and hold a baseball bat he was dubbed a Chicago Cubs fan. He never quit being a true fan even when the curse of the Billy Goat was visited upon them in 1984 when they were a few outs away from the World Series and old Leon Durham let a ground ball go by him so the winning run could score, then they lost game seven to have their season end. He never quit even when his heart was broken in 1989 when they lost to the underdog Giants and let another World Series trip get away.

Melissa and Jonathan were dating at the time and she couldn't understand why he was so sad because it was only a game, but he told her that with the Cubs it's like being in love with the truest love of your life and having your heart broken. Mitch still cheered for the Sox, even in 1986 when their flirtation with destiny ended with Buckner Ball. Baseball was the truce between Jonathan and Mitch; it was the one thing they could count on to cheer them up when they were angry at each other. The two of them talked baseball along the way, for they had a lot to catch up on and they had a lot to complain about because the Cubs were starting off to another disappointing season.

They arrived in a small Colorado town called Monument just outside of Colorado Springs. It was one of those places that Mitch had found on one of his trips out west and it was not a typical ski town, it looked like an old mining town that had just recently entered the twentieth century. It was filled with family oriented people that didn't let the outside world interfere with their lives, for they had a strong bond and they took care of each other. They also welcomed anybody that wasn't trying to sell them something; especially their own version of God, this town had no need for that bullshit, as members of the town made very clear.

Mitch had been visiting this place since the late fifties, and at one time knew everybody there, for this town never grew much because it wasn't the perfect ski town, but it was the perfect family small town. There was one place in particular that Mitch always visited, the Whiskeytown bar, a place that had been around since the mining days in one version or another. The current building it occupied was only fifty years old, but his place had been around for a long time even as a salon inside a tent during pioneer days. Mitch knew the father and son that ran the place and like most of the people he knew they had been friends for a long time.

After the weary travelers settled in their hotel room they went to the Whiskeytown to have dinner and see some old friends. When they arrived Steve and his son Jason were working the night shift since it was Thursday and Thursday through Saturday always had live music. The joint was rustic while still keeping the mining town feel and this was part of the allure of the place. It was wide open and the stage was pretty big for a bar that wasn't designed to be a concert hall. As soon as Mitch walked in the father recognized him immediately and walked over to say hi.

"Mitch, you old bastard, it's been far too long since you've visited," Steve said.

Mitch shook the hand of his old friend and replied, "Yes it has, but I have other friends to visit so it takes a while to get back this way. However, I'm here now and need a beer from your rusty taps."

"Now I don't need to hear about all the girlfriends 50 years younger than you, and for the record my taps are not rusty, they're just aged well so as to add a good flavor to the beer."

"That's one of the main reasons I keep coming back here. You have good beer that not watered down alcohol like Coors Light. If you're going to drink beer then drink one that you can taste."

Steve just looked at his friend with a big smile and responded, "Hey we only serve good beer here, don't speak about such evil things like Coors Light. You would not see so many customers if we served bad beer. So what are you doing here and who are these people that you have with you?"

"This is Sherry Melissa Felder, a friend of mine who is accompanying me on my journey across the country, and the other person is my grandson

Jonathan. We are taking a trip across America and we just couldn't come to this part of the country without stopping by the Whiskeytown."

"You know you just can't pass through without stopping by. So this is your grandson all grown up from the picture you carry of him. I'm glad that he was willing to come on this trip with you," Steven said.

"Me too, and since he's never been to this place I thought it was only right to visit so they both could see one of the best places in the world," Mitch replied.

"There aren't too many places that truly feel like home and are truly American so let me get you a table. You can eat and drink on the house and later we will catch up on old times. Stacy here will take care of you."

As they were getting settled Jonathan finally asked, "So Mitch is there anybody we're going to encounter on this trip that you don't know?"

"Jonathan, I'm old and I've been to a lot of places so there are lots of people that I know. We will probably encounter a lot of them along the way and there are some people that we meet that I just wanna get to know," Mitch replied.

Finally, Melissa spoke up after being silent for almost the entire trip to Colorado, "I think you're doing this on purpose because you know this is the last time you're going to see some of these people, but just in case you didn't notice, the cocktail waitress seems to like you even though you're old enough to be her grandfather."

"Well my dear, young people always like me and I never look like that creepy old guy who's feeling their butt. Look at me, I still have it where it counts, I'm still good looking and I'm still charming." Mitch replied.

Jonathan gave his grandfather a dirty look and replied, "Well I still think you flirt too much for a man your age. After all, you're still a border line dirty old man."

"Maybe, but I will bet you ten dollars that I can go home with that waitress tonight."

Melissa started to laugh at Mitch's feistiness mixed with a little Clark Gable charm and then Jonathan said, "Thank you for giving me images I really didn't want to have, but I will take that bet if you want to lose ten dollars."

Mitch just smiled at him as the waitress made her way back over to the table never keeping her eyes off Mitch. When she got there she spoke up and said, "So do you know what you want yet? Everything on the menu is good."

"How about something that isn't on the menu, is that good as well?" Mitch asked as he gave her his charming smile.

"You can do a special order, and believe me if you order the right thing we can make it good," she said.

Mitch smiled and winked at her while Jonathan shook his head in disgust. Melissa could only laugh at the situation being a victim of the older man's charm. This was the first time that she had laughed in a couple of days and she took a particular delight in seeing Jonathan suffer from his grandfather's rebellious actions.

All through dinner and a few rounds of drinks, she and Mitch flirted with one another. It was harmless even for her, but she knew there was something about the older gentlemen that she liked, mainly the fact that he was fun to be around.

When they were done with dinner the live band played a classic rock set of slow soulful music, most of the songs Mitch did not recognize, but he knew a good beat to dance to. He asked the waitress to dance and proceeded to lead her onto the dance floor, also nudging Jonathan to do the same with Melissa.

The last thing Jonathan wanted to do was dance with her, and she didn't care to dance with him, for she was still mad at him for what he had done days before. With enough prodding from Mitch and the waitress, Jonathan and Melissa followed them to the dance floor.

Jonathan looked at Melissa as they started dancing and said, "Well, let's just get this over with."

She looked at him and stared him directly into the eyes and didn't say anything. He just shook her head at her and they continue to dance. Finally he spoke up and said "So are you going to continue to not talk to me?"

"You know you really are a bastard sometimes, you think everything is about you. Maybe I'm not mad at you, but don't prefer to say anything to you right now. Not all of my feeling are directed towards you, you should have learned that by now," she replied.

"Alright, don't get excited, I'm not trying to get you mad again, I have had about enough of you being mad at me for something that wasn't meant to hurt you," Jonathan replied.

"You never think about things like that. You might have perfect intentions, but you never think how a person might really feel. You and I have been down this road before and I still don't think you get it. There are some things that are private and just because you know them doesn't mean everybody that we might be close to has to know these things as well."

"Fair enough, but if you want to keep throwing it back in my face the fact that I'm an inconsiderate bastard and I don't care about you, fine. But we both know that no matter how much of a stranger he really is to you he'll have some insight for you when it comes to guilt."

He paused to collect his thoughts and then said, "If you think that I don't really care about you then I wouldn't have been there every step of the way when she died, and I wouldn't be here with you now even if my grandfather really needed me. I would've said to hell with it, she can kiss my ass because I don't want to be here if she is. My only concern is that you don't let your own guilt destroy you. I know what that feels like because that's what I've been doing all these years. It's hard to admit it, but I'm admitting it with you."

Melissa gave him a surprised look because she couldn't believe what she was hearing; Jonathan was never serious and never full of compliments. When they were dating, her main complaint about him was that he was never serious enough, that he never wanted to be honest about anything, especially how he really felt about her. However, at that one moment she could see it in his eyes; she could see the truth that before she could never be sure of; she could see that he still loved her. Melissa finally saw that he was being honest with himself so he could be completely honest with her; until now he had never been honest enough to say what he truly felt out loud.

He looked at her waiting for her to say something, but she never did, and when the song they were dancing to was ending he finally said, "If it's not good enough for you then I'm truly sorry."

When the song ended he started to walk off and leave her, but then a certain song that they had always known started to be played by the band. It was their song because it was the one that always spoke true about her and her name was the title of the song, Melissa by the Allman Brothers Band. As the song began to play Jonathan stopped and smiled because of the irony, but also because they had both not heard the song in a long time. All of a sudden he felt a hand grab his and lead him back to his dancing spot.

Melissa didn't say anything, but they just looked at each other, both of them giving each other half of smile to let the other know that it was alright to be where they were. The dance floor was filled with more people now and Mitch continued to dance and laugh with Stacy as everybody in the bar enjoyed the music. It was a sweet song that put a good feeling in the place; the patrons could not help but be in the best of moods. Mitch just smiled with the joy and looked over to at his grandson and what he already knew to be the love of his life. He knew because the way Jonathan looked at Melissa was the way he looked at Alice the first time they danced together beneath the stars on the beach in Pearl Harbor.

As everybody danced Mitch drifted back into memory to the first time he had met Alice and danced with her. The scene in the bar was familiar while the young waitress reminded him of his Alice nearly fifty years ago. This is why he held on to her tight, not wanting to let go of this sweet memory that would eventually fade away.

Melissa and Jonathan just stared at each other during the song, not saying anything. They were smiling at each other and then Jonathan leaned in and kissed her. She didn't resist or become shocked at his actions; she kissed him back and leaned in closer to let their bodies touch on the dance floor. The lonely heart travelers stood there kissing each other and holding each other tight as if they would never let go.

Mitch looked at them and smiled as his

grandson finally found the courage to show Melissa how he really felt. Before the song had completely ended Melissa and Jonathan left the bar and went back to her hotel room.

At that moment the Whiskeytown bar was like a scene out of movie where all was right with the world as the patrons danced to the simple sweet song of true love. All that could be found were smiles of joy with disappearing saddened looks of despair for the patrons on the dance floor moved like dancing butterflies beneath a summer breeze in meadow where time slowed down to match the rhythm of the human heart

When the song was ended Mitch went back to his table and sat down to talk with Steve and his son Jason, as well as the waitress. The men caught up with old times and laughed at the funny stories about their lives. The waitress could not help but be interested in the stories Mitch told, how he seem to find the best in everything around him even if he could not see it within himself.

To her, Mitch was the type of person that you always wanted to be around because he could bring out the best in people and he could never be an uninteresting person no matter the age difference between the people he was around.

The four of them talked into the wee hours of the evening, with the waitress hanging onto every word Mitch said. She did this because he was a great person, one that you always wanted to be around, although there was a small attraction on her part. Mitch told his friends at the table what was happening to him and why he was on this journey and in no small way said his last goodbyes.

"You know," said Stacy, "I see different types of people come and go in here, but never one that could keep my attention like you. There is something about you Mitch, how do you it?"

"There's no secret, I'm just me and I like to laugh while seeing people laugh around me, so I find a way to make that happen."

"Well, you've got me hooked even though you're a lot older."

"Age has nothing to do it when it comes to friends and certainly has nothing to do with being able to like someone."

"What about more than friends?" she asked.

"No, age has nothing to do with that either, but I know for me the person that could keep my attention all the time was the person who stole my heart fifty years ago."

"Oh...I guess one could only be so lucky."

"It can happen because accidents of love happen all the time when we are not looking and it's going to happen to you when you least expect it."

"You believe that, what makes you so sure?"

"I have faith and I know that you are the type of person that will never settle for anything that's not the best for you," Mitch replied as he kissed her on the cheek."

"You must think I'm some innocent little girl to give me advice like that, but I'm really not that innocent. I haven't been for a long time."

"Well that's a shame, because we should never lose our innocence completely. We need all the innocence we can get."

"Do you really believe that?"

"Yes I do, because we shouldn't be so anxious to see the horrors of this world. That's why innocence is wasted on the young. When we're young we are always trying to grow up too fast and when we're old all we want is to be that young again while having the innocence of our childhood.”

"Maybe you're right because it's one of those we can never get back."

"That's right, and it would be nice to get it back even if it was for only a little while."

When they were all done talking and the bar was closed for the night the old friends parted. Stacy hugged Mitch, kissing him on the cheek and thanking him for making her evening one of the best she had had in long time. He just simply told her that the world is a beautiful and exciting place and with that in mind she should never miss the opportunity to enjoy the world around her and that can't happen in just one place.

While old friends parted, Melissa and Jonathan were back at the hotel. They arrived not too long after their song had ended making their way into her room kissing each other passionately as if they were first time lovers again. They made their way back to bed that was somewhat messy and then Melissa stopped Jonathan. "I need to know something from you. Is this just a onetime thing or do you have any other intentions because I don't think I can go through another heartbreak with you."

Jonathan just looked at her with the intensity of passion for someone and replied, "It will be whatever you want it to be, but if you really want to know the truth, I never stopped loving you. I can't give you any better honesty than that."

She looked at him and started to cry because it had been a long time since she had heard that and she didn't want to hear it from anybody else but Jonathan. She didn't say anything to him and leaned forward to kiss him giving him her whole heart even if it was to be broken again by this the man who himself was broken and hurting inside. They fell to the bed and the lights

faded into darkness as the couple started a journey
into a lover's affair with the soul of the world.

In the next room Mitch smiled to himself as he
found the room empty and noticed that Jonathan was
with Melissa. He poured himself a glass of Whiskey
and pulled out a picture of Alice from his wallet. It
was one from when she was a young girl in love with
a young Army officer; the picture was taken at the
hospital where they first met when he was a patient
and she was his nurse. He looked at and began to cry
while tear drops fell into his whiskey glass.

9

Seeing the Light of Their World

Mitch woke up to the shattering of glass. The whiskey glass that had been lying on top of his chest finally fell over and broke as he rolled over in his sleep. He was still drunk from the night before and couldn't remember too well the circumstances surrounding his state of being, but he was caught in a haze of memory from his past finally catching up with him. As he continued on this journey, the mistakes that he had made over a lifetime were finally coming back to haunt the last days of his life, and he knew there was no running away this time. Mitch would have to finally come to terms with the things he had done and would finally have to render the past he tried desperately to drink away.

For the first time since this trip had started he knew that it was time, it was time to be completely honest with himself and everybody else. He was too old and had learned too much to be a fool, and as certain memories came to mind he made up his mind to finally deal with some things that he had not been ready to deal with until now. As he looked at the empty bed next to his where Jonathan was supposed to have slept, he knew what had happened to he and Melissa and he smiled because he was glad. He was glad to see a love be renewed and then remembered the one moment in his life when in one instance he nearly destroyed the love he had for the one true love of his life.

That moment happened for him in Las Vegas over thirty years ago with a woman that he had met a few times on business. It was the one and only time that he had come very close to cheating on Alice and breaking his vow with the one love of his life. The woman in question was not some sleazy working girl at a casino. She was a young female scientist that worked in the same department as him in the Atomic Commission, but was stationed out west. She was smart, funny, and sexy and there was an immediate attraction between the both of them, but one that Mitch had never acted upon over the years that they worked together until one drunken night of stupidity.

He could still remember her and the way she smelled. He liked her, of course, and maybe if they had met twenty years before things might have been different. He had never had to lie about his relationships with the people he worked with until that day, and Mitch could remember every detail vividly.

It was late one evening and a group of them were having drinks; in a drunken moment when they were on their way back to their rooms she kissed him and he kissed her back, not knowing why. Mitch wanted to sleep with her and they ended up in her room with their clothes halfway off and that was it. The next day they both woke up half naked realizing that nothing had happened, they had both passed out.

As Mitch would say to himself for the next twenty years while wading through his own guilt about something that didn't even happen, he had crossed a line, and it was one that he could never come back over. His drunkenness might have saved him from an adulterous act, but he committed a treacherous act of the heart and it was something he had to lie about. As Mitch was packing his bags for Las Vegas he thought about this event like it was yesterday and how it had it eventually destroyed his marriage.

Mitch never worked with this woman ever again, and she never stopped wanting to be with Mitch, as he found out years later. Although he never did anything with her, he knew he would have, and that was when the end of his marriage with his beloved wife started. Alice never found out till many years later about what happened until a letter came in the mail from the woman. In the letter she explained how she loved Mitch and had never known anybody quite like him before. Then she went on to explain what happened between them and the fact that she couldn't live with not being honest about it anymore.

The letter was intended to be received in the mail by Mitch, but Alice had found it first and after reading it was crushed in many ways for she couldn't believe that this would happen. She always knew that Mitch was a well-liked person and had the ability to seduce the women he encountered, but never thought that he really would do it.

She never thought that Mitch would do this to her, even though all his heavy drinking and loss of memory. He wasn't a perfect husband, but being an alcoholic was a problem giving way to a very destructive nature within himself. On the weekends he would literally drink himself to sleep and to the point that he could not remember what had happened the days before.

Despite all this, she couldn't believe that he would do such a terrible act, and this started the end of the love affair they once had. This happened in the early eighties after forty years of marriage, and for the first time Alice didn't want him around anymore; she finally couldn't live with him. There had been times when she was really mad at Mitch and needed to get away for a while, but she never until that moment wanted him to leave forever. When she confronted him about the letter, he didn't want to lie so he told her the truth. He tried to tell her that nothing happened, but in her anger she couldn't see past the act of betrayal; Mitch couldn't blame her.

They argued and they fought, but it was too much for Alice to bear so she told Mitch that he needed to leave for good. He did, and it was a years before he would see her again. His daughters would eventually find out what happened and why he left. Both Laura and Catherine would take a long time to find forgiveness when it came to their father, and it was a long time before they would speak to him again after he left.

Mitch was out of all their lives, and for Jonathan as a young man it was a shocking heartbreak because he idolized his grandfather and never completely understood what happened. For him in the end his youthful anger would lead to his poor assumptions about his grandfather's actions.

Mitch could remember that it was harder on Jonathan because they had been very close from the day he was born, and Jonathan never knew the entire truth so all he was left with were false notions he

conjured up about who Mitch really was. This Collins
family had one great talent in never saying the things
that needed to be said. The issues that needed true
honesty were ignored as everybody lived out their daily
lives.

Because of this, certain truths were never
revealed and false notions were created to satisfy the
answers they were looking for about whom they were
and why they did the things they did. Mitch had
always believed that his family never wanted to accept
that this could happen, that they man they had loved
and revered could not be as great as they had once
seen, but Mitch knew the hard truth that people are
never what they seem because we are all broken and
destructive in nature.

Mitch had never been back to Las Vegas since
that dreadful night in 1972 because he had always
been afraid to go back. For the longest time Vegas had
been a cursed place for him and he couldn't bring
himself to go back and face the demons he had created
for himself. He had friends there, because like many
places in western America he would go to on a regular
basis when he was still working his government job, he
would develop relationships with people that would
turn into lifelong friendships.

Vegas was no different, and he had missed the
place because it was somewhere that everyday life
never became dull. It was thriving with excitement,
and for someone that was always looking to have a
good time with people, Las Vegas was never short of
opportunity. His friends that lived there that worked at
the casinos were some of the most exciting people he
had ever met, but it was a lifestyle with these people
that Alice had never wanted any part of, so Mitch tried
to soak up every minute he could while he was there
and after 1972 he began to see Vegas as a curse

because it caused him to do the thing he dreaded the most: break a sacred vow he had made many years before.

In the back of his mind Mitch always thought that if he never went back he would redeem himself and his relationship with Alice would be saved. Twenty years later he finally knew the truth; it was his own drunken stupid actions that caused him to lose the thing he loved the most: his family. He also knew coming to the winter of his life that emotional demons had to be faced and beaten down so he was on his way back to the place where the end of happy life would begin to end. Then as he loaded up his suitcase in the car he realized we never truly lose our family, we just get separated for a while and then we have to find our way back by facing the horrific events of our lives.

For Mitch, this was the most important thing for him to do on this journey because he didn't have much time left. He also didn't want the truth of his life to be the false notions that were replacements of that which he and his family had been too scared to face before. For now, his memories would have to be replaced with what was happening currently, so he went to get some coffee for him and the weary travelers on their way to the lighted city in the desert.

∞∞∞∞∞∞∞

Jonathan woke up to the persisting knocking on the door as he lay curled up on the bed with Melissa. She was sound asleep completely naked underneath the covers as Jonathan had her wrapped up in his arms. He wasn't quite awake yet and didn't know what was going on exactly, but he got up to answer the door wearing only his boxers. It was Mitch at the door with some coffee for the two lovers.

Mitch laughed at him standing there in his underwear. "I see you had fun last night. Here is some coffee for you and Melissa. By the way, you might want to put some pants on, that look is what can get us pulled over by the police, and I don't have the money to bail you out of jail."

"Look, I can explain this, I'm sure you're wondering what's going on here," said Jonathan.

"That's just a level of curiosity I don't have," said Mitch, "and you're an adult so you do what you want to do. By the way, I have told you that with women you have to tell them what it is you really want and it's nice to see you taking my advice. So you two get dressed and get out here. I'm hungry and want to get on the road soon. Vegas is a long drive from here. Also, your boxers are on backwards, the hole goes on the front. I know I taught you better than that."

Mitch walked away and Jonathan quickly took his boxers after shutting the door then put them on straight. All he could was laugh and sigh because he knew that with his grandfather he would never hear the end of it, and for the first time in many years it felt good to know that his grandfather cared about him to give him a hard time. Even now what he didn't realize is that his grandfather had never stopped caring about him ever since he walked out when he was sixteen years old.

Within thirty minutes Jonathan and Melissa emerged from her hotel room ready to continue their journey and all Mitch could do was laugh at them. Although he was mainly smiling from the joy he felt knowing that these two had finally come this far in their relationship together.

The travelers gathered together in the old car

and the radio started to play as the car was started to an old obscure Eagles' song called "'Ol 55." It happened to be one of Jonathan's favorites and they all laughed at the irony as the car pulled out of the hotel parking lot. Jonathan drove and Melissa rode up front next to him looking at him out of the corner of her eye while slightly smiling showing the joy she was experiencing from the night before.

Mitch sat in the back and closed his eyes remembering the first time he and Alice took a drive down a country road escaping to some small paradise that only they could understand. Their paradise was being with each other and letting the world go by without notice.

∞∞∞∞∞∞∞∞

Shortly after they had been home from the war in late 1945 Mitch and Alice decided that they wanted to get married, but they had never met each other's parents, so one of the first trips they took together was to Oklahoma so he could meet her family and see the farm she had grown up on. Before they arrived at the farm she made him drive to her favorite place; it was a small creek hidden behind a rolling bend among the wheat fields of Oklahoma. They drove their car down a dirt road among the tall swaying wheat beneath a bright sun that guided them to the country paradise where she had retreated to as a young girl.

As they stopped at the edge of the wheat field ended and where the bend began to take a steep downward turn she looked at him and said, "If you really want to marry me, you know you will have to ask for my father's blessing, and you won't probably won't get it because my father doesn't like anyone that has a romantic relationship with me."

"How do you know he won't like me? I'm a pretty good guy and he should know that I will take care of you. Besides, he should just know that I love you and that should be enough," Mitch replied.

"You think that will be enough for my father? He will just hate you on general principle because you're with me," Alice responded.

"Well, I guess we will just have to elope if he says no, because I plan on marrying you anyway," Mitch said.

"Don't even say that. If you really love me then you will get his blessing or find a way to make him understand that you love me and will take care of me no matter what happens in our lives," she said to him.

"I'll make him understand, but taking care of you the rest of our lives. That might be too big of a task. Who knows where we will be in twenty years? You might go crazy and then I'll have to divorce you," Mitch said.

Alice just gave him a dirty look. "If you plan on marrying me then it's for the rest of our lives, and that's nonnegotiable. It doesn't matter whether I go crazy or not, you better plan on being with me till the end."

Mitch smiled to let her know he was kidding and said, "I'm afraid Alice Clark Abshire that you are stuck with me till one of us is dead and that's because I love you. That you better believe. If your father doesn't like me then this is what I plan on making him understand."

After he was finished he winked at her and took a sip of whiskey from the flask he always kept with him. Alice just smiled her warm smile at him; her smile could light the hearts of the vicious and it was a smile that could make anybody all of sudden feel complete joy. She walked over to where he stood grabbed his flask, took a sip, and kissed him long and hard. Then she replied "I guess a stubborn Irishman never breaks his word."

"That's right, and you better not forget it, either. I promise you that we will be together till the end," he replied.

For the next hour they drove their car beneath the bright Oklahoma sun along the county roads surrounded by wheat fields and grassy meadows. They smiled and gave each other little kisses, being young lovers full of life and promise.

Mitch remembered that day vividly and it was one of the happiest days of his life. Alice was a sweet, stubborn, and girl full of life untarnished by the bitterness of the world and the agony of the war they had lived through. He thought to himself. She was amazing because could get past all of that and still be happy. No matter what she found a way to be happy, but there was one dreaded secret she had from her childhood that could ruin everything. It would be a secret that she would have to entrust to Mitch if he was to love her every day for the rest of her life

So she told him her secret, how she was she was abused and raped by a farm hand when she was a young and innocent...how she was made into an unwanted woman and could never be desired. Mitch was shocked, how could he not be, but it didn't matter. For him she was perfect and untainted; that's what he saw in her. He saw her as the most beautiful woman he had ever known. He knew it would be hard to live a happy life with this as part of her past and even harder to have a family, but that day he devoted his life to her beneath that Oklahoma Sky He made a pledge to love her completely and sometimes without understanding and the day their children were born only increased his love for her because somehow he knew deep down ,if he just loved her, everything would always work out.

∞∞∞∞∞∞

Mitch sat back in his seat and smiled at the sweet memory that he had become lost in. and right then and there he decided that he would not break that promise to his true love despite the past that was catching up with the last days he would ever have.

After a long day's drive they arrived in the city of lights or sin city as some had come to know it. It was Las Vegas, Nevada, a small paradise filled with greed and treacherous acts, but an ironic paradise none the less. Jonathan and Melissa had never been to this place before, and for the both of them it was a place filled with excitement like a kid in a candy store. For Mitch, the excitement was washed away with horrible memories.

They drove through the city trying to decide on hotel to stay at like they were celebrities. Some of the patrons in the city even thought so as they received loud applause and honks from other cars while driving though the city. Mitch thought it was strange, but Jonathan just told him that his philosophy might be right; if you drive a classy car then everybody will think you're classy and want to be just like you.

They drove through the city for a while just admiring the sites and then finally Mitch took them to a little inexpensive hotel toward the end of the city. Melissa and Jonathan thought it was strange that he would want to stay here, but he told them that it was the same hotel rooms that he would stay in when he was out here on business. He wanted to reminisce a bit while not wanting to be too extravagant. The truth is they were the same hotels he would stay at while here in Vegas, but it was also where he had committed the worst act he had ever committed in his life, the betrayal of his beloved.

Mitch had always told himself that if he could come back here then he might have a chance at finally putting this behind him so it would not haunt him for the rest of his life. After twenty years and not that many days left within his life, he saw this as the perfect chance to come to terms with this.

After a few minutes of getting settled in, the travelers went into the city to find a place to eat since each of them was a famished. Mitch took them to the Bellagio Casino since he knew one of the chefs that had been a chef in Las Vegas for thirty years. Jonathan was not surprised that he knew somebody at the casino for it seemed that his grandfather knew everybody they encountered.

The casino was big and buzzing with events; there was so much one could do in the casino that it would literally take a day's worth of time, and that was besides the time spent on gambling. As they were walking through the main lobby toward the restaurant area, Jonathan bumped into an old friend of his that was with his band in Vegas. Jonathan knew that his friend Rick would be here and knew that he had a band competing on some battle of the bands competition because he had turned down the invitation to be here with them, but he didn't know when that would be so it was kind of a surprise to see him.

"Jonathan, man what are you doing here in Las Vegas?" Rick asked.

"Hey it's great to see you; I'm here with my grandfather visiting Las Vegas. You remember Melissa, don't you?"

Rick looked over at her and was surprised to see her here with Jonathan.

"How are you doing? He asked her. "I'm a little surprised to see you here with this guy. Are you two an item again?"

Jonathan didn't know how to answer that, especially in front of his grandfather who was laughing to himself because his grandson had been put on the spot about his relationship concerning Melissa. Jonathan just stood there and didn't say anything for a moment and then finally he started to answer the question with somewhat of a horrified look on his face. Before he could start, Melissa cut him off and said, "I'm just here with these guys for moral support. Jonathan's grandfather Mitch needed some traveling companions, so we came along."

Rick looked over at Mitch and reached out to shake his hand then he said, "'It's an honor to meet you."
Anybody that knows Jonathan has heard a lot of stories about you."

Mitch looked at him and his grandson with a strange look because he was surprised that his grandson would actually talk about him in a good way to his friends. He reached out his hand to shake the young gentlemen's hand in front of him and replied, "It's nice to meet you; I take it you are one of my grandson's music friends?"

"Oh yeah, we have played in a few bands together and I have to say he is the best piano player I have played with, but you probably already know how good he is," Rick replied.

"I have to admit that I have not heard my grandson play his best in a long time," Mitch said.

"Then I have the perfect opportunity for you to hear him play again. Jonathan, I am really glad to run into to you because the keyboard player we were going to use with this battle of the bands thing just got sick and I need a replacement. If you are here then you can be his replacement if you want. We go on in about three hours and you already know the music.”

“I don’t know about this Rick, we just got here and I need to be here with my grandfather in case he needs my help,” Jonathan replied.

Rick just looked at him with a disappointed look because he knew that with his piano playing and vocals the band would have even a better chance at winning. “I understand, but it will only be for a few hours.   If we win, which I think we really can with you playing piano, then we get a record deal.”

“What songs are you playing for this thing?” Mitch asked.

“We are doing Roll Me Away by Bob Seger and Thunder Road by Springsteen. Like I said, you already know the songs and you can even do the vocals on them. I know you passed on the chance to do this, but you’re here now. So what do you say? Do it for us, help the band.”

“Well, you don’t need to give me such a big guilt trip, but if it’s just for tonight then I guess I can help you out. I’m not going on some tour with you though, the last time we did that it ended up being a disaster. What do you guys think, you don’t mind do you?”

They both told him that he should do it and it would be a lot fun to see him be part of concert on their first night in Vegas. Mitch even told him that he should do it because you never know what dreams might come true when you’re in Vegas, but if he really embarrassed himself bad then he there is comfort in knowing that what happens in Vegas stays in Vegas.

Rick told Jonathan to meet him in the Green

room of the casino in about an hour, then left him to eat with his family. Within a few minutes of being inside the casino Jonathan had involved himself in something that would eventually change the course of his life, as things often did when visiting the city of lights.

Mitch, Jonathan, and Melissa were treated to a really nice dinner before the show started. Mitch was filled with questions for Jonathan about his music and the career he had, especially within the past few years. He had known very little about what Jonathan was doing with his life since they hadn't spoken to each other for a long time. He knew Jonathan was a gifted piano player, but never really knew how far he had come with his talent since he was a kid. Over dinner they talked a great deal about being a musician and the life that one leads when you're not famous.

Melissa got to share a little bit about what made her fall in love with Jonathan the first time she had ever met him; it had been his passion for music and the way he played for her. What Mitch never realized is that music for Jonathan made sense unlike everything else in his life that had a habit of being confusing. For the first time since Jonathan was a kid, Mitch was proud of his grandson and the passion he found for something that could give him a career, even if it was not something that could make him rich. Mitch finally saw what the love of music had done for his grandson; it had made him human, something that could make him feel emotion and feel alive while not making him dead inside.

They all laughed and talked about the love of music they all had. Mitch finally realized that all the jazz and big band music that he had made Jonathan listen to as a kid had a profound influence on him because he had a just as much of love for the big band music like Glen Miller and people like Sinatra and Martin than that of Rock and Roll. The two of them quizzed each other on their knowledge of this type of music and all Melissa could do was laugh because each one them of was challenging the other in their conversation. What the two men found is that they had more in common than they realized.

After dinner Jonathan went to meet up with the band so he could get ready for the competition. He found the band and found that he knew some of the other members that were there. There were two other members besides Rick that Jonathan knew and had played with at one time throughout the New Orleans area. The band was solid, it was good, and with Jonathan on piano they all felt like they had a chance at winning. The rest of the members even agreed that Jonathan was the best choice to sing since he had a better voice for the songs they were about to play.

Mitch and Melissa walked around for about two hours before the show started. While they walked around, Melissa recounted the tale of how she and Jonathan had first met. It had been about six years ago when she was just a freshman at Tulane University in New Orleans and had to take a job as a cocktail waitress to help support herself. She took a job in a little joint in the French Quarter that doesn't exist anymore, where they had live music on the weekends. Jonathan had been a student at LSU trying to be a baseball player; it was his last chance to make it as a ball player after he had a serious injury to his arm in high school. He had been a young pitcher who had thrown out his arm when he was young, but didn't want to admit that it was a permanent injury. After high school he went to LSU to try out as a relief pitcher after nearly two years of rehabilitation on his arm

Jonathan never made it as a ball player with the university, but what he did find was his other great love. It would become the great love of his life besides the woman he would marry and spend the rest of life with. He loved playing piano and he would play anywhere he could; sometime during his freshman year he started playing small gigs at anyplace that would let him play piano in the New Orleans area

One night when Melissa was working, Jonathan's little jazz trio was playing and it was his music that captured her heart. They met that night and soon started dating. They would go to school during the day and at night see each other when they weren't working. After a short time they found a place together and opened their lives to one another.

They were off and on again for the next few years as they tried to finish college and Jonathan tried to make it as a professional musician. He had a lot of gigs and sometimes would tour across the country, but never anything big. He made just enough money for he and Melissa while they were together, but his career never really took off except for being a studio musician on some jazz albums. They had a great life, but there was always something that could keep them apart from one another; it was her guilt and fear of abandonment, and it was his anger over his past with his family that he never had control over.

Eventually they would end their love affair, but stay in New Orleans letting their regrets rob them of emotions. Melissa would become a saddened guilt stricken workaholic managing a bar in the French Quarter. Jonathan would become a beaten down musician losing his passion to write the one true song that could inspire the world, while never being able to find his song. For the last two years they had pretty much avoided each other and let their anger for the other boil to an unforgiving contempt for love.

Mitch was saddened to hear her story and he knew all too well how deep seeded anger could destroy the true passion a person could have for something. He also knew how his grandson could be; it was that same Irish stubbornness that he had and there was no easy way to just let it go. Mitch finally told Melissa that every great thing in life has to do with timing.

If you are one second to slow or one second too fast you can miss the great things that will happen to you because our lives can change dramatically in a split second. He also told her that maybe this trip was something of good timing because all three of them were experiencing some life changing events that were good for them in the end.

They arrived at the show a few minutes before Jonathan and the band was supposed to go on. The competition was a battle of the bands event where the winner would get a record deal and the winner was picked by a panel of judges from the music industry. The competitors did not get to play their own music, but had to cover a great song that had already been made famous by another musician so they could show their musical talent by giving their own interpretation of the song. It didn't necessarily make sense, but artistic quality sometimes doesn't make when it comes to entertainment.

The event was filled with lots of people and was on TV in the Las Vegas area. There were a number of great bands and singers and they all got to do two songs unless the crowd booed them off stage before they even finished their first song.

Jonathan was a little nervous because he had not played or sung these songs in a long time, but like every musician knows, it's how much intensity and passion you put behind songs you're playing that makes them good. His band came on to a large crowd cheering them on and he could easily find Mitch and Melissa in the audience. Before he had time to panic they were ready to play so he started them off with the song *Roll Me Away* since it started with a soft piano melody. Then came the opening line and his smooth voice carried them on their way to the end. The band was in perfect sync and their passion for the song they all loved won the hearts of the judges and the crowd.

The audience was rocking with the music, forgetting all their troubles. Even Mitch was tapping his foot to keep the beat while getting excited about a song he had never heard before. As soon as they were done the audience erupted in applause for Jonathan and the band. They put smiles on the judge's faces and got the room excited, even getting a standing ovation for their rendition of Bob Seger's song.

It took a few minutes for the audience to quiet down, and then he spotted her with a big smile on her face. Jonathan saw Melissa give him the smile that made him fall in love with her while always letting him know that he was home. He leaned over to his band mates and said that he was going to change the song to one of Melissa's favorites and asked if everybody knew it. It was *Faithfully* by the band Journey. To his surprise nobody objected because everybody loved the song and since they were on such a high from doing well on the song before they let Jonathan take lead and play the song that could win them the competition. All his friend Rick told him was that he better know what he was doing.

Jonathan made the announcement that they were changing the song they were about to play and that it was dedicated to someone special in the audience. Mitch knew exactly who it was for and reached out to squeeze her hand as Melissa started to shed a few tears. Then Jonathan began the song that said all the words that he couldn't say out loud.

The song was in his way an apology for all the hurt he had caused her when they were dating and when he was drinking too much to give a damn. He knew it wasn't easy to love him and to love a musician always in search for the one his song of life, but what she didn't know was that she had always been his muse. Sherry Melissa had always been the one that made sense in his complicated life and it had been that way from the first day he had met her.

Jonathan had never been able to admit it until now, and he had never been able to tell her everything that he should have told her long ago, but this was his chance so he did it in the form of a song that she was always inspired by.

When the song was done, the crowd erupted again in applause, giving yet another standing ovation for the smooth voice Jonathan added in the band's rendition of the classic song. Melissa was crying and she blew a kiss at Jonathan from the audience and he winked at her, which always let her know that he loved her.

It took a while to get the crowd to settle down after Jonathan and the others were done; the audience wanted an encore, but time did not permit since there were two more bands that had to play before a winner would be announced. They played and the crowd clapped, but they were not as excited as when Jonathan and Rick's band played. When all the bands had played and the competition was done, a winner was announced. Based on the enthusiasm of the audience when they played, the judges awarded first place to Jonathan and Rick.

Jonathan couldn't believe it and even the rest of

the band was in shock, considering Jonathan had just been found as a replacement three hours before the competition. However, the songs they played were songs that they had all grown up with and were songs that were engrained into their very souls, so with the passion for the music they played they were able to be true to their craft and play better than anyone else that night.

Jonathan, his band mates, Melissa, and even Mitch went out to celebrate the occasion, for it was not every day that an infamous group of musicians were put together at the last minute, but were true musical artists and could pull off such a sweet success. They had drinks in one of the clubs until the early morning hours, laughed and told stories from their days of being musicians on the road, and even Mitch recounted some of his stories, having seen the greats play Vegas.

He told stories of what Vegas was like in its prime, when men lived every second of their lives to the fullest without consequence and damning those that tried to put a stop to it. Mitch told of the days when Vegas was ruled by entertainers like Frank Sinatra, Dean Martin, Sammy Davis Jr., and the king himself, Elvis Presley; when Vegas was run by men with a sense of honor despite the label of criminal.

They laughed, they cried, and the young men held on to every that the old had to speak as if it were the last piece of wisdom ever spoken. Despite the age and generational difference these young men could relate to Mitch because he never judged them for how they lived their lives. He had lived hard too, and experienced more than most men from growing up a poor fisherman's son to living through the depression, a world war that nearly killed him more than once, a life as an alcoholic, and finally as a man that had pushed his family away for a drink and a deep seeded guilt.

They all loved Mitch because he was a man of experience who liked to share his stories instead of being the parental figure that told them how to live their lives. Mitch knew better than anybody that each person had to make their own way despite the mistakes he was sure to make. The group finally parted for the morning and each man left with something better than they had had before because of Mitch, and as they were saying their goodbyes, each member of the band made sure to tell Jonathan how lucky he was for having the grandfather he had.

They all retired for the evening, or early morning as it had become, happier than they had ever been since they had started this trip and the weary travelers on the road returned to the hotel. They all had forgotten for a few hours what was really happening on this trip; they had forgotten for a short time that Mitch was dying and these joyous moments were coming to an end. Jonathan went to bed with Melissa in her room while Mitch was left to a room by himself with only his guilt stricken memory. What the others didn't know was that Mitch had purposefully chosen the room he was in because of its history.

Mitch knew that it was time to confront his demons so he poured himself a glass of whiskey, took a sip and then poured the rest of it out in the trash can where the only contents of the can was a letter. It was the letter that "she" had sent Alice nearly ten years ago explaining the betrayal of her husband. Mitch had kept it as a reminder of his faults and how a lie could tear a family apart. He set the thing on fire and prayed for the first time in many years for forgiveness; forgiveness for his betrayal.

The next morning the three of them left Vegas

to continue their journey west. They were off to see the Pacific Ocean so Mitch could see it one last time. They all grabbed some coffee and breakfast to go and drove through the city of lights as it was in its slow slumber before nightfall came again. There was an old familiar song on the radio as they drove through, *It Had To Be You.*

Mitch drove his 55 caddy through the city with a smile on his face, a smile that had not been there in a long time. Jonathan and Melissa couldn't understand what it was that made him smile, but for Mitch is was something that he had left behind.

Later that day the cleaning lady walked into the room Mitch had slept in to start cleaning. She found on the bed a pair of broken cufflinks; they had been broken the night when Mitch had gone too far with another woman. They were his favorite pair of cuff links, a gift from his wife and they had become broken during his one moment of weakness in the throes of drunken passion. The broken cuff links symbolized the breaking of his commitment to the one true love of his life. So on a sunny day in the city of lights within the last days of his life, he was finally able to let go and leave them behind with the pain that he had carried inside for so long.

10

A Brother's Love

Mitch was in a deep dream. It was the spring of 1945 in England shortly before the war in Europe was to end. The ship he was stationed on was bringing supplies to England so while he was there he got a few days leave. While on leave he decided to see his brother since it had been a couple of years since they last saw each other. He met him at an army airfield in Northern England and found his brother's flight crew was waiting for their next mission, which by this time during the war were bombing missions of over Germany.

A sergeant entered one of the officer's barracks and yelled "Lt. Maxwell Collins, there's a gentleman out here claiming to be your brother."

Max, as everybody called him, jumped off his bed in a hurry and ran out the door to see if it was actually true. It was; there was Mitch standing next to a jeep that he somehow got a hold of waiting for his brother to emerge. The two men embraced. "Damn it's good to see you," said Max. "I thought the only chance we would get to see each other again is when this whole turkey shoot is done."

"Hey," Mitch replied, "I wasn't going to miss a chance to see my little brother if I had to come back to England. I don't care if it takes me an extra day to get back to my ship. Besides, our mother would kill me herself if I didn't check up on you."

"Is she still sending you those letters blaming you for getting me in the war and trying to find a way to wound me so I will have to go home?" Max asked

Mitch laughed and replied, "I get one at least once a week if it gets through the line telling me to get her little boy home. Dad won't even write me a letter because he's so mad that you followed in my footsteps, but at least I get some mail from them. What about you, are you getting stuff from them?"

"I must get the same letter every week when it gets through," said Max, "except they tell me they love me and blame you for me being here. Who knows, maybe they will come around when we get home safe as only a hero should come home."

Mitch smiled and nodded in agreement. "Hopefully, but hey, while I'm here let me buy you a drink."

"You know we can't have a drink while on duty, we can get court marshaled," Max replied.

Mitch shook his head and laughed out loud. "Then mom will be happy that you're going home, but since I out rank you then your orders are to have a drink with your brother."

"Who am I to refuse an order?" replied Max.

The two men wandered over to one of the airplane hangars where Max's plane was located. Mitch had two paper cups and a small flask with some whiskey in it which he poured completely out into the cups for his brother and him to drink. The plane Max flew was a big four engine B-17, he was the co-pilot and the plane was called "The Moonlight Mission." It was named after the Glenn Miller song which was a favorite among the crew.

The song was one of those little reminders of how home was a little sweeter when you could be dancing with a pretty young girl beneath the moonlight sky. There wasn't a man on the base that didn't feel at ease when listening to songs like that, especially when flying missions over war torn Europe. Max's favorite pastime other than flying was listening to music. He loved to listen to the radio so much that sometimes on missions he would swap places with the radio operator so he could listen to the sweet sounds of a big band jazz assemble from the music that the crew could sometimes pick up while flying.

There was even a funny story that the men in his crew liked to tell. One night in late 1944 when they were on a mission heading home in the dead of night, Max had swapped places with the radio operator to listen to the radio as they were flying over the English Channel. He was in such a deep peaceful trance that he was not paying attention to what the pilot was doing; as they passed through the clouds the plane nearly collided with another plane coming over the top of them. The pilot could only do so much to get their B-17 safely out of the way; he needed the help of his co-pilot to steer the big plane. The radio operator had to hit Max in the face to get him out of his trance so he could get back in his seat to help the pilot get their plane to safety. The men Max flew with loved to tell that story over and over because they thought it was so funny. Max thought it was funny, too, and even had to tell his big brother in a letter about the incident before somebody that knew them both did. Everybody knows what kind of stories or rumors fly around among military men.

Max took another sip of his whiskey and then asked Mitch, "So are you still writing to that nurse you met awhile back?"

"Yeah, I write a letter to her every day even though I don't know how many actually get through, but I still write to her and I get quite a few letters from her as well," Mitch replied.

"Well, I guess it must be love if you keep writing to her. Do you have any future plans if you make it out of this?" Max asked.

"Sure I do. Go home, have a lot of great meals instead of navy rations, then I will see a really voluptuous sexy girl who will welcome me home as a hero properly," Mitch replied

"Yeah, that's you and every man in the military. Of course I know I will definitely deserve it because I look so good in a uniform, unlike my ugly big brother here," Max said laughing out loud while Mitch just smiled at his brother's sarcasm. Seriously though, do you have any real plans when you get back home?"

"If you're talking about whether I plan to see her after we are done with this war, then yes I hope so. I have to admit I love her and there is nobody I want to be with other than her."

"Wow, I can't believe my brother is admitting this. I thought you never wanted to get married or have a family. You always told me you just wanted to live one hell of an exciting life and you couldn't do that by being settled down." Max responded.

"Maybe that's true, but she's worth it and with her I can find a way to make it work. She is the most beautiful woman I have ever known and it's just one more reason to settle down with her if she will have me," Mitch replied.

"If you're that serious about her then maybe there is something about her. I have to meet this girl when we finally get home, but make sure I meet her before Mom and Dad do so I can say what a wonderful girl she is and be on your side when they hate her for being with you," Max replied.

"She is so wonderful that even our prejudiced parents will like her, and I will even bet you a bottle of good Irish whiskey that they will."

Max smiled his big sarcastic smile and replied, "I will take that bet and when you give me my bottle of whiskey please include a fine crystal shot glass to go with it. "

The two men shook hands to confirm the bet and then sirens wailed out over the base. Max's crew had been on standby because of cloud cover and now their wait was over. Max jumped up grabbed his coat and took off running to meet his crew that was getting ready for takeoff. He looked at his brother and said, "Got to go, but try and stay in touch if you can…Hey don't get yourself killed. I still want to collect on our bet."

Mitch slowly walked out of the hanger as bombing crews were quickly scattering to their planes. Mitch stopped in the grassy meadow near the runway so he could stop and see the plane take off. The second plane to take off was the Moonlight Mission and as it passed by Max stuck his hand out of the side window to wave and say goodbye to his brother. It would be the last time either one of them would see each other.

∞∞∞∞∞∞∞

With that fading memory of seeing Max for the last time, Mitch woke up suddenly from his dream.

He had had the dream before, occurring several times over the last few months, especially after finding out the news that he was going to die. He could remember his last meeting with Max vividly while never letting the memories of their childhood fade from his memory. He got up from the soft hotel bed, stared at the empty whiskey bottle on the dresser, and then got ready for the day's drive to the west coast.

The travelers left early that day and drove for almost two days to the California coast They were going to the San Francisco-Oakland bay area. Mitch wanted to take them to see the Pacific Ocean; for him it was one more chance to look out over the horizon which he had grown to love while being out to sea. When they finally got there they registered at a hotel near the beach then they walked down to the beach as the sun was beginning to set over the Pacific Ocean. It looked as if the water was melting beneath simmering flames of the night time sun. It was one of the most beautiful acts of nature that any of them had seen; all they could do was stare out over the water into the horizon.

After standing on the beach for a few moments Mitch took his shoes and socks off and walked into the water as the waves came crashing up over his feet. He did it because he wanted to feel the wave's crash up against his legs again while at the same time feeling the soft watered sand beneath his feet.

Jonathan and Melissa followed his act and did the same thing until all three of them were standing side by side in water that came up midway to their calves.

Nobody said anything for a while and then Mitch finally spoke up. "The first time I saw the Pacific Ocean was in 1942 when my unit in the Navy was sent to Hawaii for training before we were shipped off to the war. I remember it clearly because I had never seen anything like it, the Atlantic Ocean looks very different and the only thing I had seen up to then was navy piers filled with lots of trawlers and fishing boats. The waterfronts I had seen up to then were always crowded. This ocean, it's always open and seems to go on forever. It seems scary, but it's also freedom."

"Mitch, are you trying to give us a poetic lesson about the sea?" asked Jonathan. "What are you really trying to say?" Melissa slapped him on the arm and told him not to be rude.

Mitch gave a short laugh and replied, "Maybe I am, but since I'm dying I can be a little poetic so don't interrupt me."

He looked over at the other two smiled and winked at them then continued in his narrative, "I was scared the first time I went out on the ocean because I had never been on a boat on the water before I joined the navy. I had worked as a fisherman growing up, but it was mainly unloading the boats when they got back from being out on the sea. I remember thinking that if I became lost out here then I would never return, but sometimes that's not a bad thing. My captain told me once that there was an old seaman's tale that said the Atlantic Ocean would restore your life, but that the Pacific Ocean had no memory and could make you forget all your pain and sorrow. After being told that I wasn't so scared of it anymore because no matter what I saw or did in life the Pacific Ocean could make it disappear."

Melissa and Jonathan didn't quite understand what he was talking about, but both of them knew that as Mitch came to the end of his life his soul searching would only make sense to him. Melissa put her hand on his shoulder and asked him "what are you trying to tell us, I think by now you can be truthful because we have all opened up apart ourselves to one another on this trip."

Mitch looked at Melissa and Jonathan while the feeling in his left arm was slowly going away from the effects of his cancer, and as he looked at them a few tears fell from his eyes. "I wonder how true baptism really is. Can we go under the water and come back up a new person where all our sins and past experiences are truly washed away? I've never told you about my brother before, and for you Jonathan you may not even realize that I had a younger brother."

"I knew you had one at one time, but I have never known the circumstances of why he is not around or why you never talked about him."

"I've never talked about him because if I did then I remember and the past is always easier to deal with when we can forget. I had a brother named Max who was two years younger than me and he was definitely the favorite of my mother. I have not spoken his name in over twenty years and not even your grandmother knows much about him or our growing up together. The truth is, for fifty years I couldn't relive it again," Mitch said as he started to cry. He was trying to hold back the tears and turned away from Melissa and Jonathan as he stopped talking for a moment.

Melissa gave him a hug off to the side to try and comfort him then Jonathan walked over to face him. Melissa asked, "What are you afraid to relive again?"

Mitch looked at her sadly and said, "His death and our parents blaming me for it until they couldn't even talk or look at me again. Max died in 1945 during the war, a month before it would end in Europe. He was a B-17 co-pilot and on April 10, 1945 his plane was shot down over Oranienburg, Germany. After dropping their bombs the plane was shot down by German ME-262's, sending the plane in a downward tailspin while losing one of its wings. My brother could have gotten out, but he stayed inside so he could get the pilot and another crewman out before the plane exploded. They survived; he went down in flames."

Melissa and Jonathan looked stunned. For Jonathan it was like meeting someone for the first time; it was a sense of shock and amazement. Jonathan had always felt like he knew his family, but with each day that passed by on this trip he realized that he didn't know them at all, he knew only the masquerade that they had been living all these years. Finally Jonathan had to ask, "Why are you telling us this now, why after all these years, why not just let it go to the grave with you?"

Mitch looked at him with a steadfast look and replied, "Because you should know, I think you should know the truth about me and maybe you won't just rely on your assumptions when you remember me."

"Maybe I already know the truth, and you're just under the assumption that I have some false notion of you," Jonathan replied.

"Trust me; you don't know the truth because there is a lot that has never been told to you. If you really knew the truth then you'd have your facts straight about me and your family," Mitch replied to Jonathan.

To calm the tension that was building, Melissa said, "What happened with you after you found out that he died? Did your parents do something to you after this happened?"

"I didn't find out that he had died till two weeks later when we were heading back to the states for refueling. It was luck that I had been in Europe at the time and I got to see him one last time before it happened; I saw him about week before he was killed. My ship was one of the ones that delivered soldiers to the Battle of Normandy and we were left there to patrol along the English and French coast till the war in Europe ended and we could be sent to the Pacific front. My parents got the letter before I found out so I couldn't get leave to tell them myself. My mother never forgave me for finding out about his death the way she did. Of course when he joined the army right after I joined the navy she blamed me for getting him to do it."

Mitch paused a moment to wipe away the few tears he had in his eyes. "The thing is, he made the choice to follow in my footsteps and not be a fisherman by moving to Chicago for college and he made the choice to join up because he wanted to fly planes. I never had to talk him into anything. Both of my parents didn't see it that way; they thought I could stop him."

Jonathan asked, "Is this why they blamed you for his actions because they couldn't see that Max was his own person?"

"Yes and no. They didn't want to understand that, but they also thought that I had some big influence over him helping to sway his decisions. The truth is that he was too stubborn to let anybody influence him. He was the kid when we were in school that would turn around and laugh at the principal when he received licks just to spite him. My brother wanted to get away from my parents just as much as I did because the life we had with them was sad and filled with pain. I loved my parents, but I don't remember many happy times with them and neither did my brother so that's why we both left. When he joined the army my mother told me that he better come home safe or I was to blame because I got him to do it. I didn't really believe her because I thought she was just upset and worried like a mother would be, but she meant it. When the war ended and everybody was grieving over my brother, my father told me that I couldn't do that because I had to be strong for the family. He said that I was partly to blame for what happened so I had to fix everything by being strong. After that I saw them maybe a few times before they died a few years later."

Mitch didn't say anything for a while and continued to stare out into the horizon. Melissa and Jonathan didn't know what to say after hearing about the unforgiving nature of his parents. After a long pause between the travelers Jonathan finally asked his grandfather, "Is this why you have always been a hard man, so nothing could hurt you?"

Mitch looked at Jonathan and replied, "That's part of it; the other reason is that I always thought that if I could be strong and not let the love I have for something get the better of me, then I wouldn't hurt those that I truly loved. If you're going to love something then you have to risk losing it. In the end I feel like I didn't love my wife, my children, and my grandchildren enough. I traded it in for the bottle so I could forget the hurt I suffered from the loss of my brother, and my mother and father not loving me enough."

Mitch started to cry and walked back to the sand on the shore to fall at his knees. Melissa and Jonathan tried to catch him before he fell in the sand. Part of it was his emotional state and the other part of his falling was from the effects of the medication.

Mitch sat up and looked over at Jonathan and said, "I'm sorry for the hurt I caused you; I never learned how to be a father...how to be a grandfather. I did the best I could and I know that it wasn't good enough."

He didn't say anything after that while he shed a few tears and looked into the fading sunset over the water. The three of them did not say anything to each other for the rest of the night as they sat on the beach until it was completely dark and the ocean disappeared underneath the black of night.

Mitch drifted off to sleep as soon as he lay down upon his bed in the hotel room. Jonathan and Melissa stayed with him, lying together in the next bed holding one another as to comfort each other through the saddened moments of the night. The next day Mitch had another one of his days where he couldn't really get out of bed and he just slept the day away. The travelers stayed another day in bay area of California; Jonathan and Melissa just stayed near Mitch's bed to make sure he would be okay. What they realized was that these kinds of days were becoming more frequent for Mitch as he was coming to the end of his life and there was nothing they could do but be there with him.

The next day the three travelers started to make their way back East. Mitch was the only one that knew where they were going; it was a place he had not been in forty years. Jonathan and Melissa did not ask where they were going; they just stayed by his side as he continued his journey. While traveling this journey each one of them had found a part of themselves, while giving away a small part of their heart to the other journeymen.

After a few days traveling across country Mitch and his companions arrived in Louisville, Kentucky. They had been through the middle of the United States; they had driven through the heartland of America. There wasn't much in Kentucky, for them to see. However, there was one important place for Mitch that he had to visit, it was Zachary Taylor Cemetery.

They drove the car down the long winding road that stretched out through the hilly pasture of graves. The tombstones were all grayish white hinting at the worn down marble of the years gone by inside this reverent place. Finally, as they arrived and Jonathan and Melissa didn't know where they were or what they were doing there Jonathan asked Mitch, "What is this place and what are we doing here?"

"It's Zachary Taylor Cemetery and this is where my brother is buried," Mitch replied

Melissa and Jonathan both looked over at him with a look of surprise, for they both knew that this was something special, even more so than everything that they had encountered up to this point. It had been forty years since Mitch had been here and it was his making peace over what had happened.

They found the office building with a map of the grave markers so he could find the grave of his brother Max. It didn't take long to find where the gravesite was. The marbled stone was worn down so much that it was hard to see the names, and even though there was more than one name on the grave site the names could still be read so people would know the names of these American heroes.

The grave had not been decorated with flowers in a long time; Mitch knew that when he decided to come to Kentucky to see the grave so along the way he stopped to buy flowers and an American Flag. The graves in the cemetery were always decorated with patriotic décor on an annual basis, but it was simple, nothing that showed the love of family. He put his flowers and the flag at the foot of the grave and then three travelers stood there for a few minutes in a moment of silence.

Finally, Mitch said, "Most people who know me

including some of my closest friends over the years don't even know that I had a brother because I've never talked about him. My own family doesn't even know what he did to become a hero or where he's buried, and I think that's a tragedy."

He looked at Jonathan sadly and said, "Everyone should know who their family is, even the bad things about them just as much as the good. You don't know a lot about where you come from because of me, because I never wanted to talk to you about it and I should be the one to tell you just like a father passes on his knowledge to his son. Your mother, grandmother, and aunt only know bits and pieces of the whole truth because I never told them everything."

Jonathan didn't know what to say. He just looked at Mitch with a sad look upon his face and then tears slowly ran down his eyes. He had never known Mitch to be an apologetic man; when he was very young he was afraid because Mitch was a hard man and it seemed that a lot of the time he was angry. Jonathan never knew why he was this way and why it seemed when he was very young that Mitch was mad at the world. As he got older and began to understand what being an alcoholic really was, he could at least blame that on the mood swings that Mitch would go through.

However, there was still a deep seeded anger that Mitch had and that he would bring out for his family to see while the rest of the world was looking on. There were many times that Jonathan could remember Mitch getting mad at him for the simplest of things, such as not finishing his entire plate at dinner. He grew up afraid of him as he got older but then he began to see that Mitch was not that bad. He could be a very fun and loving person to be around, but there was still an anger inside of him as well as hurt that would never go away. For the first time he finally began to see the hurt and the burdens that Mitch carried with him; he saw for the first time what caused the emotional roller coaster he was on.

Jonathan couldn't say anything, and to break the silence Melissa spoke up and asked, "I think we both might have some understanding why this has been too painful to talk about all these years, but what I want to know is when was the last time you were here because this place seems very unfamiliar to you."

Mitch looked at her as his eyes started to well up and said, "The truth is, I have not been here in a very long time, not since 1952 when he was finally buried here. After his plane was shot down, two of the crew that survived were captured by the Germans and they were made to recover the bodies from the crash site. The Germans made them dig shallow graves and bury my brother and the other three that died from the crew. Years after the war had ended, the remains of these crew members were found because they still had their dog-tags on and then they were brought back to the US so they could be laid to rest. The year that happened was 1952 and there was a memorial service for them; it was last time I was here and I was the only one out of the family in attendance because I never told your grandmother about what happened. I never could."

Jonathan and Melissa looked surprised. "Why have you never been back here?" asked Jonathan. "Why has it taken forty years for you to come back to see your brother? He was your brother; didn't you want to visit him here?"

"I did, and every time I came through this part of the country I always felt the urge to come here. I never did though, because it was too hard and because I never had the courage to. It hurt too much and when that happens sometimes the easiest thing to do is to try and forget about it. I never had a chance to grieve for him because of my parents and thinking about it just made it hurt too much. Alcohol could make me forget sometimes, but it never made me forget completely. If you ever face this kind tragedy you'll understand what I am talking about."

Mitch didn't have anything more to say, he started to shed his tears as he bent down to face the grave. He ran his hand across his brother's name on the grave and then he prayed, which was something he had not done in a long time. Melissa squeezed Jonathan's hand and then they both placed their hands on Mitch's shoulder to comfort him within his sadness. After a long while, Mitch stood up and reached inside his pocket to find an old military heirloom. He pulled out some World War II Army pilot wings. It was the extra pair that Max carried in his footlocker that was shipped to his family after he was killed in action.

He held the wings for a moment and ran his hand over them, amazed that they still looked like they were brand knew. The truth was, Max never wore them because he considered the pair unlucky. One time when he was wearing them a jeep ran over his foot, breaking nearly every bone in the foot. From that day forward he never wore the wings because they brought bad luck and every pilot had their own superstition in face of the fear from dying in the air above.

Mitch had held onto his wings for over forty years. The only time he got them out was when he was drunk and in need of remembering. It was when he wanted to relive the pain over and over so maybe he could somehow wash away his own guilt. As he came to the end of his days Mitch finally realized that the only way he could get rid of the guilt was to be honest about his shortcomings and finally let go. Once he could let go he would finally be free.

He told Jonathan and Melissa about the pilot's wings and explained their significance. After so many years, to finally be set free, Mitch placed the wings on top of the tombstone and said out loud, "My brother, luck has nothing to do with it, it's all in God's hands. I know that now."

11

In Memory of the Living and the Dead

Jonathan was rattling change around in his pocket looking for quarters as he stood by a payphone near the hotel they were staying at. He hadn't talked to his mother in a while and it had occurred to him that he had not talked to her since this trip began over a month ago. He knew his mother well and she would be worried because he always made a point to call her every two weeks no matter what city he might be playing in, but this time when he called they would have more to talk about. The rest of his family didn't know yet; they didn't know about Mitch or this trip that he was taking.

"Hi Mom," Jonathan said as a woman on the other end of the phone answered.

"It's about time you called me, where are you? I know you're not in New Orleans because I tried calling that bar you usually play at and they said you were gone for a while."

"I'm on the road mom, and you're never going to believe who I am with, which is why I'm calling."

"What are you talking about?" she asked. "You're not on the road playing music?"

"No mom, I actually took a little trip with somebody, somebody you know."

"Who are you with?"

"I'm with Mitch and I have been traveling with him for over a month now."

"What are you doing with your grandfather? I thought you still didn't want to see him ever again."

"Well, I'm not so sure about that anymore, we've actually had a nice time together, but I do have some bad news which will explain why I'm here with him."

"What happened?"

"The thing is mom, he's dying."

"What are talking about, what's wrong with him?"

"He has cancer and an inoperable tumor at the tip of his spine and brain, so one or the other is going to kill him."

"Oh my God, how long are doctors giving him?"

"Apparently, he has only a few months if even that because he has refused to do any kind of chemotherapy."

"Why, if there is a chance of saving his life then he needs to do it."

"Mom, one of those things is going to kill him and he knows that, he figures why spend the rest of his days in pain from doing the therapy. I don't blame him; he knows he going to die and wants to spend the rest of his time being happy while feeling as good as he can."

"I know you're right, but I'm shocked at the news right now. It's not every day you find out that your father is dying and there is nothing that can be done about it."

"I know Mom; every day with him is one more day of having to accept it. I feel like I have wasted so much time hating him all these years that I've never gotten to know who he really is or spend time with him."

"The last month you've spent with him must have made a real difference in your relationship. I've prayed for so many years that somehow the gap between you two could be bridged."

"Yeah, there is nothing like death to do it I guess, but God has a funny sense of humor."

"It doesn't matter how it's done, because God know what he's doing when it comes to estranged relationships. So where are you guys?

"Well we are in Kentucky now; we just visited the grave of his brother."

"You went and saw Max's grave? He hasn't been there in forty years and none of us in the family have even been there. What made him take you there?"

"I don't know, maybe he thought it was time to face his demons when it came to his brother, but this isn't the only place we've been. We have been all over the country it seems like, and now we are going to Boston."

"He's finally doing it," she said mysteriously.

"What are you talking about Mom?"

"Your grandfather is finally putting to rest the pain and the hurt he has carried with him for most of his life. He is finally returning home in more ways than one. Your grandmother always said that for my dad to truly be happy he would have to face that which had been too painful to forget, he would have to face the demon that has shadowed his life since he was a small child."

"I guess he is doing it since this is his last go around. There are a lot of things I didn't really know about him that we have found out on this trip."

"We, who's we Jonathan,"

"I forgot to tell you there is a woman that's been traveling with us."

"I knew it; I knew he would pick up some slutty stranger to accompany him. He really hasn't changed I guess."

"Mom, before you get too mad at him let me explain who it is. It's not some slutty stranger; it's somebody that we all know and he met her again by accident. Before I agreed to go on this trip with him he convinced her to go with him and help out if he needed it."

"Jonathan who is she?

"Mom, its Sherry Melissa."

"Sherry Melissa, you mean the girl you dated in New Orleans and lived with for a while."

"Yeah, that's one and it's actually turned out to be a blessing in disguise for all of us with her being here."

"Am I to understand that you two are back together?"

"I wouldn't say that, but I'm glad that she is here with us and yes I was angry at first, but like I said it's a good thing that she's here."

"I remember her spending Thanksgiving with us that one time and I remember liking her very much. She had a very caring soul. Perhaps it is a good thing that she's there with you."

"Look Mom, I need to go, but I wanted to tell you what's going on. You don't need to worry, we're taking care of him and he'll be okay until, well you know. I'm doing much of the driving in his car anyway."

"Oh my God, you grandfather must be really

sick if he's letting you drive him in his car."

"I know, I was shocked as well, but it really is okay. I think he's just glad to have some company."

"Well I'm glad you're there with him, you need to be with him so you finally realize that your grandfather is not that bad of a man. He really is a good man deep down."

"I know...Also I know that you're going to tell Aunt Catherine and Grandma, but don't do anything crazy like trying to find us. I'm only saying this because I think the reason for this trip is for Mitch to do some things on his own. We are going to come home when he's ready."

"Jonathan, what makes you think I would tell anybody about this unless you said it was okay to?"

"Mom I love you, but I know you better than you think. There's no way you can keep something like this a secret and I wouldn't blame you for telling everybody. I just don't want any of you doing something crazy like hitting the road and trying to find us.
I'm telling you right now that this is on Mitch's schedule."

"Son, I wouldn't say or do anything if you ask me to. I may be a bit of a talker, but I would respect your wishes."

"A bit of a talker, you like to talk to strangers in the grocery store for hours on end. A bit of a talker is an understatement, and that's why I'm worried somebody is going to do something crazy and get in the way of what Mitch is doing. At this point, and I can't believe I'm saying this, I don't want anything to get in the way of what he is trying to do. He needs all the time he has since he doesn't have too much left."

"I promise none of us will do anything until you need us. For right now you need to be with him and you need to bridge the gap you let get in the way of your relationship. When you look back on this you don't want to have any regrets."

"Mom, did Mitch ever have any remorse for the things he did or was he too drunk all the time?"

"I know that you can't figure out whether he is really a good man or just the horrible person you've chosen to see all these years. He may not be a man of many words and some things are hard for him to talk about, but he has his moments when his love and guilt collide so you see the hurt he faces. When that happens you see the remorse and the love he has for everybody in this family; you see that the most important thing for him is to keep this family happy even if he cannot be a part of it."

"Mom, I don't understand what you're talking about. How does he do what's best for this family?"

"You'll just have to see. He will have to be the one to tell you."

"Okay fine. We like to have our secrets in this family why should this be any different?"

"Jonathan, just spend time with your grandfather and everything will work out in the end."

"Okay, Mom. Look, I'll call you from the road and tell you where we are and when we are coming home."

"I love you, Jonathan."

"I love you too, Mom. Goodbye."

They got off the phone with each other and Jonathan went back to the hotel. Laura put the phone down on the cradle and started to cry. She stood there for a few minutes and cried, not wanting to face what she was going to have to do, and then Alice walked into the kitchen.

Alice asked her, "Honey what's wrong, why are you crying?"

Laura turned around and replied, "Mom, I have something very hard to tell you."

Alice just looked at Laura with concern and replied, "What is it? It can't be that bad."

"Mom that was Jonathan. He's with Dad and they have been traveling the country together this past month and a half."

"What's going on with Mitch? Did something happen to him?"

"Apparently, he found out that he has cancer and a tumor that they can't operate on. He's going to die soon because he's refused chemotherapy to fix it."

Alice nearly lost it and started to cry. She sat down at the kitchen table to collect her thoughts. "I knew one day this was going to happen and I wouldn't be able to do anything about it," she said through her anguish. "I just thought I would have more time before that happened."

"Mom, it will be okay. Jonathan said that Mitch is visiting some places for the last time and Jonathan is finding out more than he ever had about Dad. It sounds like they're mending the bridge between them and soon they will be coming home."

"Your dad is finally facing his demons isn't he? I guess he figures it was time to put the pieces back together."

"Yeah it does. That's a good thing, right?"

"Yes, it is. I have wanted this to happen for so long and wanted to be there for him, but I know that I can't. He will have to do it on his own."

"This is pretty surprising considering how stubborn he is."

"Well, I'll let you in on a little secret. Your father has a soft side to him and his stubborn side has been disappearing more and more over the last ten years, I should know..."

"How would you know? Have you spoken to him that much since he left?"

"What you don't know is that we have been writing to each other almost every day since he left. We wanted to try and work through our problems and figured letters would be a good safe way to do it. What can I say, I still love your father despite the hurt he's cause me."

"I can't believe you never said anything about it. Why?"

"You kids don't need to know everything about my relationship with your father. Some things are reserved for just us, and the letters were to see if we could fall in love with each other all over again."

"Did it work?"

"Yes it did. Believe it or not, your father still has a very sweet side and that's what made me fall in love with him."

Laura and Alice sat in the comfort of their own silence with smiles on their faces, happy that demons in their family were disappearing.

∞∞∞∞∞∞∞

Over the next couple of days since visiting the graveyard in Kentucky Mitch, Jonathan, and Melissa traveled through New England to Boston, the place where Mitch was born. He had not been there in many years and when he did he didn't stay very long or he would pass through on his way to some other place. He never wanted to go back so he would not have to be reminded of all the hurt his family had caused. It was a place of bad memories, of a hard life that he never wanted to live again and a life that in his mind should be forgettable.

Boston was still a very old town and a place of hardworking men who worked their fingers to the bone just to keep the city alive and provide a little substance for their families. It was rich in history, especially Irish History. It was a place where the men were hard and they celebrated hard in their small triumphs that might seem trivial to the average man, but the average man was not the working man of Boston. Mitch was born into that life. He was a fisherman's son who from the time he was big enough to carry a large bucket of fish worked the docks and the steamers that sailed up and down the New England Coast in search of a way to make a living.

No matter how many of Mitch's memories faded away, he could still remember clearly the life he had in Boston and the smell of the salt air that would rush off the ocean into the old port town on the New England coast. As the travelers entered Boston all the familiar sounds and smells came rushing back to Mitch from his childhood. It had been fifteen years since Mitch had come back this way, since he had returned to his childhood home.

In his mind, after his parents had died over forty years ago, there was no reason to return, for there was nothing in Boston to return to. All he had were bad memories, and an anger that had never gone away. Jonathan drove the car past the fishing ports of the city so Mitch could see the life he had left behind. Mitch stared out into the old town and the ocean that curled alongside of the old town. For Mitch, the Atlantic Ocean was entirely different for him; there was memory that could not be forgotten.

It wasn't easy for him to come back because he had to face the one thing that he never wanted to admit. Mitch could admit to himself that he was not a great person, that he had a destructive side where his anger would get the best of him, and that he was an alcoholic that was too stubborn to give up the one vice that also made him feel better about himself. However, he never wanted to admit that maybe his parents never loved him enough, that he might have been the second favorite.

His father was a hard man and his mother was never strong enough to go against his father when she disagreed. She could never be her own person unless it was releasing guilt upon the people around her. This was part of what Mitch never wanted to admit, that his family was not perfect and some of the old habits were passed on to him when it came to his family. He never wanted to admit that he might be his father's son because he was never taught how to be a good father.

The travelers found a hotel near the ports and next to an old Irish pub called Paddy's that had been there for a hundred years. It had serviced the hardworking men of the Boston docks and the fisherman who spent half their lives out at sea. Family owned, the bar had been an institution of the surrounding neighborhoods, and the family which went back three generations knew everybody that came in on a regular basis. Mitch spent a lot of time in the place with his father and he had even grown up with one of the sons of the original owners who was killed overseas during the war.

They got settled into their hotel and Mitch decided to treat them to dinner in the old Pub and to see if there was anybody he might know from the old neighborhood. Most of the people he knew as a young man had never left like he did. Most people just added more generations in the surrounding neighborhoods. Some people moved away and some went off to war while never returning home, but most of the people he knew as a young man and the kids he grew up with on the docks stayed behind to become old men just like Mitch.

The three of them entered the old Pub to the sounds of laughter and music. There was always some kind of music group playing for the crowd, mostly amateur musicians from the neighborhood giving in to their passion for music. The Pub had not really change since the twenties and thirties in the way it looked; it just gained a few technological pleasures such as a TV and a Jukebox. It had the same pictures and some new ones as well from when local sports teams won a championship, but what Mitch recognized the most was the same old familiar smell of good Irish Beer and cigar smoke.

They took a seat in one of the corner booths and ordered some beer and sandwiches from the waitress. While Jonathan and Melissa looked around at the old pictures on the wall, Mitch went to the bar. He found an older gentleman that was tending bar and decided to ask him about some people from the neighborhood since he looked like he had been here all his life.

"Hi there, how long have you lived here in this neighborhood?" Mitch asked.

"I've lived here my entire life sir, why do you ask?"

"Well, I grew up around here before the war and I was wondering if you might know somebody that lives around here that I grew up with. He and his father used to come in here all the time. His name is Mickey O'Reilly."

"Yeah I knew Mickey, his father was a fisherman just like mine and he lived in this neighborhood for seventy years. He used to come in here on a regular basis," the older gentleman replied.

"Is he not around anymore, because you keep talking in the past tense," said Mitch.

"The thing is, he died a couple of years ago from a heart attack. He was a good man, Mickey, just like his father."

"I see, I didn't know. I hadn't seen him in forty years. As I said before, we grew up together and my father was a fisherman and worked on the docks as well, so our fathers worked a lot together."

"What was your father's name, if you don't mind me asking?"

Mitch looked reached across the bar to shake the bartenders hand and said, "My father's name was Patrick Collins and I'm Mitchell Collins, it's a pleasure to meet you."

The old bartender stared at him for moment so he could remember the names, and then finally with a smile on his face his faded memories came back.

"I remember you and your father. I think our fathers worked together as well, but I don't think I've seen you around here in almost fifty years, since right after the war. You moved away didn't you?"

"I haven't been here since my parents died. I moved to Chicago to go to college before the war and that's where I settled afterwards. I came back for a visit with my grandson and a friend of ours, so I wanted to see if anybody I grew up with was around."

"You were a few years older than me, I think, and you had a brother named Max didn't you?" the older gentleman asked.

"Yes, I did. He died during the war, did you know him well?" Mitch asked.

The older gentleman smiled and said, "I knew him pretty well back in the old days. We used to pal around when were teenagers and I think we even played high school basketball together. If I remember correctly he was one hell of a ballplayer, someone who could dominate a game all by himself. More importantly, he was a good man and a good friend."

"He was a great basketball player," said Mitch. "It's what got him into college. When he graduated high school he got a scholarship to a school in Chicago where I was going to school and that's where he went then the war happened and we both joined. You're right though, he was a good man."

"I think all of us from the old neighborhood had our lives changed when the war happened and we all joined up. There were a lot of good men that we grew up with around her that went off to fight and never came home. I was sad to hear that Max was one of them, but we made it and it's good to see you here again. Are you staying for a while?"

"I wish I could stay for a while, but this is just a short stop on my way home." The look on Mitch's face almost told of his predicament all by itself.

"Well, if you're here tomorrow then a lot of the guys that we grew up with and are still here in the neighborhoods will be here. They come in on Thursdays to play cards and pool. Thursday is our dollar beer night, and for us old timers living on pensions and social security, it's the only night we can afford to splurge. There are a lot of people that are still around that you might know."

Mitch grabbed his drinks. "Thank you for telling me, I think I'll wander in tomorrow for dinner." The two men shook hands and Mitch returned to the table. He was smiling a bit when he returned as thoughts from his youth came rushing back, thoughts of he and Max getting into trouble and playing ball in the streets, not caring what time of day it was.

Jonathan gave him a funny look. "What are you grinning at; did you get some free beer or something?"

"Better. I ran into somebody that I knew over

fifty years ago and found out that a lot of the people that Max and I grew up with are still around; they come in here on a regular basis, especially on Thursdays, so I'll get to see some of them again."

Melissa smiled at him and replied, "That's great Mitch; maybe coming back to Boston isn't going to be so bad."

"Well, it's also dollar beer night tomorrow and its good Irish beer, so if that's not a good enough reason to come back then I don't know what is," Mitch replied as he started laughing.

Jonathan smiled at his grandfather and replied, "It's a good enough reason for me, how about you Melissa?"

"Have you ever known me to turn down good beer?"

He just smiled and winked at her and said, "You're a girl after my own heart."

"You know," Mitch began, sounding like a teacher, "it occurs to me that my father taught my brother and I one important lesson and that was if you were going to drink beer, then drink good beer, and its beer you can actually taste, not some cheap watered down version of it."

The three of them just smiled at one another and then laughed at the Collins' Beer Philosophy, for it was something Mitch has passed down to his own family without realizing it. It was also something that Jonathan had taught Melissa when they first began dating many years before. It was one of those little lessons that they all carried with them like instinct, and until this day had never realized where it came from.

This was just one of many lessons that they would carry with them that their descendants would pass on. As the three of them talked the

rest of the evening over dinner it became more
and more evident what they were learning from
each other and what they would pass on to the
next generation.

∞∞∞∞∞∞

The next day, Mitch took Jonathan and Melissa
on a tour of the neighborhood he grew up in and
imparted to Jonathan, some of his heritage There
was a lot that he didn't know about where his family
came from on his grandfather's side of the family. As
they walked around the docks where Mitch's father
had worked and the port area of Boston, the history of
who they were was told in storybook fashion. Ironically
enough, the birth of the Collins family in America had
its beginning near the same area as the birth of the
American Revolution, for Mitch's parents lived and
worked close to where the Boston Tea Party had
happened.

Mitch told his tale of family history and he began
to talk of his parents, something he had not done in a
very long time. John and Mary Collins were
immigrants to this country; John came from Wicklo,
Ireland and Mary came from the countryside outside of
Copenhagen, Denmark. They had met at Ellis Island
as they were being processed as new Americans and
immediately took a fancy to one another. They were an
Irishman and Dane who fell in love, a lethal
combination of ethnicity as some would say, but they
made it work.

John was a fisherman's son who knew nothing
but the toil of long hours and long days. He carried

that work ethic with him as he came to America in the early part of the 20th century to stake his own claim of the American Dream. Mary grew up on a Dairy Farm that had been in her family for six generations, but also had learned to be a pastry chef like her mother and grandmother before her. She, like her husband, knew that there were more opportunities for her outside of her place of birth, so she came to America with her sister.

While they met as newly arrived citizens to this country and soon afterwards got married, they eventually settled in Boston so they could both find better work to which they were suited for, a fisherman and a baker of fine pastries. John, like his father, was a stubborn man and prone to fits of anger even unto his lovely wife which he doted upon. Sometimes it would be too much and his violent side would come out, leaving his mark upon her.

She, on the other hand, was just as stubborn and was not easily beaten down by anyone. They could have a terrible fight and she would give just as much back sometimes with physical pain as he would dish out. However, through all their heated moments they loved each other very much and could not spend the rest of their lives without the other.

They were also deeply religious in their catholic faith and it was an instrumental part of their life the family they would have years later. A few years after they had settled in Boston, John and Mary would have their first child, Mitchell. A few years after that, John and Mary would have their second child, Maxwell. The pregnancy with Max was so hard for Mary that she could not have any more children, or at least the doctors thought. The two of them raised their sons on the port neighborhoods of Boston as they worked hard every day of their lives and instilled the same work ethic in their sons who both worked the docks as teenagers.

Now the one thing that became most important for John and Mary in the raising of their sons was a fine American education. For Maxwell and Mitchell, education was important to their parents and they made sure that their boys were going to receive a better education than the ones they had. Their education would take place through the church, giving them a fine balance between religion and literature.

Both of the boys were bright and the chance of college was not out of the realm of possibility, but when it came time for Mitch to go to college, his higher than average intelligence allowed him to go to school on an academic scholarship, and his parents were a little surprised. They had never expected for him to be given this kind of opportunity, mainly because they could never understand how he could be so intelligent and why academic things came so easily to him since they were not this way themselves. Their thoughts were not of vanity; it was the lack of understanding that pertained to simple things and both of them never expected their sons to move away from home.

When it came time for Mitch to go to college, he chose to take the opportunity given him which would take him to Chicago. This started the first real tension with his parents. Mitch was becoming independent and leaving his family as his parents saw it. To his father especially, a man's place was with his family, for the only reason he came to America, as he would often tell Mitch, was because he had no one left in the old country so it was up to him to start a new family and America was a good place to do it.

John and Mary never wanted their sons to go far. They both learned to resent Mitch when it came time for Max to leave for college because they thought he had influenced Max's decision to go to Chicago. That was the first time that Mitch could remember his parents blaming him for what was thought of as bad luck within their family, and they could not ever forgive him for it.

Mitch and his parents talked less than they used to, and there were not that many letters exchanged between them. When Max left for Chicago, John and Mary rarely talked to Mitch, and on the rare occasion that he would come back to visit, there was nothing but a silent understanding of resentment. And with Max, it was if his parents died as well.

John was killed in an accident on the docks when a crane broke and dropped supplies that weighed over two thousand pounds on top of him and another man. Mary would die a few months later after she refused to eat and live all together until she faded away in her sleep one night. To her, she had nothing left and there was no reason to live, but both of them had given up on their lives long ago when their youngest son was killed over Germany during the war.

Mitch finished his short history lesson in a grieving tone as the three of them stopped on a bridge overlooking the ocean and ports that surrounded the neighborhood that Mitch grew up in. He was slow in his steps and the cancer was for the first time really starting to create havoc in his life, for he was having to walk with a cane now. He stopped walking and leaned on the large stone railing and looked out into the endless sea. He started to shed a few tears as was becoming his custom now when he talked of the past.

Jonathan and Melissa did not know what to say to him, for they both knew that this was his way of working out all the hurt and the pain that he had buried deep down for so long. Jonathan finally had to ask, "Did you and your parents ever make amends before they died?”

“No, we never did. We never spoke during the last couple of years before they died, not even in letters. They never even knew about their grandchildren, and I never told them because I always figured they never wanted to know, but I was wrong to do that. I did it out of anger and spite, but it’s wrong to never let someone know about their family. Regretfully, they died before I could fix that.”

Melissa put her hands on his shoulder to comfort him and said, “You’re making your amends now by admitting everything out loud, and that counts for something. If this trip is anything to all of us, then it’s about finally admitting out loud our inner demons and faults. Why don’t you visit their grave and say goodbye just like you did for Max?”

“I wish I could, but I don’t know where they are buried. My mother never told me where my father was buried, for it was only after the funeral that I received the news that he had died, and when she died it was days after her funeral that I got the call. As sad as it might sound, it was upon her instructions for me not to know, and when Irishmen are made to keep a secret, that secret is taken to the grave. My mother never wanted me to know where they were buried, but I was only called to settle their small estate. It’s funny what can happen when we never let go of our anger. Maybe that’s just one more reason why I’m taking this trip. Since we can’t visit a grave, there is one thing that we can do which is an Irish custom.”

“Does it have something to do with the flowers you bought before you took us on this tour?” Jonathan asked.

Mitch smiled and replied, “Yes it does, but there is something you should know. I’ve spent too many years hating and trying to forget my parents for the love I felt like they never showed me, but eventually we have to let go and accept one little truth. One of life's injustices is that we never get to pick who our parents are, all we can do is forgive them for the pain they cause us. If we can do that, then maybe we can learn to love something greater than ourselves. My parents let their guilt get the best of them and that's what eventually killed them. I'm still sad that things happened the way they did, but all I can do is let go."

Mitch led them to the edge of pier near the small bridge they were standing on in one of the harbors of Boston. The three of them looked out among the morning mist and fog surrounding the harbor that led out into the ocean.

"The custom I speak of is throwing all of or part of the remains into the sea, and since lilies was my mother's favorite they will have to serve as part of their remains. The custom, which comes from Celtic times, is sending the dead by way of the ferryman which will take the remains across the sea in the land of the dead. Essentially, you are returning to the sea the life it helped create."

Mitch threw the lilies over the railing into the ocean that came into port so they would be carried out to the ocean. He shed some tears and then pulled from his pocket Max's dog tags. He stared at them for a moment and then squeezed them in his hand one last time. He then threw them in the ocean for the sea to collect. It was his final gesture of letting go and setting free the pain that he had carried for so long.

Jonathan Mitch and Melissa stood on the bridge without words to be said. They all just stared out into the open water like they had done once before. The lilies Mitch threw out into the water slowly were carried out of the port as the ships were coming and going. Finally, while leaning against the rail for support, Mitch grabbed the hands of Jonathan and Melissa who were standing on either side of him and said, "I know that I've never been perfect at it, but family shouldn't be afraid to be honest with one another. I'm sorry that it has taken me so long to finally tell you the truth about my family and where I come from."

Jonathan just smiled and squeezed his hand and replied, "You're doing it now and that's what counts."

∞∞∞∞∞∞

That evening the three of them went back to the old pub to have dinner. Jonathan had to help his grandfather even though he was walking with a cane. Mitch's body was hurting all over, but he was determined to not to let the pain stop him from enjoying the evening. He knew he was dying, but he wasn't gone yet, as he silently told himself. They entered in to the light sounds of big band jazz, the likes of Glenn Miller which were the sounds of his youth.

As they entered, the older gentleman from the night before saw them walk in and greeted them. Mitch and the gentleman shook hands and then the older gentlemen helped Mitch towards the back where the rest of the old men were, the men that they had grown up with together. He never had to ask Mitch what was wrong with him and why he walking with a cane since he did not have it the night before. He already knew that Mitch was dying and his age was catching up with him. All old men and women know when their time has come, when eternal sleep is on the doorstep of one's life.

The place was full of older men playing cards,

pool, and drinking beer. Mitch recognized some of them. The older gentleman said, "Guys, we have a visitor, somebody who grew up in this neighborhood but has been away for fifty years. His father was a fisherman on the docks just like most of our fathers. It's Mitchell Collins, John Collins' oldest boy and his brother was Maxwell."

Most of the men in the back recognized who he was and he was greeted as a long lost brother and friend returning home, for true Irishmen always remembered old friends that may have been away for a while. There were many questions on where he had been all these years and what he had been up to all these years. He sat and started talking, telling tales, and catching up with old boyhood friends. He even told them about his illness and the purpose of his trip.

As all old men in the winter of their life come to understand about putting things right where they had gone wrong, they all sympathized with him. He talked about his grandson and the woman he had befriended along the way who already had become the love of Jonathan's life, and because of that he could not help but love her, too.

With a long and enduring smile he talked about his wife Alice, the most beautiful woman he had ever known and that had enchanted him so many years ago while capturing his heart forever. Mitch talked about his two beautiful daughters and his joys of being a father. With all the tales he told he was never happier or felt more complete when he talked about the people that he loved the most.

As he sat in the back and spent the next few hours talking and drinking with old friends, Jonathan and Melissa just watched him. With smiles upon their faces they sat in a small booth having a drink of their own, a taste of Irish...the only true whiskey that could

make the heart stand tall, according to Mitch. Melissa
finally leaned over and gave a Jonathan a kiss and
asked, "So what are you thinking?"

"I'm thinking that it has finally occurred to me;
my grandfather is not as invincible as I once thought.
When I was a kid I used to think that nothing could
hurt him, like he was superman or something, I also
thought that he had all the answers, now I finally see
a fragile and tragic soul,"

"Are you disappointed that he is not what you
once thought?"

"No, on the contrary, I'm glad that he's not the
image I once had for him. I'm glad to know that he has
been so troubled, that he has been hurting."

"Why do you say that, do you wish for him to
be hurting so much as some kind of payback for
hurting you as a kid? If that's it, then that's an
awful thing to say."

Jonathan gave her a surprising and dirty look
because he knew from experience her scolding when it
came to treating people badly and wanting to make
them suffer. He grabbed her hand and smiled and
then in a surprising fashion for him leaned in and gave
her a kiss.

"It's not that at all, you're misunderstanding me
so let me finish. I'm glad to know that there is a frailty
about him because the more he hurts the more he
wants to put things right. I've been mad at him for a
lot of things, but learning to forgive himself and seek
the same from the people that he has hurt is a good
thing. He is reaching out, and seeing him do this gives
me hope; hope that I am able to do the same and we
don't have to live with the hurt or the anger that we
carry anymore."

Melissa smiled at him with a few tears in her
eyes. The one thing that she had been hoping for

when it came to Jonathan, more than him admitting out loud that he loved her as much as she loved him, was that he could admit that he needed to release the anger he had held onto for so long.

"Out of all the things that I have wished for more than anything with you is that the anger you have carried with you for so long would start to fade away. I have hoped and prayed that you could find forgiveness throughout this trip. You've done that little by little, and whether you want to admit it, that man back there," she looked toward the back where Mitch was, "is part of the reason you have. It's because you have started to see the truth and not let your hurt blind you."

"I guess you're right, and maybe he's really not that bad of a person. Maybe he's just a little odd like we all are. There's a lot I still don't understand and maybe I never will."

"Or maybe you will when the time is right."

"Perhaps, but I know one thing, my grandfather is full of surprises, like this trip. Who knew you and I would be sitting here with him and the world we once knew would shatter piece by piece?"

She winked at Jonathan and said, "I guess it comes down to faith, the faith that the impossible can happen. It's the faith that love, forgiveness, and true joy will overcome. All our anger will do is eat us up inside."

"You're right again, but I know one thing, my stubbornness is not going to disappear and that means that you can't lose yours if you're going to put up with me."

Melissa just smiled and replied to him, "I don't see that happening. Besides, somebody has to keep you in line."

For the rest of the evening Melissa and Jonathan

renewed the love that they had for each other while Mitch returned to his childhood with old friends. The evening for the three of them was about remembering; remembering who they once were and what they had become so they could make better who they needed to be. After Jonathan and Melissa were introduced to the childhood friends of Mitch and Max, Mitch said a final goodbye to the old neighborhood and the old men that had served as companions in his youth. As they left the old pub they realized one certain truth" it's what we take from the past that will make us who we are in the future.

12

Young Heroes We Once Were

The phone rang in its annoying tone as Mitch woke from a deep sleep in his hotel room. Jonathan was in the other room with Melissa, so he wasn't there to get it so Mitch could sleep. All he could was wake up at 9:30 am even though it wasn't quite time yet and answer the phone. He picked up the phone as he pushed his flask of whiskey and medicine out of the way to get to it.

"Hello," he said.

"Well its, about time you answered the phone good buddy. It's me, Calvin," Dr. Whitaker said. "Oh Lord, I must be on my death bed if you know where I am."

"Well you're not there yet, but you don't sound very good. How are you feeling?"

"I'm feeling miserable because you woke me up; you should know better than to wake a man from a whiskey sleep."

"I see you're still drinking the Irish even though

I told you not to, but I don't blame you for ignoring that one piece of advice. I would if I were in your shoes."

"You do it when you're on duty, but then again I've always liked a doctor who drinks the medicine he prescribes."

"No doctor is perfect. Besides, I can get away with it at my age. All they can do is retire me, which is something I should have done long ago."

"By the way, how did you find me? I didn't think anybody knew where I was."

"I called Alice looking for you and talked to Laura. She knew you were heading to Boston, and it looks like she knows what's happing with you. I figured you would be staying at a hotel in your old neighborhood so I called around and found you. It only took me three hotels to find you."

"How crafty of you! So apparently my grandson has a big mouth. I'm not surprised he told his mother, and that means everybody knows now."

"Probably, but that's not a bad thing. I do know that everybody is concerned, and Laura asked me what she could do."

"Did you tell her anything about me?"

"If you mean did I dispense with the details of your illness, no. You should know better than to think I would violate my patient's confidentiality."

"I know that, but what was your answer to my daughter's question?"

"I just told her that all she could do was be there when it really got bad, and you needed help from everybody."

"I guess those days are here now."

"Is it getting worse, to the point that you're losing control of your reflexes?"

"Yes," said Mitch, "it's actually getting to be

most of the time now. Jonathan has been doing most of the driving because I go through days where I cannot feel anything in my hands and legs. I've also been walking with a cane."

"So it starts for you now. This will the worse part of it and fairly soon you will not be able to feel much of anything, so that means you will not be able to walk or get up. Soon you will need full time help and the road will not be the place for that."

"How long till that happens?"

"It could be anytime now, a few weeks, a few days, it could be any day. It's time to think about getting home so you can get the help you need."

"I'm almost done and then we will be heading home. The pain killers provide some temporary relief, but I'm getting low."

"I'll make sure you can get some more, and I'll prescribe a different and more powerful medicine to help you get a good sleep. You are having trouble sleeping aren't you?"

"Yeah, how did you know?"

"I know that when the pain gets to unbearable you can't sleep and you're tired all the time. I just figured you would be in that stage right now. It's also why you're sleeping longer and why sometimes you will sleep all day. You've probably already had some days like that."

"There's not much that gets by you is there?"

"Not really, but remember I've seen the effects of this illness before and I know what you will go through before the end finally comes. I don't wish it upon anybody."

"Yeah, it's not what I would have wished for my final ending, but there are some good things to come out of it. You were right, it was time to put some things right."

"That's usually the case with the winter of one's life. By the way, the reason I called was to tell you the reunion at Arlington is been changed to Friday instead of Saturday. I wanted you to know so you won't miss it since this will be your last one to attend."

"Don't worry, I won't miss it, thanks for reminding me about the change. Have you told anybody in the group about me yet?"

"No, I figured it wasn't my place so I am leaving it to you. Anyway, I need to go. I will see you on Friday and I'll check you over then."

"Thank you, I'll see you on Friday."

Mitch hung up the phone and made his way to the bathroom so he could wash up. He slowly made it without any help, except for his sturdy cane. He splashed some water on his face and looked at himself in the mirror for a long moment that seemed to make time nonexistent. All he could see was for the first time in his life a scared dying old man that was slowly fading away in color and complexion. He was afraid that the life he had led was not good enough, that he couldn't be forgiven for all the things he had done, and the hardest decision that he ever had to make in the face of life and death.

Mitch walked over to the next hotel room and knocked on the door. As Jonathan answered the door he found the both of them getting ready for the day. As Jonathan got him a cup of coffee, Mitch looked at the both of them and said, "I wanted to let you know that there is some place I needed to visit alone, so I will be gone for a few days. If you guys want, I can fly you back to New Orleans or back home in Chicago and I will meet you there later."

Jonathan and Melissa both looked at Mitch with a strange look, both of them wondering what it could be that he did not want them around. Finally, after a moment's pause Jonathan asked Mitch, "Where do you need to go that you don't want us to be there with you?"

"It's just some place I need to go that really doesn't involve you."

Jonathan knew that his grandfather was being secretive again. He knew the tone in his grandfather's voice when there was something from his past that he did not want to share. When he was growing up Mitch would become cold and sneak his way into a bottle. When this happened the family knew that it was best to leave him be with his guilt and sorrow so he would not have to resort to anger or violence.

Melissa stopped Jonathan before he could say anything by touching his arm and then she said to Mitch, "Is everything okay, because you sound as if someone close to you has died and you need to pay your respects. If it is something like that, then we just want to know and to see if there is anything we can do for you. We just want to know that you are okay before we take leave of you."

"I'm okay, this is just something I have to do and it does involve my paying my respects."

"So did someone you know die?"

"Sort of, it doesn't really matter though, there' some place I have to visit and I need to leave today."

Mitch didn't really say anything else, he just stood there for a moment waiting for the other two to say something else, but there were no words. Melissa didn't know what to say without prying, which she felt it was not her place to do so. Jonathan had an angry look upon his face because he knew there was something Mitch was not telling him. He felt betrayed because they had all shared so much on this journey, and not to have his grandfather share with them something that was so painful was like a slap in the face in what this journey had become for each of them.

Jonathan finally could not keep silent, and as Mitch was about to walk out of the room he asked him, "So where is it that you have to go, just in case something happens to you and we have to come and get you?"

"I'm going to Arlington, Virginia to visit some friends. I will probably be there for a few days."

"Arlington, Virginia. Didn't you used to go there every year for something when I was growing up?"

"Yes, I did and I am going there again for something similar."

"What are you going for?"

"It's just something I have to do, but I will meet you in Chicago when I'm done."

Melissa knew that there was something else that Jonathan wanted to say, but it wouldn't be anything nice because he was growing impatient of Mitch's lack of answers. She interjected before Jonathan could say anything and replied "Mitch, are you sure there isn't anything we can't do for you before you go? We just want to make sure you're really okay."

Mitch smiled at her and replied, "No. I will be alright. This is just something I have to do on my own, it's something you guys can't be a part of, but I will see you soon."

Jonathan could not stand it any longer and before Melissa could stop him in his impatient anger he responded, "Enough is enough. Mitch, what the hell are you not telling us? There's something that's got you sad and regretful and I know that it has something to do with this trip to Arlington."

"Watch your tone with me; this is neither the time nor the place. For once get it through your head that you don't have to know everything."

"Is that what you've been telling my grandmother all these years about this dark cloud that hangs above your head? Did you push her away too until she couldn't stand anymore and threw you out?"

Mitch was really angry now and it was usually caused by someone bringing up the past between him and Alice. He was so angry that he tried to hit Jonathan, but lost his balance with his cane and fell. As he was being helped up he replied to Jonathan, "You bastard, do not bring up your grandmother when it comes to this. She has nothing to do it. Don't you have any respect for her?"

One of the things that angered Mitch the most was when someone was disrespecting his wife. Anybody could disrespect him, and although he would be annoyed he would never tolerate someone disrespecting his Alice.

"I wasn't trying to disrespect my grandmother, I just knew that it would get you mad if it seemed like I was. I want to know what this thing is that is so painful that you have to keep to yourself. It has something to do with your military service doesn't it?"

They got Mitch up on the bed and as he sat up he responded to Jonathan, "You're not going to understand this because you've never served in the military."

"Why don't you try me," Jonathan replied back.

Mitch was trying hard not to have to say anything because the pain he carried was his and his alone. He had opened up so much of his soul, so much of who he was on this trip. Although there was still one secret that he carried with him, and it was the one thing that he still wanted to carry with him to the grave.

Jonathan just stared at him for a few more moments as silence filled the room, drawing a shadow over the joy that all three of them had brought out of each other up to this point and leaving nothing but the contempt for not surrendering to the truth. It was the truth of who they really were; that they were all broken, filled with pain, trying to find some last redemption to make the rest of their lives worth living. Finally Jonathan said angrily, "Are you going to tell us what this about, because if this is what all of this has finally come to then I'm done and you can go off and die alone."

Melissa didn't know what to say as she sat next to Mitch waiting for him to respond. She was in agreement with Jonathan and wanted to see Mitch finally tell them this thing that caused him so much pain. For Mitch, there was no response; all he could do was sit there in a sorrowful state.

Jonathan didn't say anything else; he just slammed the desk chair in the room down on the floor in anger and started to walk out. He grabbed his things and walked out the door to find the nearest bus station. Melissa walked out after him and stopped him before he could get far from the room. She asked him? "Where are you going?"

"I told you, I'm done with this. That man is just full of secrets and I promise you this is just his way of walking out again."

"How can you say that when he has opened up so much of his life with us while letting go of his pride so he could show us who he really is? You can't see what kind of pain that man has lived with."

"What about the pain he has caused other people? This is the same kind of bullshit that he always does. He gets to a point where you might really know the truth about him and how he is, and then he shuts down and walks out."

"I don't disagree, but it's his pain and it's in his own time when he deals with it. This isn't about us, Jonathan."

"I think that's where you're wrong. You can't expect somebody to love you and understand if you're not willing to be truly honest with the people you care about. My grandmother, my mother, and my aunt, they finally had enough of it, and when they asked Mitch to be completely honest, that's when he walked out. That's when my grandfather walked out on his family."

Mitch had walked outside to try and speak with Jonathan and heard most of the conversation, especially the last part. Before Melissa could say anything Mitch said, "That's not why I walked out, and it's just what you've allowed yourself to believe because you got hurt when I left. Your foolish notions should stop right now, and perhaps you should know the truth. I walked out because at the time it was the best thing I could do for your grandmother since she was hurting and needed time to heal."

Jonathan just stared at Mitch with an angry look and then he replied, "What did you do to hurt her?"

"That's for another time, but what you really want to know now is why I never talk about my military service and why I carry with me such a deep regret. You want to know, then I'll tell you, but if I do then whether you understand or not you get to make no judgments because you have never been faced with something like this before. You have never had to make the decision on who lives and who dies, especially when they're your friends."

That was all he said then he walked back into

the room to make some Irish coffee and to sit down and tell a story that he had not ever told anybody before. It was a story that was very much a part of him and one that he carried in the deep bottomed out hollows of his heart. It was the kind of story that can only be in the heart of a man.

Melissa and Jonathan just looked at each other with amazement; they couldn't believe that Mitch all of a sudden found the courage to share his heartbreaking story, to share his pain.

Melissa and Jonathan entered the room and found a seat as Mitch was pouring some whiskey in his coffee. They didn't know what to expect from him and what kind of story this could be that would make it so painful for him to live with all these years. Mitch took a seat in the chair that Jonathan had slammed on the floor and started telling his story.

"When I was in the navy I was stationed on the USS Idaho as the engineering officer. The Idaho was a small battleship that crewed about 367 men. When I joined in December of 1941 I went through a quick nine weeks of basic and officer training. The reason I chose the navy was because I wanted to ride rather than walk, and the first place I was assigned to like most navy men was Pearl Harbor to help with the cleanup and the rebuilding of ships after the attack by the Japanese. I had never seen anything like it before. It was a beautiful place, or at least it had been, and there was so much decay and filth that it made you sick. I can remember the stench like it was yesterday and I never want to have to see anything like that again."

Melissa asked Mitch "Was that the first time you had seen death or any kind of dead bodies?"

"It was the first time, and there were dead everywhere. They were still pulling dead bodies out of the water three months after the attack. All I can tell you is that it had a haunting impact on me. On the Idaho we were never in any real battles, just some minor skirmishes where nobody was injured. We did shoot down some Jap zeros a few times, but nothing serious. In June of 1943 we were patrolling between Midway and Pearl looking for any Japanese subs that were trying to break our protective blockade that we were keeping in the Pacific around our base in Pearl Harbor. We always thought the Japanese would try another surprise attack on us to try to stop our rebuilding effort and knockout the communication lines throughout the pacific for the navy and the marines. They tried a few times with suicide run missions by their subs. On one particular afternoon we found a Japanese sub heading for Pearl and we engaged it. We were able to cripple it and sink it with depth charges, but what we didn't see until it was too late was that there were two subs. The second sub torpedoed us and nearly split us in half."

Mitch paused for a moment to collect his thoughts and take a sip of coffee. It was hard for him to tell the story even though he was not going into much detail and his eyes were starting to well up with tears. Jonathan finally asked during Mitch's pause, "Did the torpedo sink your ship?"

Mitch replied, "Eventually the ship went down, but not before they were able to get another torpedo off. The first one hit the engine room and killed everybody in there instantly. I happened to be going that way, but wasn't there yet so I had part of the blast throw me into a wall knocking me out. I think most of the crew never tried to rescue me as they were trying to get survivors out of the engine room even though there were none because they thought I was already dead. I had a lot of good shipmates die in the first blast. The second torpedo hit the main hull where our torpedo bay was, sending the bow crumbling in a blast of fire and smoke. That blast sent depth charges flying into the bridge, killing the captain and the crew that was up there. By the time that happened, most of the ship was in a state of confusion. Some of the crew were already abandoning ship before the order was even given."

Mitch took a moment to think and dry his eyes while getting a sip of coffee. While he paused for the moment there was nothing but silence in the room until Melissa spoke up and asked, "Are you alright, do you need anything?"

Mitch replied, "I'm okay, it's just I've never told anybody this story before. The only people that know it are the survivors." He looked directly at Jonathan who was staring back with a very serious look, but a sorrowful one as well and then he replied to him, "Not even your grandmother knows about this, and I suspect that she has had some idea that there was something so bad that happened to me that I couldn't even tell her. After all, she was a nurse during the war."

"I guess you had your reasons for not telling her this story, but I would still like to know what else happened out there that has made you not talk about it for fifty years," Jonathan replied.

Mitch just shook his head in agreement as the sunlight began to show through the window and the crack in the curtains. He knew that if he was to ever get past this then he had to tell the whole story. He also knew that the stubborn side of Jonathan would never again let him get away with half-truths.

Mitch continued in his story, "I didn't wake up by myself; the person who found me was Calvin Whitaker, or as you know Dr. Whitaker. He and I served together on the Idaho. He found me and got me to wake up as people were trying to get topside and start to get off the ship. The ship wasn't completely split in half yet and was still floating, but it was taking on water in the lower compartments. We were trying to get topside and seal everything off so the ship would not sink as fast and we'd have enough time to get the life boats into the water. As we were getting topside, another blast went off from another one of our torpedoes. It sent another big hole through the lower deck that pretty much split the ship in half, although we didn't know it at the time. We were on the third deck, two above the engine room and there were still about 35 men trapped on the second deck. I was the only officer coherent and there were no commanding officers around so I had to make the decision."

Mitch paused to collect his thoughts again and to take another sip of coffee, which he was out of. He shed a few tears and breathed a little harder. Jonathan got up from his seat and poured him another cup of coffee and poured some whiskey in it from Mitch's flask. Mitch took a deep breath and took another sip of coffee, then Jonathan put his hand on his shoulder to let him know that it was okay so Mitch continued his story.

"The decision I had to make was the hardest I have ever had to make in my life; I had to decide who dies and who lives. Nobody should ever have to decide that, but I had to in order to save the rest of my crew. We had to seal off the lower decks so the rest of the ship would not sink and I had to leave those men trapped so the rest of us could live."

Mitch began to shed his tears in a rapid fashion as he paused to catch his breath. He had never cried like this before and was even having a hard time understanding why he couldn't control his emotions. For Jonathan, it was the first time he had ever seen his grandfather really cry uncontrollably, but he also knew that Mitch had to deal with this in his own way so he had to let him express his pain.

Mitch finally got his emotions back in order to finish the story so he continued, "The really hard part of all that was we didn't know how big the hole really was from the last blast and that the ship would split in half so it didn't make a difference. We were able to get off the ship in life boats and 46 men survived that day. I was the only officer still alive so I was in charge. We floated for four days before we were found. I broke my leg during the first blast and because it was never set, I walk with a little bit of a limp. Those four days were the longest ever in my life because we didn't have food or much water. With the wreckage all around we were sure the Japanese would find us before the Allies did and kill us all. There were almost a hundred dead bodies in the water surrounding us and all we could do was watch the sharks slowly feed on them."

Mitch started to get up and almost fell over as he started to cry again. Jonathan caught him and sat him in the chair as he began to shed a few tears as well as Mitch's heartbreaking story came to an end. He understood why this was so hard for him, why he would want to keep it a secret. Mitch grabbed both Melissa's and Jonathan's hand and looked at them straight in the eye with tears and the most heartfelt look anybody had ever seen him make before.

He said to them, "I never wanted to be in charge of making that kind of decision again, and I have never wanted to see that much death. I have never been on boat since I got out of the navy and I never wanted to venture deep in to the water where I couldn't feel solid ground underneath me. Nobody should ever have to see what I saw and nobody should ever have someone die in their arms like I did. I had one of the crew die in my life boat slowly from internal bleeding while we were waiting to be rescued. Not all of us survived those four days, but I know that I can't go through something like that again. Maybe that is why I was always on the go and never stopped; maybe that's why I drank so much, because if I was going to die then I would be too drunk to remember. I look back and I know that I could have made better decisions that day and maybe I could have saved those men instead of condemning them to their death."

Before he could finish the rest of that thought, Melissa interrupted and said, "Maybe you could have done a lot of things better, but there were no guarantees that those men would have lived even if you hadn't sealed the lower decks. You may have had some different choices, but you did what was right to save those men you could."

Mitch tried to say something to her but she cut him off from making some stupid excuse. "You do know what it means to have no control over who dies and who lives. There is nothing fair about who does live or die. After my mother died I realized that the harder part was that no matter what you do or don't do, you have no control over what is supposed to happen. All we can do is keep trying to make the best decisions we can and have faith that it will all work out, but that's easier said than done and I had to learn that through years of anger."

Mitch didn't know what to say after that so he just cried and tried to control his emotions. Jonathan leaned in and hugged him for the first time since he was a kid. The he said, "I never got it with you, I never tried to understand why you hurt so much inside and did the things you did. It was always easier to hate you. I'm sorry grandpa, I'm sorry for letting my anger get the best of me with you."

The room filled with shadows as the sun stopped peeking through the window. The three of them just sat in the room for the longest time and shed their tears. For Mitch it was the first time in his life that he felt free, that the weight of a dark demented world was lifted off his shoulders. After a long moment he looked at Melissa and Jonathan and said, "When we were rescued we were taken back to Pearl Harbor and the only good part of that whole experience was that the hospital I was in was where I met your grandmother. When I did, the feelings I had where all I wanted to do was die because life was not worth living went away. I can honestly say that I was reborn when I met her. She was my angel and every day I have had with her made life worth living. You may not understand that now but someday you will."

Jonathan just looked at his grandfather with tears in his eyes and hugged him again. Then Melissa hugged both of the men that she had come to love very much over the past couple of months. They sat in the silence of their sorrow and joy for the release of pain that they had all carried for so long.

The next day the three of them drove to Arlington, Virginia for the reunion. It was the first time Jonathan had been so he didn't know what to expect. He was, however, curious to why the memorial was at Arlington instead of some place like Pearl Harbor. Mitch explained to both he and Melissa that since the circumstances surrounding the sinking of the ship was one of such heroic action because one ship had destroyed two Japanese submarines and went down in the process. As a result, they stopped the last ever attempt by the Japanese to invade America by way of Pearl Harbor. There was a memorial for the ship at Arlington National Cemetery as well as at Pearl

Harbor. The Idaho being sunk and losing three quarters of her crew was such a horrific tragedy and a big help in the cause to win back the Pacific from the Japanese that the Department of Defense decided to put up a small memorial in the cemetery honoring the crew in the memorial section.

He told them that it was easier for the remaining survivors to meet in Arlington instead of Hawaii. Arlington National Cemetery was also a bit of an honor, and to have a memorial there remembering the lost crew of the Idaho was something of heroic measure. Every year since the war ended and the memorial was put up in the late forties, the remaining survivors had been coming to Arlington in the beginning of the summer to remember their fellow shipmates. They all agreed that it was the least they could do since the tragedy had changed all their lives so dramatically and the incident was such a horrific one since most of the crew died.

After they were all released from the hospital the remaining crew never served together again on the same ship. Some went home, some served on other ships, some served in the office of a naval base, and there were three that served on other vessels who lost their lives in combat. They are remembered as well at the memorial for still serving their country as sailors and heroes after they had barely survived the incident with the Idaho.

The three of them arrived at the cemetery about the time for the changing of the guard; the sentries who guarded the tombs of the unknowns. There was a small group of men gathered at the back part of the cemetery where small white buildings and overhangs sat on hill tops looking out over the rows of white marbled tombstones. It was the memorial part of the cemetery where different battles and wars where remembered and honored as well as servicemen who were not buried in the cemetery.

Mitch was one of the last men to arrive as Jonathan pulled the car around to where the other cars were gathered on the drive path in front of the memorial. Dr. Whitaker came from the small crowd of men to greet Mitch as he was being helped out of the car. There were not that many survivors out of the original 46; only 21 still remained. There were not usually any visitors except the men who served on the Idaho, but every once in a while some family member would come to help one of the survivors who could not get around without help. The men had always agreed that it was a private reunion unless it was extreme circumstances where someone needed help as one often did when old age would finally overcome them.

The men who needed help in the past were gone now and for the first time in his life Mitch was the one who needed help. It was a shock to the other members of the reunion because Mitch had always been seen as the invincible one because of his heroic deeds fifty years ago. He was greeted by fellow shipmates and helped up the steps to where the memorial was. He shook hands, telling the crew what was wrong with him. He also told them the story of how Jonathan and Melissa came to be with him on this trip and why they were here.

Calvin stayed behind to talk with Jonathan and Melissa. He introduced himself to Melissa and got reacquainted with Jonathan who did not remember him right off because it had been a lot of years since they had seen each other, but after a few moments he finally realized who he was. He was one of Mitch's closest friends and one of the few who knew the whole truth regarding the guilt that Mitch had lived with for all these years. The guilt was the losses he suffered during the war from fellow shipmates to the death of his brother; he felt the way he did because there was nothing he could have done to save them.

After a few minutes of catching up Calvin finally asked Jonathan, "So I guess he finally told you what happened if you came along with him?"

"Yes he did, we had a good talk yesterday and I think I am finally beginning to understand why he has spent so many years trying to forget."

"Well, we all deal with loss in our own way; each one of these men here have lived with this tragedy and seeing the death that we saw in their own way. You are looking at a bunch of old drunks and bitter old men that have spent decades pushing away the things we love the most because our pain is too much."

"Are you trying to tell me that all of you have done despicable things trying to cope with the hurt?"

"We have all dealt with the hurt in our own way; your grandfather I think took on more of the burden because he was the last man in charge therefore having to be the one to lead us to safety. He has always felt that it was his responsibility to see everybody alive and safe while feeling that he could have saved so many more of our shipmates."

"He told us about the decision that he had to make and that it didn't make a difference, your ship went down. In his own way he unburdened himself of that guilt."

"That is part of the hurt he's carried, it was a decision to seal that part of the ship and send those men to their death, but that's only part of the story. There's more to it than that, he wasn't supposed to be a battle commander, just a mechanical officer."

"What do you mean, I don't understand what you're talking about," Jonathan said.

As Mitch was catching up with old friends and

talking with these men that he had served with, Calvin imparted a truth to Jonathan that had never been known by Mitch's family. It was a deep dark secret that only comrades in arms would know because they had been on the frontlines together and had seen the face of death together. It was the truth that most people never want known, the truth that we are never what we seem, especially to other people

Calvin looked at Jonathan and said, "What your grandfather will not tell you is that as confident as he might seem, as tough as he might be where nothing can scare him, he was afraid at the time of the battle and did not know what to do. All he wanted to be was an engineer and keep things working on the ship, never having to make the tough decisions regarding life and death in a battle. He feels like his fear got the better of him to where he made the wrong decisions and caused the needless death of all those men."

"Everybody at one time feels that they made the wrong decision. We're human, so we question our decisions and try to live with the ones that were wrong."

"Sure," said Calvin, "but it's different when you hold someone else's life in your hands. Mitch will always feel that the right decision could have saved most of the men on the ship. If your grandfather has been a little reckless in his decisions over the years, it's not that he doesn't have good judgment, it's just that he felt like it didn't matter what kind of decisions he made...they would always be wrong while causing something bad to happen to someone else."

"So by not caring enough and letting his drinking control his thinking, the decisions he made really were bad. He did it to himself because the hurt was too much to bare so why try and make the right choice."

"We are always the cause of our own personal destruction, but what you probably don't know is that your grandfather can't help but make the right decision sometimes. Your grandfather did save my life on that ship. With a broken leg he pushed me out of the way of an explosion as we were trying to get topside. He fell and caused even more damage to his leg and that's what caused it to not heal right and cause the slight limp he has. He may not see it, but your grandfather is a hero and he is the one that kept us alive until we were rescued."

"The last few days have been surreal because I've never seen my grandfather in this light before. I never knew what he did and what he's lived with."

Calvin put his hand on Jonathan's shoulder and replied, "It's usually in the end that we finally see the truth about who we are, the truth about the people we love and how we ended up where we are. I just thought that you should know all this about your grandfather."

Calvin walked back to the memorial with the remaining survivors of the USS Idaho so they could pay their proper respects. There was a small detachment of the old guard marching to where the memorial was. They were sentries from the 3rd US infantry unit performing a small ceremony for the servicemen of the Idaho honoring the dead. Part of the ceremony was the 21 gun salute and then all servicemen past and present saluted in honor of the dead. Mitch said few words, saying how thankful he was that all of them made it home alive to carry on the name of their dead shipmates, but that each day they should never forget the men who died.

They were ceremonial words that he said every year, but they were still just as true. He told the men that the right thing for them to do was to live the best

lives they could so as to honor those that did not
return home and then he thanked them for taking part
in the memorial of the Idaho. The last act they did as
the old guard was leaving was take a shot of whiskey
and toast their friends long gone. The service took
about 20 minutes but the men always stayed and
talked for a while to catch up and remember old times.
    Jonathan and Melissa were introduced to
everyone and for the first time Jonathan saw the dark
tormented side of his grandfather. It was the part of
him that was still like a scared child searching for
answers in an uncertain world. Both Jonathan and
Melissa walked away from that day with a heroic
impression of Mitch Collins; he was a man deeply
loved and respected by his fellow shipmates who in no
small way owed a part of their lives to him.
Jonathan saw all of that and something much more
important. Mitch was human and he was the same
tragic figure that he had read about in books and
immortalized in music. He loved his grandfather more
than he ever had, not out of pity, but because his
grandfather had a true quality.

13

The Only Way Home

The journey home back to Chicago was not as hard as the journey that the three of them had taken across America. It was the first time that Mitch felt truly free because he had released part of himself over the past couple of months that had been his torment for so many years. He had a smile on his face and quality about him that had not been there before; it was that of someone who didn't have to worry even knowing that his days were few. Mitch did not have a day where he was not in pain and exhausted, but it didn't matter because he had done the things he had set out to do. One final thing for him, he was finally going home.

Jonathan, Melissa, and Mitch were on the road for about two days before they arrived back in Chicago.

Every moment of the time was spent laughing and remembering the good times from years before when the family was electric and not strangers in the same house. Melissa for most part just listened intently to the stories that Mitch and Jonathan told her.

Jonathan would tell her his fondest memories about his grandfather like the fact that he never missed one sporting event that Jonathan participated in, whether it be football, basketball, or baseball. Mitch was always there and sometimes he would come by to watch practices when Jonathan was in high school just to keep an eye on him and make sure he wasn't "goofing" off. It was Mitch who bought him his first baseball glove and taught him out to pitch and it was Mitch who bought him his first football while showing him how to dodge tacklers while throwing a pass. One of Jonathan's favorite memories was watching this old man jump and roll around as if he was a kid again, knowing that it caused him pain, but that he would hurt himself just to have fun with Jonathan.

For Jonathan it didn't hurt so much anymore to remember his childhood with Mitch because he now understood why Mitch was the way he was; the slow limping faded hero that Jonathan had seen in his grandfather over the last nine years disappeared. There was a certain understanding that allowed Jonathan to become close with his grandfather again and to see the good man that he was.

The rest of the road trip went quickly, especially as Jonathan and Mitch would serenade Melissa with old Sinatra songs. She didn't even mind that they didn't sing well; for her it was just good to see them laughing and being happy. The only thing Melissa wanted from this trip was to see the two men she loved find again that perfect idea of family they had years before.

As they entered Chicago, Jonathan drove the car a little bit slower so they could savor the moments of returning home. It had been awhile since Jonathan had been home to Chicago. It had been even longer for Mitch, even though it was only a few months ago that he had ventured outside the city limits.

There was a light breeze coming through that kept the temperature low just to let them know that summer had not fully arrived yet, and the familiar sounds of the city that Mitch fell in love with over fifty years ago brought a smile to his face so he could know that he was finally home. It was those sounds of traffic and people yelling in the windy city that comforted him because he knew that he was home, and he knew where he belonged.

They did not tell Laura or Alice that they would be arriving. As Jonathan pulled the car into the old neighborhood on the North side of Chicago, five blocks from Wrigley Field, people from the neighborhood immediately recognized Mitch and his car and started waving at the long lost father who had finally returned. The neighborhood had not changed much in forty years and some of the same people who had been there since the early fifties were still there. Sons and daughters had grown up and moved away, but most still remained to start new generations. The important part about this neighborhood was that everybody knew each other and the people where there for each other when it was needed.

Some of the people honked at Mitch as he came driving into the neighborhood, and all the car horns caused such a disturbance that it brought people out their homes to see what was going one. Two of those people were Alice and Laura; there wasn't any surprise on their faces as the old car drove up, just the look of sympathy for the unexpected return.

Some of the neighbors came by and greeted Mitch and Jonathan since it had been a long time since any of them had been back this way. While Mitch shook hands with neighbors that he had known for years and greeted old friends, he could not take his eyes off one of person, his beloved Alice. She was still just as radiant and beautiful as she was the first time they met.

Laura hugged her son and hugged her father as he was helped out of the car, then reintroduced herself to Melissa. Alice was the last to greet everybody, and after she got finished hugging her grandson she greeted Mitch. There was hurt between them, but it all faded away with the sympathy for a dying man, but mostly for a man that she still loved.

As Jonathan watched his grandmother walk over to Mitch he saw something different in her eyes. He could recall years before after they had split up that the electricity in her eyes disappeared and was replaced with sadness. It had been there all these years since the day Mitch left, but in one single moment the sadness was gone and the electricity filled her eyes again.

Alice hugged Mitch and kissed him; he hugged her back tightly not wanting to let go. Everybody seemed surprised because Alice and Mitch could fight like the best of them, and to Laura and Jonathan they just assumed there was still a lot of hurt between them.

Mitch said to Alice, "I see my grandson told his mother that I was dying and she told you. Now before you ask how I know, what I know is your looks. The look you have right now is the one that says I already know and I'm concerned about you."

She smiled at him and gave a casual laugh at his knowing cockiness, then she replied, "the thing is Mitchell Collins,'" she was the only one that called him Mitchell, "I know your looks as well, and the look you have now is that you're glad to see me and happy to be home."

"What can I say? You know me better than anybody."

"There's no one that will ever know you better."

They both just smiled at each other like two young lovers who had gotten the best of each other while stealing each other's heart. Through all their faults and all the hurt that they had caused each other, Mitch and Alice were still those same two people that had fallen in love with each other at first glance, as ridiculous as it might sound.

It had been a lot of years since Mitch had climbed the outside staircase to his house that he bought for Alice, and as he walked inside the house he knew that he was finally home. It was at that moment that Mitch knew that no matter what, everything would be okay.

He was exhausted and worn down from the medicine so Alice helped him up the stairs to their bedroom. She had the same bed that she and Mitch had had for years; to Alice there was only one place she wanted him to be in his final days and it was at her side so she could take care of him.

As Mitch was getting settled, Laura and Melissa got reacquainted since it had been quite a few years since they had seen each other. Laura was surprised to see her again, but remembered that she was fond of her while being very good for Jonathan. Melissa told her the story of how she came to be involved on the trip. Laura could do nothing but laugh for she was not surprised at how her father could make friends so easily with people and get them to follow him on some adventure.

While they were talking, Jonathan came back

into the living room where his mother and Melissa were sitting after raiding the refrigerator looking for something to eat, which was not an uncommon thing to do in his grandparent's house

Laura finally asked Jonathan, "So did you see something different about your grandfather on this trip?"

"Different, how do you mean? He's the same old Mitch Collins that I've always known."

"What I mean is, did you see something in him that you've never seen before. He opened up to you and you finally started to understand what kind of person he was and who he has become."

"If you're asking me if it was a strange trip, then yes it was. I did find out some things that I didn't know about him before. Why do you ask, because you seem to know something more than you are letting on about?"

"I know my father and he usually doesn't make the effort unless it's important to him. I thought he might open up more since he's dying. If he didn't care he wouldn't have sought you out, he would have just gone off and died in peace."

"Mom, are you trying to tell me that Mitch somehow had all of this planned out? There's no way he could have known that he was going to die this way and then try to make amends with his family."

"That's not what I meant, you're right there is no way he could have known that he would die this way, but the one thing he must have known is eventually he would have to come to terms with his past."

Laura got out of her seat and to Jonathan and Melissa it looked like she was leaving the room because she was about to cry. However, as emotional

as she was over everything that was happening, she
went to get something out of the desk drawer that was
located in the corner of the living room. It was a stack
of letters and cards all bundled up in a nice neat
stack.

Laura walked back over to her seat and as she
sat down she said, "Your grandmother showed this to
me the last week. It's a stack of cards and letters that
your grandfather had sent over the past year or so.
This is just one stack out of many. They have been
writing to each other for the past nine years since they
split up."

Melissa just smiled at Jonathan who had a look
of shock on his face from what his mother had just
told him; she smiled because Mitch was full of
surprises. Jonathan had always been under the
impression that his grandparents would not speak to
each other, but his shocked look quickly turned to a
smile because after all that he had witnessed over the
past two months this was really not that surprising.

Melissa said, "Somehow I knew Mitch couldn't
just walk away from the love of his life so easily after
all the stories he had told us about the good times
they had and how much he had."

"This would explain why they greeted each other
the way they did when we arrived here," said
Jonathan. "I thought at first it was kind of peculiar."

Laura just smiled at Jonathan and Melissa then
she replied, "I was shocked at first as well when your
grandmother told me about this, but I guess even
though they felt like they couldn't live with each other
they really couldn't stay out of each other's lives. She
told me that they wrote over two hundred letters to
each other every year and sent cards to one another on
special occasions, including their anniversary."

Jonathan just started laughing and replied,

"That man never ceases to amaze me; still always full of surprises. I think he goes out of his way to make everybody think something different about him that really isn't true. It almost makes me wonder if he's not dying on purpose quite yet just so he could pull one final surprise on all of us."

"It's a little morbid to think so," said Melissa, "but after what I have seen the past couple of months in getting to know Mitch, I wouldn't be surprised, would you Jonathan?"

"No I wouldn't. Although if you're right, then I wonder what card he'll pull from his sleeve."

Laura looked at them both with a few tears in her eyes and responded, "I think no matter how much we think we know him...it feels like we don't know anything about him."

She was right and it was the best thing said of this whole situation regarding Mitch. The one thing Jonathan realized was that people were open and closed books. The open book of a person is marked by only what they want to show people and hidden carefully behind a guarded mask. The closed book of a person is what they are afraid to show because it's the truth of who they really are, and no matter how much we keep it closed, the words remain which we will never escape from.

∞∞∞∞∞∞∞∞∞∞

While the rest of the family was downstairs, Alice was helping Mitch get settled. It was hard for him to move around now, so Mitch spent most of his time sitting or lying down. His medicine did some good, but not enough, and his muscles were weak from the cancer. As she was getting him settled in bed he stopped her for a moment and smiled. She just looked at him with her knowing grin that always told him she knew what he was thinking.

He said to her, "I hope you don't mind that we came here, I just wanted to spend my last days with my family."

"Mitchell Collins you know better to even think that; this has always been your home and when we die we shouldn't be anywhere else," she paused for moment to collect her words as the tears welled up in her eyes and said, "I wouldn't want you to be anywhere else."

"Good, because there is something I need to ask you and I've been wanting to ask you this for a long time."

"You want to know if we made the right choice nine years ago, you want to know if things would have been different if you hadn't left?"

"Even after all these years you know what I am going to ask or say before I can do it," he smiled and winked at her then continued, "Yeah I want to know what you think would have had happened if that were the case."

"I can't honestly say that we would have worked it out and everything would have been okay. Maybe you wouldn't have left and everything would have been worse. I do believe that the best thing you could do at the time was to leave and let me grieve in my own way. The greatest thing you ever did for me was leaving when you did; you gave me the space I needed. Although to be honest, I would have liked you to come home years ago."

"Me too, but there is no way of knowing when one's grieving is completely over or how much is too little or too much when it comes the time someone one needs to grieve. I figured the best thing I could do was just keep in contact with you so I would never lose you."

"You could never lose me and you know why. You loved me when I thought nobody else would. The 'what ifs' over the past nine years don't matter , all that matters is that you're home now."

She bent down and kissed him and he kissed her back as if it were the first time they had met on a beach during a haze of war when she would be the one thing that could truly heal him. Alice had always been his saving grace, his guardian angel, and for her Mitch was the one person that made her believe that anyone no matter their past could find that true love.

Mitch was tired and feel asleep on their king size bed that was really too big for people that were five feet and ten inches and five feet and four inches. It was a big bed that was the most comfortable bed that either one of them had ever slept on in their lives. Even though there was enough space for two or three people between the both of them so they would not have to touch, Alice curled up beside him and went to sleep with him. It was the first time in almost ten years that the both of them had slept that close to each other while the world faded away around them.

That evening Catherine drove home from her place in Rolling Meadows. Laura had called her and told her that their father had returned home. She had already received the news that their father was dying and he was on one last road trip that would eventually end in Chicago, but like everybody else she didn't know when that journey would end for Mitch.

Alice made a big dinner for everyone like she used to on Sundays when Jonathan was growing up. It was just understood that Sundays were for the Lord and for family in the Collins' household, but this was a special occasion because Mitch had finally come home and no one knew how many days he might have left.

As soon as Catherine arrived home she found her father sitting in his reclining chair in the den reading the paper which was the usual place he could be found in the evenings when they all were growing up. Seeing him there was like a scene from the past, but a time when all was well. When she hugged her father, although it could never take away all the hurt, a life time of transgressions seemed to be wiped away with their tears. They were the tears for the lost survivor by one of life's twisted tragedies.

That night was a special night for everyone; it was a night that had not happened in many years because there was not any pain. There was only the joy of being together surrounded by the comforted laughter of family at the dinner table. Everybody ate and laughed while story after story was told. Nobody could remember the hurt that each caused each other over the years, nobody could remember the hurt Mitch had caused years before because even though the memories were still there, they all chose to reflect on the joyous times that they were having.

Mitch had never been short of stories from his childhood to his travels as a young man to things he remembered most about his grandson growing up. Everybody there knew the stories already, even Melissa, for they were recounted to her by Jonathan years before when they were dating, but there was something rhythmic and peaceful in hearing the same old stories again.

Some of Mitch's favorite stories were about Jonathan and his mischievous nature as a kid when he caught him doing something he wasn't supposed to. For example, there was this one time when Jonathan was three and somehow figured out how to climb onto the open space on top of the refrigerator to get one of his grandmother's homemade chocolate chip cookies in the cookie jar, but could not figure out how to climb down.

Mitch walked into the kitchen and caught him red handed eating cookies. Mitch didn't know whether to punish him or laugh at how resourceful his grandson had been at three years old. Jonathan tried to act like it wasn't big deal and he wasn't doing anything wrong. One of Jonathan's favorite stories about Mitch was when he was in High School playing baseball his grandfather strolling by the dugout to give his team a pep talk of sorts.

Everybody who knew Jonathan, from teachers to coaches and teammates, knew his grandfather and he was well liked. As Mitch came strolling by the dugout he said to the team, "You guys know what you came here to do so don't be watching the girls," and everybody just started laughing, but Mitch was always known for saying light hearted things to keep people from being nervous.

It was a good night of laughter and simple joy, reminding them of what family should be. For Melissa, it was something that she had never had and had wanted for so long. So this estranged family who had not spoken very many truthful words to each other over the past nine years welcomed her as one of their own. They all had spent the last few years going through the motions, hiding their pain while not having to speak to one another. Laura and Catherine barely spoke to each other before that night. They were all people of despair; they were all masquerading their joy through little conversations and Christmas cards to each other. Tonight was different; their truth finally came out. Not one of them could hold on to their anger, for it was a relief to find that joy of family once again.

Finally after enough laughter passed Mitch

while sitting at the head of the table like he had been years before dispensed with a final surprise. He said to everyone there, "I think it's time to tell some truth, what do you think Alice?"

She put her hand upon his and replied, "Why not, I think we have had enough secrets around here for the past nine years."

Mitch looked at every one of them individually and then said, "You probably already know that Alice and I have been in contact with one another quite bit over the last nine years. We have been writing to each other a lot just to keep in touch. The thing is, I know that all of you think I did this one terrible act that caused us to split up, but it didn't happen the way you think."

Alice interrupted and said, "I found out not too long after Mitch left that he didn't really have an affair, even though I got a letter from some strange woman saying that he did and had a child with her. I called her after some time had gone by and talked to her about it. She admitted to me that she lied about the affair and having Mitch's child. She just wanted to have some kind of revenge because he wouldn't do it and she had fallen in love with him. It was the desperate act of someone hurt and vindictive."

"Just because this happened doesn't mean I wasn't unfaithful to her," said Mitch as he looked at Laura and Catherine. "I should have never put myself in that situation and crossed the line with that woman. Not a day goes by that I don't wish I could change that moment, but I have lived with it ever since while seeking forgiveness every day from the one true love of my life."

"It's okay Mitch, you don't have to go into detail, you didn't do anything wrong, we should have just found a way to live with each other instead of giving up because we were mad."

"I do have to say it," Mitch replied in a regretful tone, "I was unfaithful to you and I want everybody at this table to know it. We can be unfaithful in different ways without committing adultery. I was unfaithful every time I took a drink trying to forget what my life was. I was unfaithful to you every time I wasn't here when I should've been; when I wanted to go out and not spend an evening with you. There were so many times I wasn't here that had nothing to do with my job and I missed out on so much, but mainly I wasn't here with you. If I could take it back..."

Alice stopped him in mid-sentence with everybody at the table looking at him. Laura and Catherine had tears in their eyes because it was the first time that anybody had seen Alice and Mitch admit their faults towards one another. She said, "I already know, and you've never had to say it with me. You're here now and that's what counts."

Mitch couldn't say anything else to her, for the tears in his eyes were overtaking him and Alice just smiled at him then hugged him tight trying to not let go the only one she ever loved and gave her heart to.

There was silence in the room prolonging the moment that had escaped in this family so many years before. Laura, Catherine, Jonathan, and Melissa just sat there looking at each other with smiles while they witnessed these two people rekindle a love that everyone thought had died. It was the first time in many years that any of them had seen the electricity in their eyes; it was the first time that Mitch and Alice believed once again.

After a few moments had passed, Alice said, "I guess we should probably tell you the truth about us breaking up nine years ago. The truth is we never got a divorce; Mitch just left and stayed away like I asked him to."

"We agreed that we could stay away from each other," said Mitch, "but still be married so Alice could still take advantage of our retirement, our savings and my pension. The other thing is that we never believed in divorce and just because we had a big fight doesn't mean that we should get one. We figured it was better to stay away from each other and let time heal the wounds."

Nobody knew what to say, the shock was the only thing to fill the room. When Mitch had walked out nine years before, everybody just assumed that he and Alice had gotten a divorce. She never spoke about their separation; anytime it was brought up she would change the subject or leave the room.

During all those years since Mitch's departure he was not seen much by anybody and he never came by the house again. He was at a few special occasions like Jonathan's High School graduation and some of his sporting events, but nobody really talked to him that much except for a few letters and maybe a few birthday cards to his grandson and two daughters. For the most part, he just stayed away so it was only natural to think that Mitch and Alice had gotten a divorce.

Finally, after enough silence had prevailed Laura spoke and said, "Okay, I don't get it between you two and there is something I've never understood. You will stay away from each other when you've hurt each other, but not get a divorce. You don't even have much in common, why are you together?"

Alice smiled at her daughter and asked her, "Why are we together? That's not what you really want to ask is it? Go ahead and ask what you really want to ask, Laura.”

"Okay, I don't understand why you two love each other. What is it that makes you love each other?"

Mitch looked at his both of his daughters, his grandson, and the woman that had been adopted by this family as one of their own. Then he answered, "I love Alice because she makes sense out of everything. When I first met her she stole my heart and I knew that life with her no matter what would make sense. It never made sense before she came along and afterward it always seemed to make sense. That's what did it for me."

Everyone else at the table could not help but smile at his answer because it was the most perfect of answers. Then Alice said, "I love this man because he dared to love me when I thought nobody else would."

Everybody else at the table but Mitch was a little confused by her answer. Mitch looked at her with a sorrowful look not wanting to see her have to tell everybody the secret that they had kept for so many years, but knew above all that secret had to be told to release the pain.

Catherine asked her mother "Mom, what are you talking about, why wouldn't anybody else love you?"

Alice had never made mention of her deep seeded secret, the one that could shatter her as a person. The last time she spoke about it in detail was when she told Mitch shortly before they got married to see if he would still want to be with her. She knew that if she was to give him her whole heart then she would have to tell him the one piece of shattered glass from her past.

She looked at Mitch, who with his eyes told her that she didn't have to tell her secret, but she kissed him so as to tell him that everything would be okay, that it was time for the truth.

Alice said, "When I was a young girl on the farm about fourteen I think, my father had an old ranch hand that worked the farm for a couple of years. He was handsome and rugged; there wasn't a young teenage girl that wasn't infatuated with him. He took a liking to me one summer and one night took advantage of me. I thought he was just being nice and when he got a little over friendly I protested, but he was too strong and he raped me in the barn. I didn't say anything for a while and then I turned out to be pregnant. That's when I had to tell my father and mother. The only solution in my father's eyes was to terminate the problem as he saw it, so I was taken to a midwife in the back woods of the area and had an abortion."

Mitch had tears in his eyes and everybody at the table sat there in shock once again. Nobody knew what to say and then Laura finally asked, "What happened to you after that, Mom?"

"My body healed after a long time had gone by, but there was some scarring. I didn't know if I would ever be able to have children; that's why you and Catherine were such a blessing. When something like that happened to a woman back then they were deemed undesirable, so I never thought anybody would love me because of it. I became a nurse in the navy so I could get away from the secret and so nobody would ever know. I told your father a week before we got married just to see how much he really loved me, and to him it didn't matter. I never thought anybody would love me, but he did, and Catherine when you were born it was the first time I ever saw him cry because we both knew that we were truly blessed. I love him because he loved me."

Mitch squeezed Alice's hand to let her know that

everything would be okay, that he would never leave again, and to let her know that he loved her. She looked at him and smiled and saw every joyous moment they had ever had in his eyes; she saw them replay in his memories by the affections he had for her.

Catherine and Laura could not help but cry, but they were tears of joy for seeing their parents like they used to be, two loving parents who could see the best of each other in each other's eyes. For them, it was the way it was meant to be, and for Jonathan it was a lesson in what he should really be looking for in this life instead what was on the road. Jonathan squeezed Melissa's hand, but didn't say anything when he looked at her. He didn't have to, for she already knew what he was thinking. He was thinking that everything was great for the first time in many years, and also that he had never been truly happy unless it was with her.

The night passed late into the evening with more laughter and stories. All of them even played games like they used to do as a family when Jonathan was growing up. Monopoly was always a favorite among the family no matter how long it took to play. They laughed and enjoyed each other's company and at certain moments sarcasm and the joking around came out in all of them. At certain moments Mitch would make cash register noises as people landed on his property. Normally this might seem annoying, but under the circumstances it was delightful and funny because the family was together enjoying the time they had with each other.

The next day everybody was up early except for Mitch. Alice, who had slept close to him to make sure he would be okay throughout the night, was up early making coffee and preparing his breakfast. Mitch by this point had taken to sleeping in later than usual so it wasn't anything out of the norm for him to sleep later than anyone. When Alice went up to check on him she found him on the floor barely breathing. She didn't know what to do, so as a reflex she called an ambulance to take him to the hospital.

He was still alive when the ambulance got to the house and drove him to the hospital, but barely. They got Mitch to the hospital and did just enough for him to get him stable. He was conscious enough to see the flashing ceiling lights as he was wheeled into the emergency room, but he could not speak. Alice and the rest of the family got there just after the ambulance did and it was Jonathan who brought the doctors up to date about his condition and said to call Dr. Whitaker for more information.

The end was finally here and it was only a matter of time before he would slip out of consciousness and die. The doctors gave him enough medicine to take his pain away, but they couldn't make him better or keep him away from the inevitable. For the last couple of months he tried to keep from having to be in a hospital, lying in the cold uncomfortable bed, tubes connected all over his upper body. Although there was no stopping it now; he was on his death bed, and his final sleep was near.

After the doctor got him stable, he came out to tell everybody that there was nothing more he could do except make Mitch more comfortable. His death was finally near and the curtains had started to drop, but he would be made to feel as comfortable as possible while he was in the hospital and until it finally happened.

For most of the day Mitch slept and the family stayed there with him. Catherine didn't even go to work that day. She didn't want to be anywhere else but at his side when the end came. Sometime during the day he got moved to a room so he would be more comfortable. They all knew what was about to happen while time slowly slipped away throughout the day. They each took a turn staying with Mitch just in case he woke up, including Melissa.

Sometime in the evening Mitch woke up to find his family in the room at his side. He wasn't very coherent partly because of the pain killers he was on, but it was enough to talk to everyone there. It had been a long day so far and Alice most of all was exhausted, so when the doctors came by to check on him about dinner time he told everybody that it might be a good time for everybody to go on home and get some rest.

Nobody really wanted to, but there was nothing anybody could do for Mitch, so Laura, Catherine, Melissa and Alice went back to the house, leaving Jonathan there with his grandfather. He said he wanted someone to be there with Mitch until he fell asleep, but mainly he didn't want to have to leave Mitch alone, not now when they had been through so much.

Jonathan and Mitch didn't talk much, but Jonathan did find one thing that he could share with his grandfather. The Chicago Cubs were on WGN playing the Giants at Wrigley Field. Although both of them wished they could find a way to get Mitch out of the hospital so they could go to one last baseball game, it was pretty much impossible now. Mitch couldn't move his legs; he didn't have any more strength in them and was for the most part confined to the bed or a wheelchair.

Jonathan did, however, do the next best thing to being at the ball park. He got a couple of bratwurst and some cans of Old Style Beer and snuck them into

Mitch's hospital room so they could watch the ballgame as a good Cubs fan would. Jonathan could recall the first baseball game his grandfather ever took him to at Wrigley field. They were playing the Giants and they would lose 7 to 5, but it was the most magical experience he could remember having with his grandfather. It didn't hurt that they were in a place where the purest form of baseball prevails, a place known as Wrigley Field.

As they were drinking their beer and eating their bratwurst and hoping that the Cubs could hang on to the lead, Jonathan had to ask Mitch something that had been on his mind for a while.

"Mitch I've been wondering about something ever since we left Vegas. Did you really accidentally walk into Melissa's bar and then get her to come with you on this trip? You didn't plan it or anything just to get me to be with her again?"

He smiled, but didn't answer Jonathan. He was amused that Jonathan would think that, but most amused at himself for still being full of surprises on his death bed.

"You're not going to tell me are you, but I think that you had something to do with it because you knew how much she meant to me."

Mitch smiled and asked Jonathan, "Let me ask you this, how much do you love her?

"I love her very much."

"Do you want to spend the rest of your life with her?"

Jonathan didn't even hesitate anymore when asked how much he loved Melissa, he simply replied, "Yeah, I do. She's always been the best thing that's ever happened to me besides my family."

"Then it doesn't matter if I had anything to do with it, you love her and that's enough. It's the way I have always felt about your grandmother and knowing that was enough for me."

"I can certainly say this, if this trip had not come along then I would not have had the courage to try and be with her again."

"Sure you would, because when you love someone enough you're willing to do the things that you never thought you would do. With love time is a minor inconvenience because eventually you'll find a way to be together. If you have doubts then you weren't paying attention to your grandmother and me last night."

They both laughed and continued watching the game. The Cubs would end up losing the game, but it didn't matter because the joy was sharing one last game with good food and good beer with each other. When the game was done and Mitch was starting to drift off to sleep, Jonathan started to gather his things. "I'm about to get out of here so you can get some sleep, but I'll be back tomorrow bright and early so we can see about getting you out of this place."

Mitch smiled and then replied, "There is something I need to tell you and I really don't feel like waiting, apparently I don't have much of that anymore."

"Hopefully you'll have a little more time."

"I don't know about that. Time is always an unfriendly stranger to the old and the weak. I think I can definitely qualify as both right now."

"What else do you need to say?"

"One little piece of advice from this old man, something I wish my father had the courage to say to me."

"This sounds like one of your long speeches, but that's okay. I think you're entitled, though. Anybody that has to eat this hospital food has every right to make whatever speeches they want to make. "

"You think this is bad, you should have tried the army rations during the war. That's a bad taste one can never forget, but that's not what I wanted to talk to you about." Mitch smiled and patted Jonathan's hand which was holding onto the railing of the hospital bed.

"When I'm gone I don't want you to feel sorry for me; I've had a great life and I got to spend forty seven years with your grandmother. How many people get the chance to spend that long with the great love of their life? I've made mistakes, most you know about now. If I have any regret, it's not letting go when I should have. It's time for you to let go and live life the way it was meant to be lived."

"I'm not holding on to anything and I'm not going to feel sorry for you."

"I know you better than that, I know how you are; you're just like me when it comes to holding on to your pain. It's the hurt you've had for most of your life; from your life not turning out the way you think it should have, and the hurt from the people you love the most letting you down. I am partly to blame for that, but there is something you better learn. Family may be the first to let you down, but they will always be the first to pick you right back up when you need it. That's what I have experienced in the last few months. I can tell you that I'm sorry for everything I've ever done to hurt you, but that's not what you need to hear. You need to hear this even if you don't want to, let it all go Jonathan because you shouldn't have to sit in a hospital bed thinking about all the time you wasted feeling sorry for yourself and the life you've had to live when you could have done something about it.

Jonathan turned his head away so he wouldn't

have to show the tears that were in his eyes as he sat down in the chair next to the bed. Mitch coughed a bit as his breathing got heavier. Jonathan in a saddened tone said, "If you think I blame you for anything, I don't. I have regrets, but I can honestly say that I don't hate you anymore Mitch."

"I know you don't."

"Damn you though for making me love you, it was a lot easier to hate."

"Your grandmother once told me the same thing, but she couldn't help but still love me. The thing is though, I couldn't help but love her, too, and loving her was always better."

"I don't think I have anything to let go, but I wish some things could've been different."

"We all wish that about certain things in our life…You may not think you've held on to anything that needs to be let go, but someday you may think different and when that time comes don't be afraid. Have the courage to admit the anger you have and then let go of it because it will just tear you up inside. I have watched you all your life and watched you keep that chip on your shoulder from people who have wronged you in some way. Just let it go Jonathan."

Jonathan started to say something but Mitch wouldn't let him. He knew that Jonathan would get defensive and say some smartass comment out of anger, but wouldn't let him without finishing what he needed to tell him.

"Don't say anything; just listen without saying a damn word at least once in your life. If you don't want to admit it then don't, but you already know the truth and you know what I am saying is right. Don't let your pain or your regrets consume you. You're better than that, and if you learn anything from this journey then learn from what I have lived."

"Maybe the only thing I can learn from is my own experience."

"Then learn from living a life of good experiences, not a life filled with pain that you cause within yourself."

Both men just looked at each other without saying a word. Mitch coughed and fought to breath normally, but he did just enough to keep speaking. "I have never really talked about your father with you, but you should know the truth. We didn't agree on anything and I thought he was young and foolish. I was wrong. He lived life by his own choices making them by conviction and without excuse. He didn't have to go to Vietnam, he could have dodged the draft, gone to Canada or something of that nature, but he didn't. He believed in service, even service in something that he didn't necessarily agree with, but service unto something greater than himself. He let go of any hatred or dissent he had so if nothing else he could serve and help the men he served with. No matter what he was free inside and he was a good man. Because of his conviction and the service he chose I have the deepest respect for him. I don't know if I ever had that much courage of my conviction."

Jonathan with tears in his eyes replied to Mitch, "Maybe not always, but you made it home when it really counted. You saved each one of us from living with the pain of our own misguided notions."

"Maybe you're right. The last thing I am going to tell you is this. Even if you don't see it now, don't wait for the winter of your life to make things right. You're smarter than that...you're better than that and if you're looking for some way to be redeemed for the hurt you might have caused then redeem yourself by loving that beautiful lass that's been standing by your side for the last couple of months. That kind of love can save you more than you know, especially when you see your whole world in her eyes. It saved me fifty years ago when I met your grandmother.”

Jonathan squeezed the hand of his ailing grandfather to let him know that he understood what he was saying. It was hard to hear it from the man that he had loved and hated, but he understood even if he was not ready to accept it.

He replied, “Are there ever any simple answers in this life? You seem to have only complicated ones.”

“There are never simple answers unless a simple life can be invented, but we both know there is no such thing. The truth is, life is just one big complicated mess, but somewhere we can find the good things, the things that can truly make us happy. Somehow we swim through all the confusion and heartache to find our happiness in whatever form it comes.

Mitch smiled at Jonathan as his breathing got heavier and he had to adjust the nose tubes. He squeezed his hand and said, “Go home and get some sleep, and I’ll be here tomorrow.”

Jonathan bent down and kissed the top of his grandfather’s head and then replied, “I love you Grandpa, just so you know. I’ll be back tomorrow.”

The two of them parted and as Jonathan was leaving Mitch drifted off to sleep with a normal breathing rate. It was the sound of a tired old man, the restful pace of a life lived, and the end coming near. Jonathan turned back to see Mitch in his peaceful state, something that he had rarely seen in Mitch; it was something that had only come about in the last few weeks. Jonathan could not help but smile, peace was long overdue with Mitch.

14

The Meaning of Family

No one in the Collins' house got much sleep the
first night Mitch was in the hospital. Everybody was
up early and exhausted, but it was mostly emotional
while everybody just waited. The waiting was for the
inevitable, for they all knew that the days with Mitch
were few and every moment with him would be even
more precious than before.

Jonathan woke up early not really being able to
sleep peacefully even with Melissa next to him. All he
could do was think about what Mitch had told him,
knowing that it was a final lesson from his teacher of
life; he knew that there wasn't anything more he
could say that had not been said. It was a heavy
feeling to know that the end was finally here and all
they could do was wait to hear it out loud.

That weighted feeling was felt by everybody at
breakfast that morning, especially by Alice as she
prepared Mitch's favorite breakfast meal knowing that

he would not be there to enjoy it. While they ate breakfast there were not many words exchanged by the family.

So when the hospital called in the early morning during breakfast no questions of why were asked. Everybody knew what the call was about and that their waiting was finally over. Mitch had died in his sleep during the night; he did not feel any pain or was conscious enough to be aware of his death. He just slipped away peacefully into his final sleep.

Alice, Laura, Catherine, and Jonathan went to the hospital as tears filled their eyes; they were all an emotional mess and grieved in their own way for it was hard to accept that he was finally gone. Alice more than anyone else grieved hard for the love of her life, for the time they would never get to spend together ever again.

Arrangements were already made with the hospital and a funeral home on what to do when Mitch had finally passed away and to prepare for a memorial service. There wasn't much to be done. Everything had already been set in motion when it came to Mitch being laid to rest. Everybody was mainly there for each other, to comfort each other when they needed it the most. For Melissa, she knew that all she could do was be a shoulder to lean on for Jonathan and say goodbye to a very good friend that had opened her eyes to the trueness of life.

Phone calls were made to friends and family so everybody would know what had happened. Thomas and Rebel were the first ones to be called, as well as Dr. Whitaker. An announcement was made with his obituary within all the various newspapers in the Chicago area so friends and people that knew him would know and could pay their final respects. His graveside memorial service would be in four days, but there would be a special memorial gathering for him in one of his favorite spots to visit. It was an Irish Tavern a few blocks from the Collins house in the neighborhood that he had lived in for the last forty six years.

The place was called O'Malley's and Mitch had known the owner and his son since he moved to this part of Chicago with his beautiful wife. It was a like a home away from home for people in that neighborhood, a gathering place for folks looking to relax and unwind from a hard day's work and watch whatever ballgame was on TV. Mitch had always called it the club because it was like a social club for the working class and he always saw the same people in there, most of whom were friends.

Jonathan could remember going in there with his grandfather while growing up and getting Cherry Cokes with real cherries to garnish it with while Mitch would get a glass of whiskey or a good Irish beer. It was part of their time together where they could watch baseball or football together and play pool. A lot of nights Mitch could be found there playing cards with friends when he finally retired. Jonathan also remembered winning fifty dollars one time when he was a kid playing one of those scratch off games that he was never allowed to play, but his grandfather would let him play anyway. His mother was never supposed to find out, but she did anyway and Mitch got yelled at about teaching Jonathan how to gamble. Although as mad as she might have been all she could do was laugh and get over her anger because it was a chance for Jonathan and Mitch to be together. No matter what trouble the y could get in it didn't stop them from spending time together in O'Malley's doing the same thing anyway.

The family thought it would be a good place to

have a memorial gathering for Mitch, and Gus
O'Malley and his son were happy to open up their
place to people so they could remember a dear friend.
The place was simple and familiar, which was perfect
for remembering Mitch; he wouldn't have had it any
other way.

When the day of the funeral arrived, nothing was
spoken as people got ready for the funeral. The family
went through their melancholy routine up to the time
of the funeral. They had a graveyard site in one of
Chicago's oldest cemeteries where the Collins family
had plots in. Mitch would not be buried at Arlington as
upon his wishes, he wanted to be buried at home near
his family and be laid to rest next to his beloved wife.
The gravesite service was only for immediate family
and close friends.

There was other family that had made it for the
funeral. They were Catherine's two children Michael
and Eliza, cousins of Jonathan who were a few years
younger than him and that he had not seen in quite a
few years. They had been close as children growing up
and playing in the backyard of their grandparent's
house, but as they got older they drifted apart. It had
happened about nine years before when the family had
been split apart by a lie and their misguided notions of
one another got the best of them.

However, on the day of the funeral it had all
been wiped away by their sorrows for the old man they
loved deeply passing from this life to the next.
The service was nice and the words from the priest
inspiring. He talked of living the best life that we
could and that hope for the living is much more than
a word on a wall or pretty language inside a poem.
Hope is something that we have to live every day, for
its power does not come by speaking mere words.
Hope was something that we had to fight for and

that can never be taken away if we don't let it.

The priest who had known Mitch for many years said that Mitchell Collins was a true example of hope because he lived it every day despite the mistakes he made, especially in the final days of his life by putting things right within in his life. Alice commented to her children and grandchildren that Mitch would have liked the words. The service was not very long and ended with a military ceremony for a fallen hero. The 21 gun salute was startling but appreciated, and then a folded flag was presented to Alice by a captain in the navy telling her that a regretful nation will mourn the fallen hero while thanking her for his years of heroic service.

Alice had been crying a little bit all day, but after the flag was presented to her she broke down in uncontrollable tears, saddened that the moment was real and that Mitch was truly gone. His death had not really hit anybody in the family yet because they had been expecting it, but now that he was finally gone it was hard to accept. Their little moments of joy with him the night before he went into the hospital were now becoming a distant memory just like the individual memories they all had of Mitch.

After the graveside service they all went to O'Malley's for the memorial gathering, to eat and remember Mitch. Each one of the family members had their own special memory of him and he meant something different to each one of them. However they all had one common thing regarding Mitch, they loved him and were changed profoundly by him.

There were lots of people that came through O'Malley's that day to pay their respects to the Collins family. Neighbors and friends from the old neighborhood, coworkers from Washington who had made a special trip for the memorial gathering, and young men and women that Jonathan had grown up with were all there to remember Mitch. They were all people who had become better off by just knowing him.

There were thousands of stories told about him; some were funny, some were sad, and some were about his generosity towards people. He was always a giving man and when a friend needed a little money to get through the week he was always there for that friend. O'Malley was good example, for when he was down on his luck it was Mitch who helped him out one time with a little money to keep the Tavern open for people in the neighborhood so they'd have a place to gather. Tickets for the Cubs game could be found with Mitch for a lonely kid who just needed to enjoy a baseball game or a father who needed to find some tickets for his kids. Many of those same people were in the Tavern that day remembering Mitch and saying goodbye to their friend.

Then there was Stacy, the waitress at the Whiskeytown in Colorado, who sent a letter to Mitch thanking him for the money he had sent her to help with college as she finished her nursing degree. A lot of the young men and women who were there were people that Jonathan had gone to school with and they were just as much friends with his grandfather as they were with him. Mitch being old didn't seem to matter to any one of them; they just enjoyed his company and the words of wisdom he would give them. Mitch in his later years would always be a good source of information on the lessons of life, which he gladly shared with many of Jonathan's friends. It didn't matter where it was, whether it was on a football field or a golf course; he could always inspire the joyful pursuit of things and give a little wisdom about the human journey.

Mitch just had a way about him that could make anybody like him and when he was gone those same young people grieved for the loss of this man just as much as anybody else. As Jonathan found out that day by all the visitors at O'Malley's, Mitch was very much loved and revered by people. They would all agree that the world would have a great loss without Mitch Collins.

As hundreds of people came through that day to pay their respects there was a little request by Alice for those that could stay. Mitch, being the Irishmen that he was, always liked the song Danny Boy, and thought it was a great honor to have sung for someone upon their death. As sad of a song as it might be, it was a great song of remembrance. Alice asked Jonathan to sing and play it on the piano and for everybody to hold up glasses while singing in remembrance for him.

Jonathan found the old upright piano in the back low lighted corner of the tavern and began to play and sing Danny Boy. Everybody in the bar held their glasses high to toast their beloved friend for the last time. There were tears that were shed and smiles of joy for the good memories that Mitch had inspired among friends and relatives as the entire tavern sang out loud. It was a good moment and nobody had any doubt that Mitch was smiling with joy from heaven above.

A few hours later the tavern began to clear and Jonathan had a chance to catch up with his cousins who were both living in different states. He mainly wanted to mend the bridges between them and become close again like they were when they were kids. Both Michael and Eliza told Jonathan that they had gotten visits from their grandfather months before and were able to spend a few days with him mending the relationships that had fallen apart. Mitch had visited each one of them to the do the same thing he had done with Jonathan, to find a way to fix what had happened between them.

Michael and Eliza didn't know that he was dying at the time when he had visited each one of them, but they both said that his visit was a good thing. After hearing about the road trip with Jonathan, Michael and Eliza both realized what he was doing. Jonathan had always been closer to Mitch because he was practically raised by him, but Mitch wanted all of his grandchildren to know that he was sorry for the things he had done and that he loved them all just the same. Jonathan was a little surprised by hearing this, but he also knew how Mitch could plan things out. He wouldn't be surprised if Mitch minus the dying part had it all planned out, especially bringing his family back together because he was always full of surprises.

While Jonathan was talking to his cousins Alice walked up behind him and said, "Your grandfather left this letter for you and I was left with instructions not to give it to you till after he had passed away."

"What's in it?" Jonathan asked curiously.

"I honestly don't know Jonathan, he left it for you and what's inside that letter is for you only. I just wanted to give it to you now because it's time you read it. There is no telling what your grandfather left for you in that letter so I guess you'll just have to find out." She didn't really know the contents of the letter, but she knew Mitch well and it was probably some final words of wisdom.

Jonathan found a quiet booth to sit in by himself and sipped his Irish whiskey slowly as he opened up the letter. It was two pages long and written in Mitch's messy writing.

Dear Jonathan

Years ago someone once told me that the only thing that keeps us from living an extraordinary life is our own fears. What is it that we fear the most, it's what we don't know? Although, we're not really afraid of failure, but that we might be successful because we already know how to fail. We never truly understand what it means to be successful, so of course we can't help but be afraid of it. In the last year or so I realized what made me successful. It wasn't money or a job, or some kind of medal for bravery. I was successful because I had a loving family and I had the one great love of my life, your grandmother; that was all I needed. I never knew that until I almost destroyed it.

Now you might wonder what I feared the most in life; it was that I could never have those things. When I did have it, not knowing what I truly had caused me to destroy it and I did it with a bottle and my own guilt. The reason I'm telling you this is because I don't want to see you walk the same path as me. If you have learned anything from me on our journey then learn from my past and what I had to go through to put it right.

Over the years I have traveled the road seeing different things that I had never seen before and searching for answers. What I found and what you will find eventually if you keep traveling the road is that there are no answers out there, they're inside you. Somehow we always know the right answers, but they don't become clear enough until we are ready to accept them as the truth.

Life is filled with heartache and we all eventually become the broken hearted losing sight of our successes. That's why you see so many people filled with sadness going through the motions until they can't feel anything anymore. Although, you have to believe that life can be better than what it seems and that hope is something living and more than just empty words we say to ourselves to feel better. Our lives shouldn't just be the sum of all of our parts. Our lives should be the whole thing, filled with both joy and sorrow so we can find in the madness of our wretched lives what success really is.

The only thing I can tell you about beating fear is that you have to keep facing and fighting it until eventually it's gone or it can't be ignored. Those who live ordinary live are the ones who can't do that. There is nothing more I can tell you that you don't already know, and you don't need me anymore. Maybe you never did, but I did need you to be with me on this journey. I couldn't have faced the things that I did without my family and you helped me realize that. Thank you. Although, perhaps we did need each other while on this journey, but now you'll have to be the one to figure out if that's true.

You have a choice to make on how you want to live your life; whether you want to let of your fears and the anger that eats you up inside or defeat it so you can have something extraordinary. You are coming to the age where you should have figured out what kind of life you want and how to get it. When you're my age it is a little too late. Hopefully, you will learn something from all this and maybe you can put my final words into action. That would make this old man proud. I love you very much and I am very proud of the man you have become.

~ Mitch

Jonathan just stared at the letter for a few minutes after he was done reading it with tears in his eyes. He couldn't help it, he was sad and more than ever because his grandfather wasn't there to tell him these things in person. All he could do was sip his whiskey and mourn for the loss. He had learned so much from Mitch since he was kid, some good things and some bad things, but more in the last couple of months since they had been thrown back together by a tragic fate. He tucked the letter away in coat pocket for safekeeping and didn't do much for the rest of the day; He simply retreated to good memories to find some kind of comfort.

The next day friends and family went back to their normal lives. Michael and Eliza returned to their homes in other states while Catherine returned home to Rolling Meadows and to her job. Laura went back to work as well; she had become a school teacher and had to prepare for summer school. Alice saw Thomas and Rebel off at the airport and then went back to doing what she did best, helping in some kind of charitable fashion for people who needed it more than her. As Mitch would have wanted it ,everybody went back to their normal routines and he simply became a reflective thought to everybody.

Jonathan, not knowing what to do now, knowing that his life had been changed profoundly, decided to go back to New Orleans so he could get back to some kind of a normal life. He assumed that Melissa would go back as well and they'd have a relationship again, trying to figure what place they had in the other's life. As he was packing his things in one of the extra bedrooms Melissa walked in.

She looked at him with concern, for she knew that he would be sad for a long time. And that it would take a long time for him to work though his grief. She asked Jonathan, "Are you packing for New Orleans?"

"Yes. I figured the best thing to do was to go home and that's where I live. Are you going back?"

"I haven't decided yet, it sort of depends on you though."

"Well, if you want to know whether I think we should start dating again then I assumed we would. I thought after this trip we might try and make a go again."

"That's not what I was wondering, but I do want to know why you want to go back to New Orleans."

"Well the music is there and my so-called career. I just assumed you'd be there."

"Do you want to be with me again, no matter where it is?"

"You're going to make me say it, aren't you?"

"Yes, Jonathan, I need to hear it."

"Okay, I want to be with you no matter where you are. I just want to be with you."

"Good because I have something to tell you and I don't know how you're going to feel about us after I do."

"Is this bad news?"

"I think it's a little bit of good news, actually...I'm pregnant and I'm a few weeks along."

Jonathan stood there for a moment with a look of shock, but he also knew it was very possible that it could have happened. He didn't know really what to say as he sat down on the bed. Melissa walked over and sat down next him.

"Say something," she said.

"Well I'm not going to ask how it happened because we both know how it happened. When did you find out?"

"The other day when Dr. Whitaker arrived I had a feeling I might be, so he examined me and sure enough I am."

"Does anybody else know besides him?"

"No, I wanted to tell you first and I didn't want to do it the day of funeral. However, I do need to know where this leaves us now."

"If you want to know if I am going to walk out and forget about it, then no. We're going to raise our child and we're going to be together when we do it."

"If we do this, is it only for the child?"

"No I'm going to do because I love you and although this is a bit of surprise it doesn't change anything about how I feel about you. I love you and I want to be with you; I want us to make this family work."

Melissa kissed him and hugged him. "Okay, then let's make it work...let's make this family work. You and me, I guess that's the chance we're going to take."

"You and me, Melissa. I'm choosing you and me and that's the only choice I need to make."

"So where are we going to raise this kid, where's home going to be?"

"I hadn't thought that far yet, I guess New Orleans."

"I was thinking of Chicago."

"Why Chicago?"

"Because its home and your family is here. They're going to need you, and to be honest I've grown quite attached to your family. So why not move here?"

"Do you even want to live here?"

"I'm not crazy about the harsh winters, but home is where your family is and that's here now so the rest doesn't matter."

Jonathan squeezed her hand and kissed her. "So I guess you and me have returned home now?"

"We all have to sometime, as a wise old man said to me once. I'm just glad that home is with each other."

"Me too!"

They laughed with each other and held each other for the rest of the day, letting the joy of living come back again. They made their plans for the future right then and there lying on the bed while holding each other tight. They made a pact with each other that day that home would be with each other and they would pursue their dream with each other. They promised to one another that they would grow old together and when they came to the winter of their lives they would not have regrets or fears, only the a sense of a life lived with love and fullness.

∞∞∞∞∞∞∞

It was in the early morning as the sun was beginning to rise when my father finished his story. My mother was already up making coffee for the two men she loved more than anything. What started out as just another one of my father's long winded boring stories turned out to be the most important story that I needed to hear. I learned something about my family and the way I saw things seemed to change overnight because of what my father told me.

I still didn't understand my father completely, and maybe I never will. He even said that he still didn't completely understand Mitch when he passed away and perhaps we are never meant to understand our family in full. That's part of loving someone, because real love is about loving without complete understanding. What I did find out was that my father understood me all too well and he was right, I needed to know this story about my family at this point in my life. Not for some school assignment, but because of who I was and what my family would become for me. It would eventually set me free just as it did over twenty years ago with my father and my mother.

As my mother brought us both a cup of coffee he looked with a tear in his eye and said, "There is one regret I have and that's not telling you more about your great grandfather over the years."

"Why didn't you?" I asked my dad.

"Because it hurt and because I was still angry about everything."

"Angry for how things turned out?"

"I was angry because he died and he wasn't here for some of the most important moments of my life. You being born and me getting married are just a few of those moments."

"Are you still angry now?"

"Yes and no. My anger just comes from missing him every day and it's been replaced with a sadness that I never talked about him enough. It took a while to get past the fact that I didn't have that long with him, but I was there with him right up to the end. I got to see my grandfather be the best that he could be and get past the worst of himself."

"You know, I just realized that you have been telling me more stories about him over the last few years than when I was a kid. Is this your way of getting over it?"

"Yes it is. It has taken me a long time to settle these issues within myself. I find a peace now by talking about him and sharing with you what he shared with me, so I will be telling you more stories as we go along."

"I would like that, Dad. We need to talk about these things more and more so we never let what happened with you and Mitch happen with us. I don't want to go through years of hating each other and not speaking to each other."

"I don't either, Sean, and that's why I'm here talking with you now. It never has to be too late with us."

I hugged my father for the first time since I was a kid, not because I was sad and wanted to feel better, but because he was my dad. I loved him despite all the bad things between us and I knew that he was a good man. He had learned from his grandfather. My mother couldn't help it, she just hugged us both knowing that all of our lives would be changed once again by this story. My mother had one true quality about her that she had learned from Mitch, she learned how to bring out the best in people and to make them feel good, of course if you ask me I think she's always had it.

So as I sat at the front of the room in my humanities class I came to the end of my story. It took me two class days to tell it, but nobody seemed to mind because it was that good of a story. It was true and struck an emotional accord with people; I saw plenty of people with tears in their eyes, including my professor. My mother and father were there as visitors sitting on the top row with tears in their eyes. I even looked at my girlfriend who was crying, for she was seeing something different about me. She was seeing something good in me.

I was different, but in a good way after hearing this story about the best man that my father ever knew and who changed the lives of the people he cared for the most in the best possible way. I looked at my girlfriend with a better understanding than I had before and she knew it because she was changed by the story I told. I loved her and knew that by looking at her without any fear, perhaps the same way my parents did with each other 21 years before. When our lives are changed in a profound way then we begin to see more clearly.

After Mitch died I was born nine months later, and as soon as my parents knew that I was a boy they immediately wanted to name me after my great grandfather so I became Sean Mitchell Collins. My parents settled in Chicago and both of them gave up the road for careers in teaching others what they have learned. My father became a music teacher and my mother taught little kids because somewhere in all the madness she realized she had a real heart for children.

Alice would pass away a year and half later. She wasn't ill at all, but it was her time, and if you ask my family the thing that killed her was a broken heart. She just missed my great grandfather too much so one night in her sleep with a small simple smile on her face she peacefully died in her sleep. My father's cousins eventually moved to the Chicago area, getting married and having children of their own and making our family bigger.

Catherine and Laura became more than sisters again, they became best friends and when they took over Christmas festivities after my great grandmother died, it was always one hell of an adventure. Always a good adventure though, because Christmas was always Alice's favorite holiday and she made everything wonderful. She made it wonderful from the fresh baked Christmas cookies and sour cream cinnamon rolls that always let us know that Christmas arrived; she made it wonderful because she brought the family together for one of life's most joyous occasions. Laura and Catherine picked right up where she left off and Christmas has always been the best time of the year where everyone can feel the true meaning of home.

My parents, as sappy as it might sound, made it work and the chance they took on each other was the best one they ever made. I have never seen two people who love each other more and dote on each other like each day is the last they will ever have. It's actually kind of inspiring to watch. Now if you were to ask them why they love each other then they may not have a clear answer, but they know that it makes sense and that's all they have to know.

There are a lot of things that we can take from this story. My father and I both learned something different from it. But, there was something in common that we found in his story And it's in what my father told me he really learned from his grandfather.

It's not important how we die, but how we lived our life. Holding on to fear and anger or even regret never leads us to anything extraordinary. We should remember the dead, but they are never truly dead as long as we do remember them. We have to remember beyond the tears we shed for our loved ones that are gone and their faded photographs we hold in our hands. We remember them in the laughter of the stories we tell about them. And we remember them through wisdom they gave us.

We may lose our family for a time, but it only helps us to find our family. The only true success we have in this life is living beyond the fear of what we may lose and where we find the love of family and friends. We all return home to those that love us the most, which will be our family in some form. When I see my success, I see my loving family and that's when I know, I've come home.

"Only write from your own passion, your own
truth. That's the only thing you really know about, and
anything else leads you away from the pulse."

~*Marianne Williamson*

www.ingramcontent.com/pod-product-compliance
Lightning Source LLC
Chambersburg PA
CBHW032111180726
48284CB00002B/528